MW00416270

FLYING HOME

a mother's conflict between dreams and duty

ANGIE MOSES

Cover art by Caroline Coolidge Brown, www.carolinecbrown.com.
Cover art photo by Kevin Chelko, www.foodshooter.com.
Copyright © 2012 Angie Moses
All rights reserved.
ISBN:1475196083
ISBN-13:9781475196085

LCCN:

DEDICATION

To the not-so-super moms
who fall short of perfection
but keep on loving anyway

ACKNOWLEDGMENTS

Thanks to my husband Mike and my two sons Dylan and Austin for encouragement and laughter. Thanks to literary agent, Sally Hill McMillan, for validation. Thanks to the astute readers and advisors who contributed to the book: Peg Robarchek, Didi Romanek, Erik Fatemi, Heather Atkinson, Dr. Tracie Lanter, Officer Mark Cook, Officer Will Faulkner, Sally Meredith, Jen Atkinson, Kimberly Ogas, Christina Lewis, Tracy Grubbs, Debbie Booze, Brenda Allison, Jodi Roth, Mary Andrews, Jane Copeland, Anne Cathey, Penny Noyes, and Bobbi Campbell.

SECTION I
SPARROW

House sparrow, Passer domesticus: Common North

American bird. Dull, gray breast and shrill, monotonous chirp.

Loose-knit nesting colonies. Typically monogamous.

1

No one in Holly's present life suspected her of color theory, not the other carpool moms or the neighbors or Peter and Ethan's teachers. Languidly, Holly sketched a color wheel into the dust of her computer screen. Even her husband Ted had forgotten about her hidden skills, regarding her as little more than a talented grocery-list doodler. Rhinestones Vitalize Boy George's Yellow Overcoat. Using her special mnemonic, Holly labeled each dusty wedge with an initial, RVBGYO—Red Violet Blue Green Yellow Orange. Only one group of people still remembered the artist formerly known as Holly Dover. Only one group of people knew that long before Mrs. Holly Reese had settled into her present world of Play-Doh and play dates, young Holly Dover had camped in a more Bohemian world of oil paints and turpentine. This group of people came from a time long ago: they were her friends from high school.

Nostalgia then, not just for old friendships but also for a lost identity, nudged Holly towards e-mailing YES to her fifteen-year high school reunion. But embarrassment about how little she'd accomplished in the past six years pulled her back towards a NO. Holly had no success stories to bring to the reunion, no hints of being anything more than a boring mom with boring hair.

She'd set a goal to complete a painting by the date of the reunion, so she could casually mention to any classmates who asked: "Why yes, I am still pursuing my art. In fact, I just finished a landscape that I hope will become the first in a series of paintings with aerial viewpoints." But Holly had nothing—just a six-year old sketch and a few thoughts about how she'd pit

1

yellow-green lawns against red-violet houses, letting these color wheel opposites duke it out.

Travel logistics reinforced her inclination to stay home from the reunion. Ted had a trade show that same weekend, leaving Holly to solo-parent the seven-hour drive from Charlotte to Northern Virginia. Such a trip, alone with her two raucous boys, would be harrowing enough to cause facial tics.

Of course facial tics might make a good conversation starter with her fellow alumni: "Why yes, John, I do have a problem with facial tics, and speaking of ticks, do you and your wife have any pets?"

She smudged away the lettered wedges from the dusty monitor. The date to get discounted reunion tickets had come and gone. Now the pressure to decide about the reunion came from her high school friend Kate Arrington, whose nagging e-mails demanded a head-count two weeks ahead. Kate, now Kate Jones, wanted to go ahead and reserve a table at Casa Maria's, their beloved high school hang-out that used to offer bottomless chips and a generous carding policy. On the Friday night before the reunion their group of friends planned to gather for a pre-reunion fiesta.

Tonight Holly planned to e-mail her final reunion decision to Kate, though she still didn't know what that decision would be. The computer played its start-up song, "Somewhere over the Rainbow." It didn't just play those first two measures, which Ted might have tolerated without always groaning and drumming his fingers. Instead Judy Garland's melancholy voice belted out for an entire eight measures, clocked by Ted at 21.5 seconds. Holly sang along. If they ever made a sequel to *The Wizard of Oz*, she'd be a shoo-in for the fat, aging Dorothy.

After her moving solo, Holly sank down in the black swivel chair and soaked in the marvelous, splendid, beautiful, wonderful, blessed sound of silence. She had found Brigadoon, the magical island between nine and ten o'clock, when the kids were in bed and Ted was out of town and she could ignore the million other things she should be doing. In Ted's ugly home office, she ignored the computer equipment that junked up her periphery and focused on the monitor, now royal blue. Just for tonight this 9 by 12 inch space was hers, and she didn't have to dust it or share it with anyone.

She found Kate's e-mail and hit Reply.

April 11, 1998
Dear Kate,

Holly stopped typing. Her gaze fell away from the computer screen and down towards her roll of post-childbearing fat. With both hands she squeezed the bulge between the waist of her pants and the elastic of her bikini underwear. This handful was reason enough not to see high school friends. Why did she even bother with bikini underwear? Why not accept her fat housewife status and wear granny underwear like her mother? Within the panty area of her mother's underwear, sheer, loosey-goosey nylon showcased her mother's aging cellulite, and along the panty perimeter, gray elastic showcased the bulges at her waist and thighs. It was Nice 'n Bulbous Underwear—for the woman who wanted to say, "Sorry honey, but I just don't care."

If only Holly didn't care, like her mother, who left Holly's father when Holly was 15 in order to "end her tenure as a domestic slave." Her mother left domestic slavery for career slavery, becoming a real estate agent chained to her beeper. Did her mother start wearing the granny underwear then? Or did she start wearing it long before, perhaps making it a contributing factor in her deteriorating marriage?

Besides the roll of fat, Holly's hair hung in her face, flipping stupidly at the ends. Back at Washington High School during the glory days, she'd had interesting Farrah Fawcett hair. She'd been one of the homecoming princesses, all with Farrah Fawcett hair, who waved from the convertibles that circled the football field. She'd been the one awaited by Alex Meyers, heart throb of the tenth grade.

The high school memories strutted out in white disco suits from their shrine in the back of Holly's brain. She typed them to Kate:

Remember the homecoming parade sophomore year? Remember spending the night at Pete LaSalle's in order to finish the homecoming float? How Alex and Sue got into a paint war while they painted the yellow submarine and accidentally splattered my Paul McCartney face? Remember skinny dipping in the LaSalle's pool and Pete's peter? (I just laughed out loud. I hope I didn't wake up my own boy Peter, who's sleeping down the hall.) Remember how Sue woke us up at three o'clock in the morning after cramming for her World War II test, shouting, "Enola Gay! Enola Gay! Hey everyone, I've learned how to ask if you're gay in Spanish. Hola, Holly, ¿Enola gay? Buenas Noches, Kate, ¿Enola gay?"

The shrine held another Sue-memory, less gay, which Holly didn't feel like writing about. When Holly's father died, less than a year after her parents' divorce, Sue and their other high school friends attended the funeral, filling up two pews. It was strange to see them all in suits and dresses, crying. In the hallway afterwards Billy Holton brought out a roll of toilet paper from the men's bathroom because he couldn't find Kleenex, and everyone laughed. Then Sue started a round of Mr. Dover stories, beginning with how Holly thought it was cool in the eighth grade to wear her dad's large white t-shirts cinched with a silver belt.

Holly's high school friends knew things her present-day people didn't. They knew about her dad's death, and they knew that she and Alex Meyers had a good thing going on.

Did Alex have a roll of fat too? Would his brilliant blue eyes still penetrate her like the laser eyes of Gengar the Pokemon? Holly snorted at her knee-jerk source for poetic comparison: preschool superheroes. "Alex, darling, your eyes are as bright as Gengar the Pokemon's." Her cartoon simile would surely impress Alex, who was now an English professor.

If only she could watch the reunion from behind a cracked

door. Maybe she and Kate could find a nice broom closet somewhere at the back of the Sheraton ballroom.

Kate's presence at the reunion guaranteed at least one other stay-at-home mom in the crowd. Together they could give matronly hugs to all their career-oriented classmates and bore them with their mommy talk: "Hey everyone, who here saw the one where Barney and Baby Bop helped the custodian get ready for his violin concert?"

Holly and Kate had been best friends ever since the first day of first grade. Holly's family had just moved to town. Her mother was having some new tennis ladies over for coffee and needed Holly to walk home from school by herself. Only Holly turned left outside of the elementary school instead of right and began wandering into an increasingly unfamiliar neighborhood. She couldn't find the yellow house with the motorcycle or the white house with the purple flowers. Her heart started beating faster, and she started to cry. When Kate tapped her on the shoulder, she screamed.

"Sorry," Kate said. "It's just me. You're in my class."

Holly sniffled. "My new house has disappeared and I don't know how to find it."

(The line became a running joke when they got older: "My A in chemistry has disappeared and I don't know how to find it." "My boyfriend has disappeared and I don't know how to find him.")

That day Kate invited Holly to come home with her. Fortunately Kate's mom was able to find Holly's new phone number in her book bag, and fortunately Kate's mom wasn't an ax murderer.

When they eventually reached Holly's mom and she came to pick up Holly, her mom said to Mrs. Arrington, "I'm so sorry to have troubled you. I thought I made the directions crystal clear, and we're just off the same street as the school. But I swear, Holly can't remember her own name half the time."

Once in the car her mom yelled, "Damn it, Holly, I told you to go RIGHT. Do you even know your left from your right?"

A cough barged into Holly's memories. Peter was coughing

again. The bugle call of mother-duty blasted into her ears, and poof, her Brigadoon evaporated. She'd forgotten to give him his cough medicine before putting him to bed. He'd been so whiney and she, so tired, that she'd done the drive-thru version of bedtime—kiss-kiss, pat-pat, no story, good night. The bedtime books, she'd told Peter, had gone on vacation and refused to be read until they'd gotten their proper rest. Holly had managed to jet out of Peter's room without yelling but also without giving him his medicine.

She went to the boys' bathroom and got the Robitussin bottle off of the Crest-spattered counter. How hard was it to spit into the sink? She had to look up the dosage every time. Now came the most counter-intuitive act known to motherhood: waking a sleeping child. She'd have to wake him in the dark, just enough for him to swallow the red, stain-happy syrup, but not enough for him to speak, ask questions, make comments, or voice complaints.

Holly listened in the hallway. The coughing had stopped. Her services weren't needed after all. With the Robitussin bottle in hand just in case, she returned to the computer to the treat of completing her task.

Anyway, enough nostalgia. I was writing to say...

Peter coughed again, this time hacking for several seconds. One tiny completed task—was it too much to ask? She wasn't asking to go to the spa. She just wanted a few moments to write a stupid e-mail after a fourteen hour day of feeding her boys, grooming them, bathing them, driving them, cleaning up after them, answering their questions, acting interested. She picked up the plastic Robitussin bottle and banged it on the keyboard. The syrup made sloshing sounds while a barrage of letters, numbers, and punctuation marks fired onto the screen.

';lhy65esaw34456yh-=]nm,.

Blah, Blah, Blah. What difference did it make? The plastic

medicine cup danced off the bottle cap onto the keyboard. Holly crushed it and flung it across the room, only she threw the lightweight cup too hard and strained her shoulder.

"I have a stupid life," she said out loud.

Holly stomped into Peter's room with the Robitussin bottle but once there realized she now had nothing with which to measure it. There was always one more thing to do. Back in the boy's bathroom she opened the cabinet underneath the sink, its doors also Crest-splattered to match the counter. She knocked around various plastic containers until she found another medicine bottle with a crusty, old measuring cup. She grabbed the cup and banged the cabinet doors shut, not caring who woke up. The crusty little cup came clean as she rinsed it under the faucet.

She set aside the cup on the dirty sink counter and put her hand under the running water, which slowly turned from freezing cold, to warm, to hot, to burning hot. She held it there for as long as she could bear until the pain of the near-scalding water calmed her. Her fingers, when she pulled them out, were bright pink, and she sucked on them until the burn subsided.

Now resolute, Holly poured the half teaspoon of Robitussin and carried the cup into Peter's dark room. He drank it down, dribbling only a little. Right away he nestled his sleepy head back into the pillow. Holly fingered away the medicine from Peter's chin and licked her finger. She felt his forehead for fever and kissed his gold-spun hair that smelled of baby shampoo. Asleep, Peter didn't threaten to engulf her. At night, this raging, Class 5 rapid settled into a gentle pool that was easy on the nerves. During these nighttime checks, Holly appreciated the smallness of her boys, and subsequently, the villainy of her anger towards them. Peter couldn't help it that he had a cough. All he required was some simple cough medicine. Kids with cancer required handfuls of medicine every night and they had no hair to kiss.

"Thank you," she whispered to some vague deity. "Thank you for two healthy boys. I need to be more thankful."

Back at the computer, Holly erased the mish mash of letters, numbers, and punctuation marks and resumed her e-note to Kate:

Anyway, enough nostalgia. I started writing to tell you that I can't come to the reunion and to ask if I could mail you the class nametags I volunteered to make, but then I decided that I desperately need an evening out with grown-ups. I need to laugh about the good ol' days. I'm coming, even if the car trip kills me. You can just scrape me out of my minivan, put a little lipstick on me, and carry me to the party, bride-of-Frankenstein style.

I've been having fun making class nametags and looking through yearbooks. I've decided to put your ninth grade picture on your nametag, the one with your braces, crescent roll hairdo, and shiny disco vest. Just kidding. But you'd better be nice to me because being the Nametag Queen does give me some leverage.

Did you get an e-mail back from Alex Meyers? He wrote me saying that he definitely is going to make the trek from Alabama, but his corporate ladder wife won't be with him because she's on a six-month assignment in Honolulu.

Is Jimmy coming with you? Let me know the details about the Friday night get-together. Can't wait to see you.

Love,

Hol

2

The first e-mail from Holly, which appeared late one evening after six years of silence, had shocked Alex Meyers. Without lead-in or fanfare, Holly wrote to ask if he and Emily planned to attend the reunion. Alex wrote her back immediately, saying that he definitely planned to be there, though he hadn't until that very moment given it any thought. Holly waited until the following evening to respond and thus set the pace for once-a-day correspondence over the past several weeks. What started as innocent chit-chat—"How's Emily's job?" "Have you heard that Billy Holton got married?"— quickly became more personal with comments such as, "I bet Emily loves living with such an accomplished back scratcher." Then Holly said something that taunted Alex like a matador waving a red cape.

"Ted's never around," she wrote. "And when he is around, he's not around emotionally."

Without waiting the customary day before responding, Ted charged forward, steam puffing from nostrils, and typed a six-word reply that began a great rush of revelations.

If e-mail weren't their method of communication, the rush might never have started. E-mail allowed Alex to be daring. He typed the six words on the screen and clicked "send" before thinking through the consequences. If he'd written Holly a regular letter, he'd probably have changed his mind somewhere between putting the letter in an envelope, finding a stamp, and carrying it to the mailbox. If he'd been with Holly in person, he'd never have risked the face-to-face rejection. But with e-mail? A simple click of the mouse and out the six words flew.

"Are you happy in your marriage?" he wrote.

Holly responded by suggesting a chatroom discussion Sunday at 11:00.

Now, one hour before their scheduled chat, Alex Meyers arrived at his little rental house in Henrietta, Alabama. He'd just dropped off his wife Emily at the Atlanta airport so she could fly back to Hawaii, where she was working 14-hour days on a Hyatt Hotel project. They'd endured the obligatory weekend at their Buckhead home just outside of Atlanta by sitting in front of the television, sorting mail, and cleaning up a fallen tree limb.

Alex plopped his suitcase onto his bed, emptied the top layer of clothes, and pulled out from the bottom a small painting. He traced the orange and blue lips of the face that resembled an African mask. The canvas had bubbled between the staples on the sides and curled along the edges on the back, but the front surface was still in good shape. Eventually he would find a frame for it. Emily had never asked which friend painted the picture, which Alex had dragged with them on each of their moves; she just knew she didn't want "such amateur work" hanging in their home. After much searching over the weekend, Alex had found the painting squirreled away in the basement underneath some old frames and manila folders.

Now that Alex had what amounted to his own bachelor pad, he could decorate however he pleased. Only twice had Emily visited his rental house at Huffton College, which was the only school that had offered him a tenure-track position as assistant professor. She came the first time to help him move in and the second time for an English department Christmas party that first year. But ever since, for over two years, they only saw each other in Buckhead, every weekend at first, then every other, and now with Emily's project in Honolulu, only once a month.

He therefore had complete freedom to hang the painting Holly had created back in high school. He held up the colorful canvas against a wall in his bedroom and then in his kitchen, but the wall in the living room above his futon looked best. After leveling it on a nail, he walked around his tiny house, admiring the picture from different angles. Then he knelt on the futon and once again touched the orange and blue lips.

He could still see the painting from his office when he booted up his computer. To prepare for his e-mail chat with Holly, he took out a yellow pad of paper and jotted a few phrases to describe his marriage: Relational Demotions; Common-law Divorce; Sexlessness. He went to the kitchen to grab an Amstel Light, and right when got back to his desk, Holly's words appeared on the monitor.

"Hey Alex, are you out there?"

He took a long gulp of beer. "I'm here," he typed. "So, Mrs. Holly Dover Reese, the question at hand: Are you happy in your marriage?"

Her words returned rapid fire. "Beat around the bush, why don't you? I don't know, Mr. Alexander Caleb Meyers. Do you think June Cleaver was happy in her marriage, or do you think she secretly wanted to run off and join a jazz band?"

"I think June wanted to join a jazz band *and* I think she was mad as hell about having to wear pearls and high heels while she cooked."

"Lucky for me I don't own high heels anymore, I never owned pearls, and I don't cook much beyond frozen food."

Alex glanced at Holly's painting on his living room wall. "Do you ever daydream about running off to SoHo to become a painter?"

"Sure. A girl can have her fantasies. But I have a few tiny details holding me back—a husband, a house, and 2.5 kids. Did I tell you about our .5 child? We keep her in our dresser drawer."

"She sounds cute. But really, Hol, why aren't you painting?"

"Because I have constant kids, and when I have a break from my constant kids, I'm exhausted."

"Doesn't Ted help with the kids?"

"He tries to, but he has to travel so much. I'm pretty much a solo act."

"Can't you find childcare? You're too talented to give up your painting."

"I don't want to pay someone else to raise my kids, although they could probably do a better job. Ethan is in preschool two mornings a week, but that time gets frizzled away with cleaning and errands. I had actually set a goal for myself to paint a painting by the time our reunion got here. I thought I could work after the kids went to bed, but I don't have a space to work and something always comes up. I'm always just too tired. I've become a tired, old lady. My excuses are lame. I know. I'm sure I'll get to paint someday, but now just doesn't seem like the time. I guess I still have five days before the reunion, right? Maybe I can whip up some token thing. Anyway, what about you? Are you happy in your marriage?"

"Yes, what's-her-name and I are very, very happy. Edith? Emma? Oh yes, Emily is her name. I hardly ever see her. Did I tell you her project in Honolulu will last for SIX months?"

"How often do you get to see each other?"

"Once a month she flies back to Atlanta for the weekend, and I drive there from Alabama to meet her at our half-empty house, which we still own for some reason, though neither of us lives there. Or at least that's what we did the last two months. We talk on the phone a couple times a week. She's very focused on her work."

"Must be frustrating."

"You mean sexually? Yes." Alex pressed Send.

Holly didn't reply. Alex peeled off his Amstel Light label. She still didn't reply.

"Just kidding," he wrote. "Connecting with Emily has become labored. We miss out on so many things in each other's lives. Little things. For instance, I'm sure by the time I talk to Emily I'll forget to tell her that I got carded last night at the grocery store. Or I'll forget to tell her about this student in my American Lit class who called Steinbeck's *Cannery Row*, 'Canary Row.' I laughed so hard I dropped my notes on the floor. Instead of down-and-out men, I imagined yellow canaries lined up on a fence, whistling."

Finally Holly responded. "You mean that book isn't about birds? Well, I guess I can scratch it off my reading list. I'm sorry it's hard with you and Emily right now, but I suppose the six months will be over before you know it. Funny, when Ted and I do see each other, I don't ever bother telling him the little things.

If I try, his eyes glaze over. I'm sort of like his au pair—he doesn't want to hear about the little triumphs and trials of carpool and homework; he just wants to know that I'm doing my job managing the household."

"Hey at least you have a role. I don't know if I have a role in Emily's life anymore. Maybe I never did. She's so independent. She also thinks I'm unreliable, too pie in the sky, so she doesn't depend on me for anything. Emily is a concrete thinker (an architect—ha ha); she has no time for philosophy or poetry; she should have married an MBA type."

"Ted should've married an MRS type. He can't understand why I'm not totally satisfied with my house in the suburbs and my new minivan. He thinks I've got it made—a woman of leisure with a Dodge Caravan, for crying out loud. For my birthday last year he gave me a family pass to the zoo. It was almost as crass as a toaster. He thought he was being so sensitive to my need to get out of the house."

"Remember the Van Gogh book that I got for you at the National Gallery?"

"It's one of my favorite gifts ever. It has the highest ranking in my house which is *not* the coffee table. No, Vincent stays on the nightstand by my bed. Do you remember what you wrote on the inside cover? 'Let's always take time to gaze upon beauty—together.'"

"The together part never quite panned out, huh?"

Holly took a good ten seconds to respond, and Alex longed for an Un-send button. He took a long swig of beer.

"Why did we break up again?" Holly finally wrote.

His fingers hammered at the keyboard. "The first, second, or third time? Only you know the answer, as instigator of all three break ups." Send. He thought he had evicted the hurt a long time ago, but it had merely been curled up in a corner of his heart.

"Maybe I was stupid," she answered.

"Damn straight," he typed, but he paused before pressing send. Holly's four words emitted an after-echo of regret, which offered a hand to his hurt. She was inviting him to a new, unnamed version of their relationship, beyond the mistakes of the past, beyond the flirtations of the present. He erased his surly response.

"I was stupid too," he wrote instead. "I settled for Emily when I still wasn't over you." Click and send.

Alex drained the end of his beer and hurried to the kitchen for another one, but when he got back to his desk, Holly still hadn't replied. Maybe Holly hadn't been confessing regret for breaking up, just regret for not making the break-up stick the first time. Maybe she meant she was stupid to lead him on all those years. Alex had downed most of his second beer by the time Holly replied.

"Sorry I took so long. My boys got into a fight and I haven't been able to settle it long-distance. I need to go. I think there may be blood. Let's talk soon."

3

The boys' skirmish concerned a Star Wars tie fighter.

Peter bubbled with explanation. "Ethan stole my tie fighter and busted the wing. See? I didn't mean to hurt him, but it's my tie fighter."

If it had merely been his x-wing, Peter might have let it slide, but his tie fighter? Well, anyone could understand.

Ethan sat on a little painted chair, only the chair and Ethan lay horizontal on the living room floor, like an astronaut except for the screaming. Holly lifted Ethan and let him sob into her shoulder. What should the appropriate punishment be? She wished there were a chart: the breaking of one tie fighter equals three spanks, or three minutes in the time-out slammer, or for the advanced parent, a chores-for-cash fundraising campaign to pay for the broken ship. A chart, though, could never account for all the technicalities. How and when should the parent dispense punishment if the defendant had incurred booboos and was sobbing on her shoulder? And what of the ship owner's nasty retaliation?

Once Ethan calmed down and Holly declared him concussion-free, she banished both boys to solitary confinement, duration undefined.

The boys' brawl had ended her chat room with Alex, and she felt relieved. She wasn't sure what to write in response to Alex's confession that he wasn't over her and that he'd "settled for Emily."

Holly walked downstairs to the laundry closet in the kitchen. From the closet's bowels she gathered up her reunion nametag supplies and set them out on the kitchen table.

15

Although the next nametag to make was Alice Johnson, in black velvet bodice and matching headband, Holly flipped through two more Xeroxed yearbook pages until she got to the M's. She cut between two columns of senior portraits and maneuvered the scissors around Alex Meyers, whose light-colored suit stood out from all the dark ones. Even from the tiny black and white Xerox, even from under his big swoop of blow-dried hair, Alex's eyes beckoned. Holly glued Alex Meyers onto the white card and printed his name with a black calligraphy marker. She blew gently on the ink and then kissed the tiny freckle above his lip. Why did she break up with that freckle?

Her to-do list peeked out from under the nametag pile:

-Groceries
-Peter's ladybug costume
-Nametags
-Painting

She added to the list, "Lose 25 pounds."

Outside the kitchen window a gray sparrow plopped down from its magnolia nest to a patch of greening grass, where it pecked around for worms. Graceless, it flapped over to a more promising hunting ground by the purple iris. It pulled up a juicy one then zipped back home to the tree.

Holly's life didn't differ much. Zip to the grocery and back home, off to carpool and back.

The sparrow's staccato flight had one purpose—caring for babies. No time for soaring like the raptors she learned about while chaperoning Peter's field trip. In the Raptor Center film, the lone Harrier Hawk soared fiercely and elegantly across the sky, and the two Peregrine Falcons dove at 200 miles and hour to catch their prey in mid-flight. When she saw the actual birds, though, convalescing in their Raptor Center cages, she felt sad seeing those fliers not fly.

What was she doing bird watching? In addition to the tasks on her list she needed to do a load of underwear. Ted had yelled at her that morning, launching into his full-on laundry speech.

"I'm down to my Santa Claus boxers," he said. "Why can't you keep up with the laundry? My mother used to go to school and work and do the laundry. You used to meet gnarly deadline after gnarly deadline, and now you can't even keep up with the laundry. Step number 1, wash. Step number 2, dry. Please Holly, I'm just asking for clean underwear."

Ted never understood laundry or children or the baby fog that had descended on her the minute she had Peter. In the thick of the baby fog, laundry took at least 10 steps: Step 1) Separate laundry, 2) Quiet crying child, 3) Load washer, 4) Feed crying child, 5) Load dryer, 6) Change crying child, 7) Fold laundry 8) Entertain crying child, 9) Put away laundry, 10) Begin crying yourself, about how little you've accomplished.

Yes, she had insisted on quitting her job as an art director to stay home with Peter. Yes, she had insisted that she should raise Peter, not a daycare. But she hadn't expected the terrible baby fog. Peter's thick neediness had overshadowed her own, like cold air lording over warm, so that her life became saturated in every corner by her role as mom. The soupy fog barely allowed her to see an inch ahead, and the house became a make-shift bunker strewn with baby debris. In her state of near-sighted survival, Holly couldn't always get around to laundry. She learned the sniff and recycle method of underwear selection, but Ted had not.

As Peter grew into a toddler and the fog lifted, Holly began thinking that daycare wasn't such a bad idea and that advertising was the greatest job on earth. Then Ethan came along, not really planned, not really unplanned, and once again Holly had to relearn simple household tasks. With two babies, laundry required extra strategic analysis of feeding and nap schedules, of safety issues during those unsupervised moments, and of cost effectiveness—how dirty were the clothes anyway?

Now that the boys were three and six, the baby fog had dissipated into a mere child haze, but the laundry still piled up, and their home still fell short of Ted's American dream.

Holly didn't imagine that Alex Meyers was persnickety about laundry. His room in high school had been such a pig sty, strewn with clothes, sports equipment, textbooks, and who knew what else. She never understood how Alex managed to reel in from that scum pond the third highest GPA in their class.

In Holly's laundry closet, she'd recently installed extra shelving, baskets, and a bulletin board. The closet not only overflowed with an arsenal of laundry products but also school newsletters, carpool schedules, broken toys, phone messages, and mail. Maybe the laundry piled up partly from her fear of the crouching laundry closet, which waited in darkness to ambush her with obligations.

Juxtaposed to her administrative debris, Holly's college diploma hung on the laundry closet wall. It made her laugh. Her knowledge of art history, computer graphics, and printmaking didn't help her one bit when it came to deciding whether Ted's white and navy striped shirt should go in the light load or the dark one.

Below her diploma she'd recently thumb-tacked her oil pastel sketch. A few days after she'd gotten the reunion invitation, she tracked down the sketch in the attic and brought it to the laundry closet. She'd drawn it six years ago while in her last trimester with Peter. The style was bold and cubistic in a palette of plum, chartreuse, and white. The title, "Home," was written boldly across the top. Dave, a copywriter from work, had taken the photo during a hot air balloon ride that happened to pass over her house. Holly never found the photo, only the sketch with its oval cul-de-sac, triangular roofs, patches of green lawn, and glaring white driveways. Although age had yellowed the drawing paper and humidity from the dryer had warped its surface, the aerial viewpoint and color blocking still pulsed with fresh potential.

"You're too talented to give up your painting," Alex had written.

But Holly hadn't gotten around to gathering art supplies or buying a canvas. Now, the sketch mocked her sorry time management, derided her world of housekeeping drudgery, and mourned her life before children.

"JUICE," someone pleaded, someone surely crawling through the desert on hands and knees.

Holly turned to face a sweaty Ethan.

"Mo-om, juice."

No please. No would you mind. If Holly were moaning on the floor with blood gushing from her head or if a green alien were standing at her side, the boys would still barrel into the kitchen yelling "mo-om," a two-syllable, lowercase version of Mom that was more accusation than name. Sometimes Holly made the boys go through the manners hoop, complete with what's-the-magic-word. Other times she interrupted what she was doing and acquiesced to their wishes.

This time she sing-songed her response. "You are not down here, Ethan. You cannot leave your room, Ethan. You broke Peter's ship, Ethan."

Ethan tiptoed back upstairs. Holly ran her thumb over Alex's nametag.

Peter waddled around Eckerd's in his ladybug costume. The camera needed film for Peter's spring program at school, and since Ted didn't have time get it on his way from work, Holly had to drag Ethan and Ladybug Peter into the drugstore. They were already running late because she'd had technical difficulties with the antennae. Dinner had been cheese slices and bananas in the car.

They arrived at the school stage ten minutes late, which meant Mrs. Jamison had to rearrange the kindergartners, again. Mrs. Jamison had a hard job, putting up with parents like Holly.

After dropping off Peter, Ethan and Holly walked up and down the aisles and into the lobby, but they didn't see Ted anywhere.

Ethan tugged at Holly's pants. "Lights go out, Mommy! Lights go out, Mommy! Lights go out, Mommy!"

"Okay, okay," she said to Ethan. "I see two seats over there in the middle of that row. Your father obviously has more important things to do than show up at his son's very first school

19

program. He can sit by himself, or stand in the back." Then she mumbled to herself, "Or hang himself from the rafters."

The fifth graders opened the show with a rambling birds and bees number. The bees dispersed and then circled around the giant, lumpy flower. By the third bee circle, Ethan got bored and began kicking the seat in front of him. He loved repetitive sound. He could repeat a sound or a phrase up to nine times before he would naturally stop on his own. Thankfully his threshold wasn't thirty-nine, or even ten, or else Holly would presently be curled up on the floor of a mental institution pulling at her ears.

After Holly asked twice for Ethan to stop, he kicked again, causing the guy in front of them to turn around and give Holly the hairy eyeball. If the guy hated children, why had he come? Obviously he'd never had children of his own; he'd probably never been married; he probably still lived with his mother at the age of forty-six. What right did this maladjusted mama's boy have to judge her parenting skills?

She put her hand firmly on Ethan's shin, but he kicked once more, busting through her barricade, making vicious contact with maladjusted guy's seat. The guy turned again and said, "For the love of God." Holly stood and yanked Ethan onto her hip. Since the kindergartners were last on the program, she knew she had time to deal with Ethan and still get back for Peter's number. Everyone glared at Holly as she scooted to the end of the row and Ethan cried, "No Mommy. No Mommy. No." Judging from the looks, these hostile people all must have been parents of fifth graders, who were currently taking bows. Apparently none of their little birds and bees had ever pitched a fit in public.

Out in the lobby Holly spotted Ted leaning against the red cinderblock wall, talking away on his mobile phone. When he saw them, he smiled and waved. Did he not see Ethan's writhing body? Did he not see the fire shooting out of Holly's head? Ted gestured with his hands to take Ethan, but Holly ignored him, whipping past him into the girls' bathroom.

She jerked Ethan into a stall, took down his pants, and smacked his bottom until it became red. Ethan wailed. On the backswing of her last smack, her wrist banged the toilet paper holder, and her wounded yell echoed off the bathroom walls. She shook out the pain and turned to Ethan. The smallness of the stall made it difficult, but she managed to squat down and clamp her fingers into his shoulder. In a Mafia whisper three inches from his terrified face, she said, "Don't you ever disobey me like that again. If I say don't kick the chair, you'd better not kick the chair. You are such a... You're making us miss the program. You ought to be ashamed of yourself. What do you need to say to me? Huh?"

He was unable to talk between tearful breaths.

"You're in time-out. You stay in here until you can say sorry."

Holly exited the stall, leaving Ethan with his pants still down. She wet a paper towel and dabbed at the blood on her wrist. The blood was minimal but the wound ached. Holly looked at her watch and listened for a while to Ethan's crying.

"Ethan, I'm waiting. You'd better say you're sorry."

When he didn't come out, she splashed water on her face and refreshed her face with lipstick and eye pencil. When he still didn't come out, she looked at her calendar at the week ahead.

The door to the girls' bathroom slammed opened, and Holly froze. In walked the moms of Justin and Frank, Peter's best buddies since preschool and Holly's carpool mates.

"Holly!" Sharon sang.

"Hey Sharon. Hey Ann. Ethan's in time out. Excuse me."

Holly reentered Ethan's bathroom stall and locked it. There she covered her anger with a public veneer, transforming herself from Crackhouse Mom to Grandma Mom, the indulgent babysitter who got a kick out of children's' shenanigans. She pulled up Ethan's pants, gently wiped his face with toilet paper, and kissed his ticklish neck until he began giggling. Holly carried Ethan to the sink area where Ann was reapplying lipstick. Sharon was now in one of the stalls.

"Ann," Holly said cheerfully, "How are you? I love your shirt."

Ann turned from the mirror. "Hey there. Oh my gosh,

Holly, Peter was such a cute ladybug! Where did you buy his costume?"

"I made it, from fabric scraps and aluminum foil."

"You're amazing. And Mrs. Jamison—how in the world did she pull off a routine like that with 26 barely-socialized kindergartners! They were great, weren't they?"

"Wait," Holly said, "the kindergartners already went? I thought they were last."

"Oh that's right. Ya'all were late. It was a last minute change. They announced it backstage when we first got here. They decided the fifth-graders' flower prop would work better for the kindergartners than the first graders' oak tree, so they switched the order."

"Oh," Holly said, "I didn't know. I missed the whole thing."

She'd missed her kindergartner's first real stage performance because 1) she'd gotten him there late, and 2) she'd been busy spanking the hell out of her three-year old. Peter and the other garden bugs had been working on their song and dance for an entire month. So glad she'd gone to the trouble of buying film.

Sharon joined them after eavesdropping from her bathroom stall. "What a shame," she said with a condescending head tilt. "Gerry got some good video. We'd be glad to make you a copy."

Clearly, Holly was not an Honor Student Mom like Ann or Sharon. She'd figured this out the one time she went out to Starbuck's with them. Ann, a mother of five, ordered herbal tea because she didn't partake of caffeine. Neither did she partake of epidurals or McDonald's. Holly, on the other hand, had dozens of Happy Meal toys that she kept in jumbo coffee cans. Sharon was a different kind of Honor Student Mom. She did the room mom thing, the Mary Kay thing, and, Holly found out that night at the coffee shop, the executive wife thing, throwing all these fancy parties for her husband and his business associates. All this she did without ever appearing flustered and without ever forgetting anything. Of course, Sharon had the cash-flow to hire a housekeeper, plus her close-by mother was always willing to babysit. Holly's mom not only lived seven hours away, but she worked 24-7 and always managed to mention that she was not a little kid person.

Holly found Honor Student Moms everywhere she went. She'd found them in her short-lived playgroup, where Peter was the only toddler interested in touching all the lovely, breakable knick-knacks. She'd found them swarming at a church she went to one time, where they bragged like Christmas cards about their children's mastery of baby sign language and playpen time. Most likely, Kate Arrington was also an Honor Student Mom. In her latest e-mail about the reunion Kate said she was "in love with her tiny bundle of preciousness," a phrase that had never crossed Holly's mind. "Bundle of energy," yes, but not "bundle of preciousness."

Holly said to Sharon, "I'd love to get a copy of Gerry's video. Thanks. We had a little melt-down here." She opened the door to the hallway. "I drive tomorrow. See you all bright and early."

Out in the lobby the minute Holly saw Ted, any remnant of cheerful Grandma Mom dissolved.

Ted had been watching the girls' bathroom door while trying to wrap up his call with Bill Douglass. Ted was sure he'd won the upgrading bid for their Charlotte headquarters—how could anyone go with Data Solutions over him? But Douglass hadn't yet signed the dotted line, so Ted needed to walk the second schmoozing mile. He needed this account. His boss Pierson had made his expectations clear at Ted's annual review. Ted needed to land Douglass and Clearwater Distribution in Knoxville. One might think eight years meant something, even after a slow year, but Pierson's new accountant only cared about recent stats. Tom Jarvis, who'd been with the company even longer than Ted, was let go last month and replaced by a recent college grad; Jarvis was still out looking for work.

When Holly and Ethan came out of the restroom, Ethan

had calmed down, but Holly still looked agitated. She always looked agitated. Maybe Ted had looked at her wrong or maybe she was having her period.

"We missed Peter's song," Holly hissed.

"Bill?" Ted said into his phone. "I'm sorry to interrupt, but I'm going to have to call you back Monday morning. Thanks so much for being willing to continue our meeting over the phone. I'll make sure to fax those …"

Holly shoved Ethan into Ted's leg, so hard that Ted's hipbone banged into the wall. "He's all yours," she said as she stomped past him.

Ted closed his eyes and fought to keep his voice steady. He had to win this deal with Douglas. "Bill? Sorry. So, yes, I'll fax over the projections on Monday morning. Thanks so much. Take care. Bye." Ted clicked off his phone, placed it back on his belt loop, and made a note in his day planner. Sometime over the weekend he would have to produce out of thin air the supposed projection graphs.

Ethan tugged at his pants leg. "Daddy let's go. Daddy. Daddy."

Ted looked down at his brown pants leg. Ethan had left behind a sticky patch of snot. "Look at what you have gotten all over my pants. I just got these back from the dry cleaners. Doesn't your mother wash your hands?"

Ted walked Ethan into the boy's bathroom. As Ted washed Ethan's hands, Ethan's sad eyes met his in the mirror.

"It's okay, buddy. All clean." He dried Ethan's hands and then used the damp, brown paper towel to wipe off his pants, leaving behind brown fibers and a wet spot. Ted sighed.

"Sorry Daddy."

Ted put his arm around his son. "So what have you been up to today? Have the Power Rangers gotten into any good fights?"

Peter knew his mommy was mad, m-a-d mad. His daddy

24

drove him and Ethan home after the show. Daddy missed his ladybug song because he said he had to make a living. Peter was glad his daddy made a living. A dying would be sad, like what the caterpillars had to do. A living was what the butterflies got to do. "Butterfly flying onto my nose. Butterfly flying onto the rose." He knew all the words to the fourth graders' song.

It was okay his daddy missed his song because Peter had forgotten some of the words to his own song. "Grouchy, Grouchy, Ladybug, Ladybug, wants all the aphids for herself." He remembered ALL the words now.

His costume sat on his desk chair near the nightlight. One antenna was broken. If Justin and Frank brang their costumes over, they could play ladybug wars!

His mommy and daddy were talking in their room, but he couldn't hear what they said. They both sounded m-a-d mad. Mommy must of saw how Peter forgot the words to the song. She must be telling his daddy about it.

After putting the kids to bed, after lying to Peter about seeing the ladybug number, Holly flopped spread eagle onto their bed. Ted was arranging his clothes for the next day, as he did every night, even on the weekends. He placed his black sports shirt over the back of their blue leather chair, check; he bi-folded his jeans and put them on the seat of the chair, check; he centered his boat shoes between the legs of the chair, check-check. All was perfectly aligned.

"You bailed on us again," Holly said.

Ted spun around. "Bailed? I was there wasn't I? You have no idea how I busted my ass to be at Peter's program. I asked Bill Douglass, *the president*, if we could finish up our meeting over the phone while I drove to the school. He looked at me as if I'd lost my mind. We were right in the middle of negotiating an upgrade on all his hard drives for the entire company, an enormous amount of money."

Above Ted's dresser hung his cheesy sailboat poster in its brass metal frame. Underneath the photo it said, "Americas Cup 1991, Water Wind Wings." Holly's funky metal sun hung on the adjacent wall, dripping with globs of soldering and swirling with blowtorch blues and browns. Their bedroom décor aptly represented their dissonance. Both pieces of "art" came from their pre-marriage days and both had been demoted by the spouse from the living room to the bedroom clearinghouse. Both inspired fierce love in one and fierce hatred in the other.

"I'm sorry if Peter is an intrusion to your career," Holly said. "Does it even bother you that you missed his ladybug song?"

"I hate that I missed it, but I have to do my job so that we can eat and have health insurance. It's a juggling act. Do you have any idea how hard it is to juggle so much?"

"No. I have no idea because I just sit at home all day eating bon bons."

"Holly, I didn't mean that you don't juggle a lot too. It's just, I can't do it all."

"I can't either, especially when I'm like a single mom."

"Oh please, not the single mom thing. I don't get it. I work my ass off so you don't have to work *and* take care of kids, yet you say you feel like a single mom."

"No, you don't get it."

She got up and walked towards the bedroom door. On her way, she kicked Ted's boat shoes out of alignment.

In the garage, Holly banged open the sliding door of the minivan and climbed into the middle seat. The space between Peter and Ethan's car seats provided just enough room for Holly to wedge in her body. Her crystal prism hung from the rearview mirror. She said to it, "Why did I let myself become pregnant?"

The crystal prism had always hung from her rearview mirror—first in her mother's rust-colored Plymouth, then in her

sky-blue VW Rabbit, and now in her high styling kid-van—
except during her shotgun wedding when she wore the crystal on
a silver chain around her neck. Her father had intended to give
her the pendant for her sixteenth birthday, but he died four days
before.

She felt that her father embodied the crystal, and though
she wasn't Catholic, she accepted this transubstantiation like a
Mass-taker from way back. It's not that she expected her father
to answer her in some booming Wizard of Oz voice. And even if
he did answer, she didn't think he had any more to say now than
when he was on earth, anything beyond "I see" and "I'm sorry
about that." Still, she just knew in her heart that he was listening
and nodding compassionately.

She continued with the well-worn tirade. "Ted and I should
have been more disciplined. It's not as though we were
hormone-dominated teenagers in the backseat of a car. We were
28-year old adults, with mutual funds and college degrees, who
knew all about delayed gratification. I waited twenty-eight years,
dated lots of guys, including Alex. Yes I'll go out with you, yes I'll
laugh with you, yes I'll drink with you, but at the end of the date,
no, no, no. Why was I so stupid with Ted?"

From her middle seat vantage, the dim garage light colored
the crystal triangles black and blue, the perfect colors for her self-
castigation liturgy.

"Ted seemed like such a prize. I won the Ted contest in the
church singles' group. Of all the hungry women, the handsome
and mysterious Ted Reese chose me to give his reticent smile of
approval. Yes, yes, yes, I said, and so did the pregnancy test. I
was so vain. So stupid."

When she found out about her pregnancy, Holly had sat in
her VW Rabbit at 2:00 in the morning, parked in her driveway
because she didn't have a garage. The streetlight had turned a few
of the prism triangles yellow. She complained to the crystal about
how Sue had sex with lots of guys in high school and college but
never got pregnant. (These days her tirade excluded Sue, since
her husband died of leukemia.) But Holly? Holly got pregnant
with the first guy she ever slept with.

27

"I would have been better off as a single mom," Holly continued from the backseat of the minivan. "If I hadn't married Ted and were a working single mom, at least I'd have a good excuse for missing Peter's ladybug song and yelling at Ethan and having a filthy house. I'd have a good excuse for feeling so utterly alone. What am I saying? I am utterly alone. I am a single mom. I'm a single mom and I'll never depend on Ted again." She shouted, "Never Again."

The door from the kitchen to the garage opened and Ted stuck his head out. He looked around the garage. "Holly?"

She slid open the van door.

"Holly? What are you doing in the van? Who were you talking to?"

"I was just talking to myself. I'm the only one who really listens."

Holly knew better than to tell Ted or anyone else that she talked to a necklace and that the necklace listened and that it was really her father. Though really, how was this any crazier than talking to a priest or an advice columnist?

"Yeah," Holly said as she stepped out of the van, "I'm just a crazy person talking to myself."

Ted held the door for her while she walked into the kitchen, as if it were totally normal to be escorting his wife from her camp-out in the garage.

"Look, I've been thinking," he said "tomorrow morning I want you to take the credit card and go shopping (which Holly translated as: here is my plastic peace offering). Buy something flattering for your reunion (as opposed to the something frumpy you normally wear). I'll babysit the boys (be a babysitter, not a father who wanted to spend time with his sons). You deserve a break. (I'm being magnanimous, but I'll probably expect sexual favors in return.)"

Holly thanked him, but his gesture of reconciliation left her sadder than if he'd just stayed silent. With silence she could still hope that he'd finally heard her when she said she felt like a single mom. With the shopping offer, though, Ted showed he wasn't any closer to understanding her struggles. The shopping offer, like the zoo pass before it, betrayed his stubborn belief that a good diversion was all Holly needed. He couldn't see that what she really needed was a companion to alleviate her isolation, to share her failures, to remember her competence before kids. What she needed was a soulmate, perhaps with a freckle above his lip.

4

Alex found his senior yearbook underneath some literary journals on one of his ubiquitous black bookcases. The yearbooks hadn't really qualified as essentials when he moved to Huffton College two years ago, but he'd packed them anyway alongside such necessities as his two place settings of dishes and silverware. Maybe Alex had a sense then that he'd be cramming not just essentials in his tiny rental house, but an entire life completely separate from Emily and her career at Barrett and Row Architects.

Washington High School, 1982-1983. Alex settled into the black futon and opened to the senior superlative spread. Along with "Most Likely to Succeed" and the other real categories, there was an inset with mock superlatives. Alex and Holly won "Most Likely to Get Married... Divorced... Married... Divorced," in honor of all the times they'd broken up and gotten back together. A small photo showed a cross-armed Holly with her back to Alex, who begged on bended knee. Alex hated the photo, except that it was a great shot of Holly's back side.

Their first break up had come in the middle of tenth grade at Sue Granger's party. After months as HHF's (hand-holding friends), Alex French-kissed Holly in front of a driveway full of friends as they sat on the hood of the Granger's station wagon. His friends whooped and hollered, which felt great until later when he and Holly were alone underneath the willow tree.

Holly said, "I'm not really ready for all that mushy stuff, are you?"

"Nah."

"So, you want to just be friends?"

"Sure."

But the summer before their junior year, after Holly's parents divorced, Alex and Holly got back together, and during round two, they rushed past the HHF stage.

Holly and her mom had moved to a townhouse a couple blocks from Alex's house, and Holly began sneaking over late at night. Alex might have returned the sneaking, as would have been the gentlemanly thing to do, but Holly's townhouse wasn't set up for it. Her second-story bedroom faced the road and lacked the standard tree limb leading to her window. Alex's bedroom, on the other hand, occupied the corner of a walk-out basement, which had sliding glass doors opening onto a back yard patio. His mom and dad and sister were all upstairs. Holly would tap on the sliding door until Alex woke up, and then they would sit together on the gold vinyl sofa in the rec room.

Their meetings followed two unspoken rules. One, they never planned them ahead of time, perhaps because that would seem too presumptuous. Two, they never ventured from the gold vinyl sofa into, say, Alex's bedroom, perhaps because this too would seem too presumptuous. Instead they stuck to unplanned trysts on the gold vinyl sofa.

From sliding glass door to gold vinyl sofa, they adhered to a ritual. Alex would kiss Holly's cheek and hold her hand as they crossed the moonlit linoleum and as he turned on the lamp with the pom-pom shade. Holly would set down her house keys on the driftwood table. Then they would sit on the gold vinyl sofa, which Alex's mom had exiled to this land of teenage basement-dwellers from the more fashionable upstairs. Its embossed surface was cracked and full of small holes, unredeemable by vinyl repair kits, and the once perky shine was dull after years of people peeling their skin from it.

They never had sex on the gold sofa. Maybe exposing that much skin to the vinyl seemed the sure path to an early flaying. Maybe Holly just wasn't ready. Maybe Alex felt afraid Holly would think he had a one-track mind, which of course he did. Maybe they were both just too afraid of pregnancy.

Regardless, this old sofa was the wardrobe to Narnia,

leading Alex to a secret world of intimacy, which, however innocent, imprinted Holly Dover on his heart forever. On some of these secret nights Holly and Alex didn't even kiss but just talked or watched TV like an old married couple. Sometimes Alex scratched her back or played with her hair.

But one September evening at the beginning of their junior year, everything changed.

Holly came over with a plate of homemade chocolate chip cookies. "Smell," she said, as she unfolded the towel that covered the warm cookies. He inhaled the chocolate steam as if it came from a bong.

"You made my favorite," he said, "at two o'clock in the morning. I can't believe your mom didn't wake up." He took the warm plate from her, cupped her chin and gave her a long, juicy kiss.

"We need milk," Holly said.

They held hands and teetered up the stairs like drunk people trying to stay quiet. Of course the basement door to the kitchen creaked. Of course Flash barked. Alex knelt down to appease the dog with a cookie, but as soon as Flash quieted, Holly burst into nervous, snorty laughter.

"Shhh," he said, smiling, but her shoulders kept shaking.

As Alex set down the cookie plate on the edge of the counter, a cookie slid off, much to Flash's delight. Alex grasped both of Holly's hands and leaned his forehead against hers.

He whispered, "If my parents wake up, we're dead."

For a few seconds Holly feigned seriousness then snorted again. Alex put three fingers over her lips, and she took exaggerated breaths through her nose. But when her giggling started again, Alex grabbed her hand and pulled her across the kitchen and into the pantry.

He pulled her flush up against him. She quieted. Parts of their bodies that had never touched before, touched. Alex felt bewitched and embarrassed by his body's involuntary reaction. He tried not to move. Then, without any lead-in, bursting forth from the stillness, Holly's historic restraint became unhinged, and she loosened her hands, hips, t-shirt, and bra. Her teeth were clenched—he never forgot that. This frantic needing made him wild. There was no time to fully undress and no room to lie down. He thought they could manage standing up. He was about to attempt the feat when he heard his mom's voice and saw a strip of light underneath the pantry door.

"Alexander, is that you?"

He pulled away painfully and turned on the pantry light.

"Yeah, it's me. I was just..." he zipped up his pants "... just getting some napkins for my cookies. Just a minute. I think I see some back here."

Holly put on her shirt and stuffed her bra into her pants pocket. Alex signaled for her to stand behind the door. He turned off the light and walked out, leaving the door open with Holly hidden behind it.

"Why were you in there with the door closed?" his mom asked.

"I don't know," he said with his best teenage belligerence.

His mother walked around Alex and turned the pantry light back on. She grabbed the doorknob just inches away from Holly's hip. She stood in the doorway and began scouring the shelves on the right side of the pantry. Was she looking for hidden drug paraphernalia? Did she suspect he'd chosen the kitchen pantry to shoot up?

"What's the problem?" Alex asked in a voice that no longer sounded anything but petrified.

His mom didn't answer but took two steps further into the pantry to examine the back wall of shelves. Then she turned to the left side of the pantry. Alex knew he was busted. He would be in so much trouble. His parents would probably ground him for a month, and worse, the night time visits would stop. But just as his mom was about to look behind the door, something crashed on the other side of the kitchen.

His mother dashed out of the pantry. Over near the door to the basement, Flash was growling at a broken plate and cookie crumbs. His front paws and chin lay flush against the floor while his bottom and wagging tail jutted up in the air.

"Flash," his mom said. "What in the world have you got?"

His mother and Alex walked over.

"Oh man, that stupid mutt ruined my cookies," Alex said, trying to sound annoyed but knowing that the stupid mutt had been a dues ex machina sent from above.

"Where'd you get the cookies?" Alex's mom asked.

"Holly brought them to me, today, at school."

"Alexander, it's 2:15 in the morning. Why are you up so late?"

"I was studying for a history test and I got hungry. Geez, I was just looking for a napkin. What'd you think I was doing?" More belligerence, it was his best defense.

"Just clean up the mess and go on to bed. Good night."

Alex cleaned and listened for several minutes before going back to the pantry. Holly had slumped in a pile on the floor. Alex lifted her chin and pretended to wipe sweat from his brow.

"I'd better go," she whispered.

In silence they tiptoed down the basement stairs to the sliding glass door. They didn't hug or kiss, and for the first time Alex whispered "I love you." Holly squeezed his hand but didn't reply.

That night was the very same night Holly's dad died in a car accident on Raymond Pike. When Holly arrived home at three o'clock in the morning, her mom was up waiting for her because she'd been awoken with the call about Mr. Dover. In hindsight, Alex believed Holly felt a triple dose of guilt—for not being there when the call came, for sneaking out behind her mom's back, and for almost going all the way. Part of her penance, it seemed, was to initiate break up number two.

Break up number two lasted all the way until the end of eleventh grade. All junior year Holly had pretty much ignored him until one night at Sue Granger's May Day party. The weekend before, Alex had taken Kate Arrington to the spring dance, and though he had no intention of taking her out again, their date had gotten Holly's attention. She came up to him on Sue's staircase and sat very close.

She put her hand on his knee. "Did you and Kate have a good time at the dance?"

"I guess. It was a nice passing of...*The Hours*," he said, making reference to their AP English reading, *Mrs. Dalloway*, which Virginia Woolf initially entitled *The Hours*.

"Oh geez," Holly said. "All those references to time. I can't wait to be done with it."

"I love it," he said. "How should we spend our time? Great question. Clarissa Dalloway spent a huge amount of time getting ready for her little dinner party, an event that wouldn't exactly change the world. Yet gathering people together like she did, like Sue is doing tonight," he motioned to the crowd in the basement, "it's a really important way to spend your time, don't you think?"

Holly grabbed Alex's hand. "Go for a drive with me."

They snuck out of the party and parked at a Burger King.

"Alex, I miss our talks about literature. I miss your hands. I miss laughing at your stupid jokes. I know I was awful to you when we broke up. My mom was furious about me sneaking over to your house and I was depressed about my dad. But I want to be with you again. I mean, I know you and Kate may have a thing so I don't want to mess that up..."

He cut her off with a kiss that began round three of their relationship.

Round three lasted until the night of their senior prom. After prom breakfast at Kate's, Alex drove Holly home, and in the driveway of her townhouse, for the third time, without much explanation, Holly broke up with him again. She gave some lame excuse about going to different colleges. Alex had felt her pulling away for a month or two beforehand: she'd become less available on the weekends, and sometimes she almost seemed embarrassed by him. Probably she'd been waiting to get through prom before dropping the bomb.

Over the next few years during college breaks, they had a few flickering moments, a long hug here, an emotional conversation there, until their junior year in college when Alex met Emily.

Alex set down the yearbook and grunted. How did he end up in this lonely house with a wife half a world away?

5

In her dream, Holly met Alex at the Tyson's Corner Hilton. He wore the tan suit from his senior picture, and he had his dog Flash with him. Alex started making out with Holly in the restaurant booth. He climbed on top of her, and just as she started to worry about the other diners, the booth turned into the gold sofa in Alex's basement. Fully clothed, Alex began rocking on top of her, faster and faster, until Peter's voice broke in.

"It fell in the potty!" Peter shouted from the hall bathroom.

"Ookie," Ethan yelled.

Holly opened her eyes. Her alarm clock read 6:30 am. Peter and Ethan were obviously up. Ted's side of the bed was empty since he was still in Nashville. Today was…Thursday, the day before she would get together with Alex. Whatever Peter and Ethan dropped in the potty, Holly didn't care. She closed her eyes and let her dream linger on her skin.

Alex had sent an e-mail the night before: "Hey Hol, let's grab a drink Friday night after the Casa Maria gathering, just the two of us. How about the little restaurant at the bottom of the Tyson's Corner Hilton? That's where I'm staying. I'll buy you your old favorite, a cranberry spritzer. We could add vodka."

The talk of spritzers was a decorous formality draped over his hotel proposition, like the useless sheet of tissue sent with a wedding invitation. Holly sent back her equally decorous RSVP: "I'd love to have spritzers together."

Ethan yelled from the bathroom, "Flush it! Flush it!"

"Don't flush!" Holly yelled as she yanked off her covers and raced towards the bathroom. When she got there, Peter was swirling the toilet water with a long plastic sword, trying to trap

Ethan's red toothbrush against the side of the bowl.

"Stop," she said. "I got it." She grabbed the toothbrush with her bare hand. "I don't want to know what happened. I don't care. I want you two to go play downstairs."

After washing the toothbrush and the plastic sword with watermelon hand-soap, Holly looked into the boys' mirror and tried to fluff her country-curtain hairstyle. Her pouf valance bangs fell back into place across her forehead, and the side panel drapes, with ruffle bottoms, fell back down to her shoulders. She tucked the sides behind her ears, which looked like two gaudy tiebacks. Alex would never be interested in starting something with Holly Sue Jo Bob. Not that he for sure wanted to start something—maybe he really just wanted to have drinks. But *if* he wanted to start something, he would surely change his mind when he saw this farcical square dancer.

Get thee to a cuttery, she thought. If her neighbor Judith could babysit the boys, Holly could slip off to a cheap walk-in salon and still stay within Ted's reunion budget.

Judith Ferrell, her sixty-something neighbor, was a woman of leisure who loved Holly's boys. She often babysat for free, but only during the daytime. At night, Judith drank. More than once Judith had staggered over in the evening and chatted loudly with a slur that went way beyond her Southern drawl.

When Holly called her that morning, Judith said, "Sure honey. A girl simply has to get her hair done before her reunion, so she can impress all the boys. Besides, I wanted to come over and show you my new Jonathan Miller outfit. It's darling, and I got it on major sale. I'll bring the boys' lunch. Oh, tell Ethan and Peter I have a little surprise for them."

Judith brought over pimento cheese sandwiches and the game Cooties, which she'd picked up at a garage sale. The Jonathan Miller outfit was a hideous rhinestone number. "It's so you" was all Holly could say about it. Judith and the boys quickly engaged in Cootie building while Holly slipped out to the minivan.

On 97.3 they played "Stayin' Alive," and Holly sang along with the Bee Gees. The prism danced on its nylon string.

Sunshine refracted through the crystal cuts, and dozens of tiny, flickering rainbows waved around the dashboard. Her father was the strobe light to her karaoke performance.

At the hair salon, Holly looked at sexy hair books while she waited for the twenty-something stylist with the clunky shoes and slinky dress. Karen was her name. Once in her chair, Karen snapped the black plastic smock around Holly's neck and agreed that the style on page 23 would work well with Holly's square face. Karen held the entire outcome of Holly's reunion in her scissor-wielding hands.

Underneath the smock Holly folded her hands together as if in prayer. Five-inch strands of blonde hair snowed down around her, along with any chance of a rescue by barrettes. The sounds of quick, reckless snipping accompanied the hair droppings. Did the model on page 23 look hip, or did she look like an angry man-hater? Karen never spoke the entire time she worked, which Holly translated as, "Oops."

Finally, the snipping ceased, followed by rigorous kneading and goop. Karen spun the chair towards the mirror. Holly slowly raised her head.

This time, the mirror had something nice to say. Holly looked artsy and so much younger. What a really nice mirror!

Holly tipped Karen $5, which at the Clip and Save was 50%. Next stop, the mall to find cheap funky jewelry for her black dress.

She and her hair swaggered towards the Belk jewelry department. But on the way the Victoria's Secret mannequin in turquoise bra and panties seduced Holly. An hour and $150 later, Holly left the mall without any jewelry but with the turquoise underwear set and a maroon teddy, purchased with non-traceable cash she'd gotten from the mall ATM, "spending money for the reunion" if Ted were to ask.

Ted called from Nashville on Friday morning. "Are you all

packed for your reunion?" he asked.

Holly swallowed. Her maroon teddy was all packed. Her turquoise bra and underwear were laying out on her bed. "Almost," she said. "The boys are ready, but my suitcase has a little way to go. I got my hair cut really short yesterday."

"Uh-huh. Hey, have you gotten a chance to pick up my dry cleaning?"

"No, Ted, I've been by myself all week, managing the kids *and* trying to get ready for my reunion. You have several clean shirts in the closet."

"Just not my blue Geoffrey Beene. I have a big meeting first thing on Monday."

Holly looked at the clock. "Maybe I can squeeze it in this morning."

"Thanks. Are you excited about seeing your high school buds?"

"Yeah. Kate and Sue and...some other folks are meeting at a Mexican restaurant tonight. Casa Maria's. We used to hang out there all the time in high school. They have the best salsa in the world."

"Is your old boyfriend going to be there? The absent-minded professor?"

"Alex? I think so. Then on Saturday night, Kate and I are going to be each other's date because her husband Jimmy can't make it either."

Ted whispered to someone, "Sure, I'll be there in a sec." To Holly he said, "Uh-huh. Kate and Jimmy will be there..."

"No, not Jimmy, just Kate. Anyway, the boys are looking forward to spending time with Grandma. She wants to take them to the Air and Space Museum if she can get a contract signed today on a big house. Otherwise the boys will play lots of video games while grandma works."

"Hang on, Holly." She heard Ted cover the phone and say, "It's in a folder on Sonya's desk."

"So," Holly said, while Ted continued talking to his colleague, "I'm going to do a striptease dance at the reunion. I think my classmates are going to love it."

"Uh-huh," Ted replied. "Excellent. Well listen Holly, I hope you have a great trip."

After hanging up, Holly got the kids situated in front of the television with juice boxes and granola bars, counting on the magic of *Barney* to anesthetize them while she showered and dressed. Television was the extended family Holly didn't have. Since there were no grandmas or cousins living in her house, or next door, or down the street, she relied on her Great Aunt Television to help with the kids. The kids behaved beautifully for their Aunt, hardly ever fighting in her presence, hardly ever moving in her presence. Aunt Television had such steady control over Peter and Ethan. What would Holly have done without her?

True to precedent, Aunt Television held the boys, and Holly took a long hot shower without interruption. Afterwards, Holly towel dried her new short hairdo and wrapped the towel around her body. She looked in the mirror to fluff the spikes the way Karen the hairdresser had.

She gasped.

A giant, red disaster blazed on her cheek beside her nose. Not just a zit, this was the zit that ate Tokyo. No, it was too big to even be classified as a zit. It was a cyst deserving its own name—Mars, the red planet. Not since she was pregnant with Ethan had she gotten such a doozy.

She let her towel drop to the floor and looked at the rest of her body. Besides the two points of attraction, Holly didn't have much except girth. She regretted everything she'd ever eaten. But eating had been the one part of her life she could control. Her wall to wall children could invade her privacy from room to room to even bathroom, but they couldn't invade her mouth; they couldn't prevent her from rewarding herself with small bursts of epicurean pleasure. Eating had taken the place of smoking after she'd gotten pregnant, and unlike smoking, eating was morally and socially acceptable. She could have her cake and be a good mom too. But now she cursed those years of having her cake.

Alex might be able to look past the cake-lovin' bod, but how could anyone get past THE ZIT. Who was she kidding?

Alex would take one look at her and laugh. No, he was too kind to laugh. He would take her to the Hilton restaurant as planned, and for an obligatory 45 minutes they would talk and sip spritzers while Alex tried not to stare at her cheek. Then Alex would claim extreme exhaustion and say good night.

Well, if Alex wasn't able to accept her new little zit pal, then it just wasn't meant to be. She wondered what she meant by "it." A fling? An affair? A divorce?

If per chance they did get past THE ZIT, her new turquoise underwear would help. She went to grab the underwear off her bed where she had laid it. The panties were there, but the bra was not. She looked in her suitcase, her dresser drawer, the bathroom, and the laundry tub in their closet. No bra. Possibly it had gotten caught up with the laundry load still in the dryer.

In towel and turquoise painties, Holly headed downstairs.

"Boing, boing, boing," Holly heard from the powder room.

"Barney and Baby Bop love jumping!" Peter said.

"Boing, boing, boing," Ethan repeated.

Inside the powder room Peter and Ethan were making their plastic figures jump up and down, up and down. Upon closer inspection, Holly saw that Barney and Baby Bop were jumping on a makeshift trampoline made of one turquoise bra stretched between the bathroom doorknob and the toilet handle.

"What the hell have you done?" Holly shouted.

Peter quit making Barney jump. "It's a trampoline. See the springs?"

They had drawn black magic marker "springs" around the edge of each cup, and even without untying the knots that attached to toilet and door, she could see the rippled, stretched-out elastic of the shiny bra straps.

"It's ruined. RUINED. You stupid …get up," Holly yelled. "GET UP, I said."

The boys stood. Holly squeezed both their chins and made them look up at her. "That's what I was going to WEAR today. To my REUNION. Why did you think it was on my bed? Huh? I spent a fortune. I wanted for once in my life to do something for me, but you idiots always have to…" Holly roared a subhuman roar.

"You're hurting my chin," Peter whimpered.

"Damn right. Now go to your rooms. I don't want to see your stupid faces. NOW or I'll spank the crap out of you." She pushed Peter's face away and accidentally scratched him.

"Owww," he wailed. "You hurt my chin." He ran out of the bathroom.

Ethan lagged behind. "GO," she screamed.

Holly tried to untie the bra. "I HATE my life."

Her anger stole her dexterity and she could not undo the knots. She slumped down beside the toilet with her back against wall. "I hate my life. I hate my stupid life." She banged her head to the rhythm of her chant. "I hate my life. I hate my stupid life." With each dull thud she transferred the violence she felt towards her kids back onto herself. What kind of mother was she? The boys were an intrusive, snot-nosed presence in her life, but she had no place calling them names or grabbing their faces. They were just little kids. She was afraid she was becoming abusive.

Eventually the pain she inflicted against her head helped restore her equilibrium. She looked at her watch and saw that it was 10:30, her intended departure time. She untied the bra, which she threw in the kitchen trashcan, and calmly walked upstairs to check on the boys.

Peter lay on his bed holding Big Bear. He'd been laying there forever. He looked at his Pokemon poster on the wall. Gengar's big red eyes pointed down at his bed. His friend Justin had a big brother, Jake, who knew everything. Jake said if you felt cold, it meant a gengar was in the room stealing your heat. It must be true, because Peter felt cold, even under his covers.

His mommy came into his room. She said, "Peter, honey, I'm sorry I was mean." But Peter and Big Bear did NOT turn around. She sat on his bed and scratched his back. "I don't blame you for not wanting to talk," she said and kept on scratching. "How is your chin? Can I see?"

Peter turned over and his mommy looked at his boo boo. It didn't hurt anymore, but she went to get a Band-aid anyway. It was a Pokemon Band-Aid with a bunch of little Pikachus.

"Mommy, sorry we were bad."

"You're not bad. I'm sorry I called you an idiot. Mommy just gets frustrated when everything she does gets messed up and she can't do anything according to plan. Can you forgive me?"

"Yeah," he said.

"You're a great boy. You deserve the best. The truth is, I'm just an idiot mom."

Peter thought for a moment and then said, "But you're good at drawing."

"Yeah, I'm good at drawing."

Ethan walked into Peter's room.

Mommy said, "Ethan, I'm sorry I yelled at you."

Ethan said, "That's okay. Have you seen my gray Power Ranger?"

Ethan ALWAYS lost his toys. He did NOT take care of his things.

Holly, wearing old graying bra and panties underneath old t-shirt and jeans, loaded up the minivan. The trunk was piled with preemptive car-trip items: pillows, stuffed animals, toys, books on tape, food. She had tried talking Ted into purchasing a portable VCR for the trip, but he said it was too expensive.

Delayed departure time: 11:45.

It had started raining, and Holly stood under the protection of the trunk door, trying to think of anything else she might have forgotten. She looked one more time in her purse for the reunion ticket.

Ethan flew around the back of the van. "I want gum," he said. "Peter said you have gum."

He yanked so hard at Holly's purse that the strap ripped off of one side. Her purse fell into a puddle, spewing sunglasses, tampons, and the coveted pack of gum.

Ethan dove for it.

"No way, Ethan." She grabbed his shoulders. "No. Leave the gum alone. Damn it. How many times have I told you not to grab my purse strap? What else are you guys going to ruin this morning? Get in your car seat, NOW."

She gathered up her purse contents, slung her broken purse onto the passenger seat, and cranked up the ignition.

"Seat belt!" Ethan cried.

Holly turned and gasped at his unbuckled car seat.

"I forgot..." she stammered. She got out of the driver's seat and slid open the van door. "I got so flustered..." She buckled Ethan into his seat. "Ethan, you completely unravel me. Geez."

"Sippy!" he demanded.

Holly rolled her eyes. Always one more thing.

Ethan's yellow sippy cup should have been back in the trunk with all the other preemptive car trip items, but she couldn't find it. "Did you take it from the to-go pile?" she asked. "The one by the door?"

"Juice. Juice. Juice."

Holly stomped back inside the house and found the sippy cup on Ethan's bed, where it had leaked onto the bedspread. Toys had reappeared on the floor despite her multiple sweeps. The toys always returned. Again she gathered them into Ethan's basket to avoid a housekeeping lecture from Ted upon their return. A loud honk sounded from the garage, meaning Peter had gotten out of his booster seat. Holly dashed back to the garage, but the only damage was a blaring car radio that she turned off.

"Peter, you are not allowed to get out of your booster seat. I swear." She handed Ethan his sippy cup. "Listen boys, if you behave, we can listen to *Winnie the Pooh*. Okay? The more you behave, the quicker we can get to Grandma's house."

Holly glanced at the rearview mirror to make sure Peter had latched himself in. In the mirror she caught sight of THE ZIT. The sweat and grease on her face made it shine like a

Christmas ornament. Holly screeched out of the driveway and sped away from her house.

Rain began to really pour. Holly turned on the headlights and windshield wipers, but the old, dull wipers just smeared the water.

They sped through town and onto Odell Highway, booking along until they got behind a muddy green tractor going 30 miles an hour. The driver wore a black rain slicker and straw hat, and he looked nonplussed about the rain. The minivan and tractor crept over two hills before a break came in the double yellow lines. Holly pulled into the passing lane. She saw an oncoming car, but it seemed a long way off. As she reached neck and neck with the tractor, Ethan shrieked a nerve-shattering shriek.

"Give it to me," Ethan yelled.

"NO," Peter shrieked.

A small, hard object hit Holly on the side of her head behind her ear. She swerved right, almost side-swiping the tractor, then overcorrected by jerking the steering wheel to the left. Through the blurry windshield she saw the oncoming car.

6

Holly awoke, entombed by darkness except for the sad glow behind her. Angels spoke in hushed voices. A white shroud lay heavy on her body, and metal bars ran along her sides. She was afraid to look through the bars, imagining thousands of identical tombs on her left and right. Yet this graveyard smelled oddly like Listerine, more sterile than the afterlife she'd imagined. And death had not brought an end to her pounding headache.

"120 over 70," the angel in white whispered to the other, their backs towards Holly.

"Atta girl," said the one who wore purple flowers instead of white. "Lovely pulse."

Not lovely, awful, pulsing pain into her head. Too much pain for heaven.

Plastic tubing joined her arm to a pole, tethering her to this earthly world. The plastic tubing told her she'd not made it to heaven after all, just a hospital. The world would hold onto her a while longer, subjecting her to its atrophies, including windshield wipers that quit working the exact day of a rainstorm.

That was her first memory, the dull windshield wipers. She was supposed to replace the wiper blades when she got her oil changed, but she was proud just to have taken care of the oil. The wiper blades had merely smudged the fat raindrops onto the windshield.

"And the boy in ICU?" the nurse in purple flowers asked.

The nurse in white answered, "Bagged and tagged, I'm afraid."

Holly's stomach dropped and she clenched her fists. The second memory hit: her tires screeched, the lake rushed madly towards the nose of the van, and her crystal necklace swung off the rearview mirror, stopping in midair, just like her memory. Were the boys with her? What boy in ICU? What boy was bagged and tagged?

She willed her fists to become Salvador Dali clocks, melting onto the mattress. Her eyelids oozed shut.

Burnt orange vibrated inside her eyelids, the color of the earth's molten core, the color of daytime. People spoke in daytime voices now, with no attempt at angel whispers, especially the loud man nearby. She opened her eyes. The sunlight tunneled into her pupils and detonated in the center of her forehead. She reached for her head and found a small bandage surrounded by short greasy hair. Her long blonde hair was gone.

The loud man at the end of her bed talked on his cell phone, his back towards her. At one time she had thought it a good idea to marry this man, who liked to talk loudly on his phone in public settings. The ever-important Ted Reese still looked good in dress shirt and slacks, but naked, not so much. Ted hadn't gotten fat, just cylindrical. Add a mustache and specs and he was a young Teddy Roosevelt.

"Elizabeth," he said into his phone, "you're not coming because of a real estate deal?" He was talking to her mother. Her mother prided herself on 24-hour accessibility.

Another voice came from the doorway. "Knock, knock," the voice said.

Holly shut her eyes. Knock, knock. Who's there? Orange. Orange who? Orange like the inside of my eyelids. The visitor was Sue Granger, her old friend, but Holly didn't want to talk to Sue or Ted or anyone else. Instinctively she wanted to stay "asleep," curled safely under the white sheets, where no one would ask anything of her.

"I have to go, Elizabeth," Ted said. "Sue Granger just showed up. Strange—she was able to take time off work."

Did he have to act ugly to her mother? Did he have to raise his voice while her head throbbed? She heard him shuffle away from the end of the bed to the door.

"Sue," Ted boomed. "Hello there. It's so kind of you to come all the way from DC. Holly will appreciate it. She's still sleeping—has been since yesterday. Holly's mother is going to check in by *phone*. She's in the middle of a bidding war on a whopper house in McLean."

"Brrr. That's Mrs. Dover for you. I guess she planned to drag Ethan and Peter to these negotiations while Holly did reunion stuff?"

The reunion. She was heading to her fifteen-year high school reunion. Hi, I'm Holly Reese, stay-at-home mom, defunct artist, squanderer of potential. And you, you're a brain surgeon? Well good for you, bitch.

Ethan and Peter. They were going to stay with her mom during the reunion. They must have been in the minivan.

Ted answered, "Elizabeth doesn't hesitate to drag the boys with her while she wheels and deals," Ted said. "The boys don't mind. They get to play their Gameboys for long stretches. How long was your drive to Charlotte?"

"I made pretty good time. Left this morning around 9:00, so…five hours, fifteen minutes. D.C. traffic's a cinch on Saturday."

A machine beeped and Sue gasped. Long steady beeps continued.

"I'll run grab a nurse," Ted said.

Where would he grab her? The nurse came in and made the beeping stop. In a sweet, preschool teacher's voice she announced that she was checking Holly's IV to make sure it was "snug as a little bug in a rug." She lifted Holly's elbow ever so gently, ever so lovingly, but then the secret sadist ripped the tape from Holly's arm. Holly suppressed a scream and pictured her blonde arm-hair all over the tape. When the nurse jiggled the needle further into Holly's vein, Holly hoped no one saw her jaw clench. The nurse re-taped the needle and reverted back to sweetness and light. "She's all set now, ready to roll."

48

"I *hate* the beeping machines," Sue said after the nurse's footsteps trailed away. "Before my husband Jack died we lived at the hospital for three and a half weeks. I learned to handle the smell of vomit, I learned to eat the hospital food, which sometimes looked like vomit, but I never got used to those damned beeping machines."

Holly had never heard Sue talk about the beeping machines. When she talked about Jack, she liked to talk about the less depressing times during their three-year marriage, like the time Jack met the president and called him Bill.

"The beeps are very unnerving," Ted agreed. "I'm so sorry about your husband. Holly said he was a real character."

"So," Sue continued, "I got Holly this green plant instead of flowers because flowers always made Jack sad. I'll set it over here on the window." Sue clomped across the room in what Holly pictured were mannish power shoes. "When the flowers withered after three days, they reminded Jack that three more days had passed with him still in the hospital. Holly probably doesn't need a stupid plant—I don't even know if she wants visitors—but I had to come, and I had to bring her *something*. Ted, I'm so sorry about the accident."

Bile surged into Holly's throat. The word "accident" recalled the sickening memory—screeching tires, lake, flying necklace. Her head got sweaty. This scrap of memory terrified her.

"We got the news last night while we were waiting at Casa Maria's," Sue said. "Kate cried and Alex Meyers choked on a tortilla chip and coughed for like ten minutes. We were all in shock."

Alex Meyers, Most Kissable Freckle.

"My mom was the one that called me. Holly's mom had called her. At least Mrs. Dover found time to do *that*."

Ted snickered.

"Even before I told the others, I decided I had to drive down to Charlotte. Holly and I go way back. Kate said she wanted to come too, except she's breastfeeding. Do you people in North Carolina not breastfeed? Kate can't travel and breastfeed? She's so lame."

Kate Arrington, Holly's best friend from high school, chose not to visit her in the hospital because the trip would disrupt her baby's precision feeding schedule. Holly's own mother also chose not to inconvenience herself. It was just as well. Holly didn't want to talk to anyone about the accident, least of all Kate and her mother.

"It was really kind of you to drive down," Ted said, "and all by yourself. I hate that you'll miss your reunion tonight."

"They'll just have to mail me my Queen of the Reunion tiara. Kate and Alex both sent cards. Alex dropped off his card at my mom's house early this morning, but Kate, of course, asked me to drive all the way to her house to get her card—because of the *baby*. I'll set them here beside the plant."

A card from Alex Meyers. Did he sign it "Sincerely" or "Love"?

"Tell me what the doctor's are saying," Sue said.

Ted cleared his throat. "Because the minivan hit water instead of a hard object, the airbag never went off. So Holly's head banged against the steering wheel. It's only seven stitches, but the concussion's pretty bad. The CAT scan showed a small blood clot, which should resolve itself without surgery. But she keeps sleeping, and she hasn't talked yet. I'm getting a little worried."

Sue paused, "They don't think she'll have permanent, or rather, ongoing, um, cognitive issues, do they?"

"Temporary cognitive issues, killer headaches, some dizziness and nausea, hopefully nothing permanent. It's weird that she won't talk."

Footsteps entered the room. Holly continued her "sleeping." A droplet of sweat ran down the back of her neck.

"Sue," Ted said, "this is our son Peter. Can you say 'Hi' to Ms. Granger?"

"Hi Ms. Granger," Peter said in his proud gravelly voice that strived for adult formality but remained kindergarten cute. Peter was okay.

"It's good to meet you Peter. Your mom and I have been

friends since we were about your age. How are you feeling?"

"I got a strap burn. I thought seat belts were good for you, but really, they can burn."

Peter and Ethan had definitely been in the minivan when it nosed toward the lake.

"Does it hurt?" Sue asked.

"A little."

"Tell Miss Granger about how brave you were," Ted said.

"I got my booster seat and seat belt undone all by myself, underwater, and I climbed through the window."

"Wow, I'm glad to meet such a brave boy."

"Thank you," Peter said.

Sue hesitated. "I'm sorry about Ethan."

A pause filled the room, like a moment of silence. Holly's brave boy, Peter, had rescued himself, but Ethan wouldn't have known how. Oh God, what had she done? Had the nurses been referring to Ethan when they talked about the boy in ICU? Was Ethan "bagged and tagged?" Panic rose in her chest. Ethan didn't know how to undo his car seat. How high did the water get? Why were the windows open? Oh God.

"Peter?" Ted said, "Would you mind going back to the lounge with your Gameboy? Thanks, buddy."

Ted didn't want to talk about Ethan in front of Peter. Holly suppressed a scream.

"Sorry," Sue said. "I obviously don't have kids. From my experience with Jack, I got so used to talking head on about illness and death. Sorry."

Oh God.

"They have Ethan downstairs in the…" Ted's voice went high.

"I'm so sorry, Ted. Why does bad shit have to happen to a three year-old?"

Oh God. Ethan was downstairs in the morgue, bagged and tagged. She had driven him into the lake. How long had he struggled underwater before he gave up? Oh God. She refused to hear any more. Holly turned over onto her stomach; the sheets and pillow rustled in her ears. Rustle, rustle, rustle.

"Holly?" Ted roared. "I think Holly's awake!" He shook her shoulder. "Holly? Are you awake? Honey, can you hear me?"

Holly kept still. Still "asleep." Unable to hear that Ethan was dead.

Ted was glad when Sue left to check into her hotel and when they found an *Andy Griffith* rerun for Peter in the lounge. Ted just wanted to sit quietly with Holly, alone. He felt completely exhausted. He'd gotten the news Friday afternoon during a meeting with Torrence Pipes and caught the next flight from Nashville to Charlotte. For over 24 hours he'd interfaced with airlines, doctors, policemen, and now visitors. The night before he'd slept maybe an hour with Peter, who had begged to sleep with him.

A drop of blood had soaked through the bandage where Holly's hair met her forehead. The shaving and bandaging must have been easier with Holly's new haircut. He'd been a little miffed when Holly cut off her hair without telling him, but the new haircut did make her look cool, like the Holly he first knew. Ted lowered the rail so he could sit on the side of her bed. He lifted Holly's limp hand to his lips and kissed her wedding ring. They'd only been dating a month when he found the one carat marquis of perfect clarity and color, but he didn't give it to her right away. He waited until several months later.

Holly was so different than the other girls he'd dated: than Courtney, the happy slappy preschool teacher who chalked up his dad's latest affair to "just a midlife crisis"; or Cheryl, the accounting major who wanted to watch TV every weekend; or Margaret with the quilted Bible cover and little-girl headbands. Holly, on the other hand, was an artist who smoked and wore gypsy earrings. She took Ted to the Russell Museum sculpture garden and asked him questions no one had ever asked him. Her red living room had a giant daisy she'd painted on the wall and stacks of books and a crazy music collection.

Please, God, let her be okay. Her face was so pale. Please God.

For months Ted kept meaning to take the minivan into the dealership to replace the recalled tires, but Ted had been crazy busy, juggling a million contracts, trying to build up his stats. Still, he should have made the time so Holly and the boys wouldn't have had to drive in the rain on bum tires.

Please, God, let her be okay.

Daddy and Peter left the hospital for the night. The car ride scared Peter, just like it did that morning and just like the night before. Ms. Granger called him a brave boy, but he didn't feel brave now. He told his daddy again and again that he needed his booster seat. Tonight his daddy yelled to shut up about the stupid booster. His daddy said "shut up" *and* "stupid."

Peter's mommy had yelled at him pretty good, too, right before the crash. He shouldn't of throwed his Obi Wan at Ethan, even if Ethan did take his Pikachu and throwed it at Mommy's head. Peter was bad sometimes and sometimes his mommy didn't like him. She never saw the bad things Ethan did. Ethan was always taking his stuff and breaking it. Peter felt bad, though. He wasn't suppose to hate people but sometimes he HATED his brother and sometimes he even hated HER.

Right before they crashed, he heard the choo choo train and said the sneezing rhyme, "Ahh-choooo, God bless youuu." He never forgot to say it, never once. Sometimes his mommy forgot, but he never did.

Then the van squeaked real loud. It hit the lake. It wasn't hard but it wasn't soft. Peter's forehead almost hit the back of Mommy's seat and his shoulder hurt. He felt water on his legs. Did he pee? No. The lake was coming into the van. It smelled like pee. "Mommy!" he yelled, "Help, Mommy." But Mommy didn't answer. He knew how to undo his booster seat. It was easy. Just push the orange button and pull the straps over. He couldn't see the button under the water but he knew just where it was. Presto! The water was cold. It covered all of him except his face. He reached for the head thing on the front seat, the seat with the airbag where they weren't allowed to sit, and pulled his way to the front seat. Mommy was sleeping in the water and her arms floated. "Wake up, Mommy." She was always so tired. Peter crawled out of the window and sat on the door. The window was rolled down inside the door. He was sitting on top of the window!

The fisherman came toward him.

"Hang on, I'm coming," said the man. He was kinda running in the water and splashing and swimming. At first he had a fishing pole, but then he dropped it in the water. Bye bye fishing pole. The man got to the van and asked Peter, "Is it just your mommy in the van?"

"My little brother is in the back. He can't undo his car seat yet, like me."

The man smushed Peter to one side and climbed in through the van window, feet first. He kneeled on the front seat and leaned over to Mommy. All Peter could see was his big butt. His big butt went into the water and then soon Mommy floated out of her side of the van.

"I'm bringing your mom around to you. What's your name?"

"Peter."

"Peter, I want you to hold onto your mom's collar and try to make sure her mouth and nose stay out of the water. I'm going to scoot around you again and get your brother."

His mommy had a bleeding booboo on her head. She was still sleeping. Once, the water made her head turn and she throwed up water. Peter didn't know it was possible to throw up in your sleep. One time he throwed up in the middle of the night, but he woke up first, grabbed his tummy, and then throwed up. Peter held on tight to his mommy, just the way the man said. His mommy's nose went under once, but just for a second and the man never saw.

The man pushed Ethan out through Peter's window, and

the man came out too. He smushed Peter again and it hurt his side but he held on to his mommy's shirt. Ethan was sleeping too. The man carried Ethan like a rock-a-bye baby and began to kiss him on the lips. Maybe he knew Ethan. Lots of people knew Ethan. He kept giving Ethan little kisses all the way to the shore. He put Ethan on the sand and put his ear on Ethan's lips. Did the man want a kiss back?

The man came back to the van and got Mommy and carried her to the beach, where he put her right next to Ethan. He didn't kiss Mommy. Peter felt something on his leg under the water. He reached down and felt a strap and pulled it up. Mommy's purse with the gum. The man got back to Peter.

"Peter, I want you to get on my back."

"I found Mommy's purse!"

"Here, you hold onto my shoulders. I got the purse."

"Betcha can't kiss me piggy back."

"Listen, when I get you to the shore, I want you to lie down against the back of your brother to keep him warm. I'm going to walk up to the road and flag down some help."

Peter didn't want to lie down in the ookie sand but he obeyed. He was tired. Ethan felt very cold. Peter snuggled against him and took a little nap until he heard the sirens.

After Ted and Peter left, Holly looked across the hospital room at the navy duffle bag Ted had brought her. The corner of a Ziploc baggie poked up from the partly open zipper. She'd overheard Peter and Ted discussing it: someone, she wasn't clear who, had put in a Ziploc baggie the contents of her black leather purse, which was now ruined by lake water.

She remembered something. Even before the lake, her purse had already been ruined. Ethan had ripped off the strap trying to find her stash of gum. This was before she ran inside to fetch his yellow sippy cup, which she'd found wedged between Turtle and JuJu, part of the stuffed animal ensemble on his bed.

No matter how messy the rest of his room got, Ethan always lined up his stuffed animals in the same order. Oh God. Would they start referring to his room as "Ethan's old room"? What would they do with all his stuffed animals? What would they do with Ethan? She pictured him in the morgue downstairs. Oh God. She had to get away from the morgue.

Holly yanked off the tape around her IV. The needle slid out, smooth like a trombone, leaving just one droplet of blood that she dabbed with the white sheet. From peeking at one of the nurses, she knew to turn off the IV with the green dial.

Nursing was the easy part. Getting up was harder. Holly's head weighed ten thousand pounds, and yellow spots clouded her eyes. She waited until the urge to vomit passed. She made her way over to the chair and clunked down. Centuries passed while she took off her hospital gown and put on the clothes Ted had packed. For several more centuries she waited in the chair, gathering strength before getting back on her feet.

She stood and waited for the bees to stop buzzing; then she walked over to gather the get-well cards from the window. Alex's white envelope said "TO HOLLY" in his left-leaning uppercase print. She put his card and the others in the duffle. In the mirror above the hospital room sink, Holly examined her appearance. Gently, she leaned over the sink and splashed water on her face. With wet fingers she fluffed her dirty hair and coaxed strands over her bald spot and stitches. Lipstick, a lake water survivor, helped with her paleness.

She practiced the confident yet slow stride of a healthy hospital visitor back and forth across her room, relaxing her eyebrows and neck, which wanted to give away her pain. She lightened the weight of the duffle bag by removing a large shampoo and conditioner. Then she opened her door and walked past the nurse's station, down the elevator, and out the front doors of Presbyterian Hospital.

SECTION II
HARRIER
HAWK

Northern Harrier, Circus cyaneus: Low flying raptor. White streaks on brown body. Nomadic nesting sites. Polygamous.

1

Holly stumbled in darkness across the Presbyterian parking lots to a Shell gas station next door. Her dry throat begged for juice, which she found in the large wall of refrigerators. Kiwi-strawberry. The clerk didn't comment on Holly's Ziploc purse.

Outside the Shell, Holly sipped her drink and leaned against the wall next to the glass doors, her duffle bag by her feet. If she had a tin cup, people might give her money. A tall, graying man stopped and said what a chilly night, kindly ignoring her vagrancy. His name was John; it said so on his nametag. She introduced herself as...Victoria, just in case he was a weirdo. They chit-chatted long enough for Holly to find out that John was a truck driver heading to Atlanta, a place as good as any. Holly asked if she could hitch a ride, and John said he'd be happy to have her company.

"Do I have a second to make a quick phone call?" she asked.

"Sure thing, Victoria. I'm not in too big a hurry."

Holly balanced her head on her shoulders and walked to the outdoor payphone. Her phone number came to her as she saw its pattern on the keypad. A down-pointing isosceles --709, a right triangle--974, a zig right, left, right--7613. The sound of her own voice came on— "We can't come to the phone right now..." She closed her throbbing eyes in order to focus on her message for Ted.

"Hi, it's me," she stammered. "I'm leaving town for a while. I have to get away. I can't face it all. Thanks for handling everything. Tell Peter I love him..."

John was leaning against his rig, smoking. Once she got

near enough to smell it, the tobacco smoke triggered the desire of her old habit. Smoking used to relax her and went hand in hand with her best creative ideas, her deepest talks, and her greatest times of solitude.

"You mind?" John asked. "I forgot to tell you I'm a smoker."

"No problem. In fact, do you have a spare?"

He shook out a Marlboro from his pack and offered her his yellow Bic lighter. After taking a long satisfying drag, her first in over six years, Holly told him she was ready to head for Hotlanta. Casually she tossed her duffle onto the front seat and climbed into the truck cab, as if she'd been hitchhiking for years. She startled, though, when John cranked up the roaring truck engine.

John seemed nice enough. In his late fifties, he'd driven a truck for 33 years because he got antsy staying in one place for long. Life on the road suited him, although he missed his new grandbaby, Charles, who was a 10 pound, 2 ounce bruiser with John's nose and his daughter's serious eyes.

"You got any kids, Victoria?"

Holly nodded but she couldn't get the words out. She closed her eyes.

"You sick?" John asked. "I seen your stitches and hospital bracelet. You act mighty puny."

Holly opened her eyes and took a puff of her Marlboro. "Oh no. I'm feeling great. Hunkey dorey. Yeah, I keep forgetting to cut this thing off. Do you have a pocketknife or anything?"

As John's fingers searched the compartment underneath the dash, unknown objects clunked around. Holly froze. Maybe he wasn't looking for a pocketknife. A small pistol could fit into this cubby, or a can of mace, or the jeweled hand of one of his victims. Holly peeked at John's face from the corner of her eye. He stared out the windshield in a creepy trance. Did the truck smell strange? She eyed the door handle.

"Here you go," John said. He placed a perfectly normal, perfectly closed Swiss army knife on the seat between them. "I knew I had a pocketknife in here,"

Holly unclenched her teeth and breathed. Her cigarette shook as she brought it to her mouth.

"I was just thinking," John said, "if you're sick, you probably don't want to be smoking. I mean, I know I shouldn't smoke at all, period, but I try cut it back when I'm sick, is all I'm saying."

She snuffed out her cigarette in the ashtray between them. It was about finished anyway. With the tiny scissors of John's pocketknife she cut off her I.D. bracelet. She cranked open her window and let the wind blow her hand backwards, then let the bracelet blow away. Bye-bye. The wind and the regal height of the truck cab gave her the sense that she was zooming above and beyond the fray. Drowsiness soon set in. She closed the window and leaned against the door.

3 hours later, when John announced that they were in Atlanta, Holly awoke from an intense nap, disoriented and newly suspicious. Not until she saw four green highway signs did she believe that they had in fact made it to Atlanta and not some back woods full of murdered hitchhikers.

They'd gotten there quickly, thanks to John's fuzz buster. At 11:30 John dropped her at the airport Holiday Inn, where he'd stayed before and eaten a mighty decent bear claw from the continental breakfast. She tried to give him a twenty out of her plastic baggie, but he refused it. John came around and helped her down.

"Good luck, Victoria."

That night Holly dreamt she wore her black reunion dress for her ride on the back of the Corvette convertible. She waved to the homecoming crowd. Alex waited in the middle of the football field. Her father drove.

"Faster, Daddy, faster."

Her father stepped on the accelerator and zoomed off the high school track, through the grassy area by the concessions, across the school parking lot, and down Raymond Pike. Her Farah Fawcett hair flew flag-like behind her. When she saw the bend in the road and the tree, she jumped off the car and rolled onto someone's front lawn, TV detective style. Her father continued speeding past the gas station towards the bend.

"STOP," she yelled.

His car crashed into the tree and caught fire. She walked down the road, watching police cars and ambulances gather. The sirens pulsated inside her chest. She crossed the police tape and looked inside the burning car. A figure lay in the back seat, crushed by metal, enveloped by flames, surrounded by demons. She expected to see her father, as was standard in the dream, but when one of the demons leaned she saw that the figure behind him was Ethan.

The yellow-eyed demon turned towards her and growled, "Holleee."

Holly awoke with a scream. The nightmare was back. She'd had it often the first couple years after her father's accident, but it had stopped by her freshman year of college. Now the dream was back, featuring Ethan.

She couldn't go through it all again—police reports, the mangled body pieced back together for the viewing, orange make-up over sunken cheekbones. This time, the casket would be junior-sized. She couldn't field the sad march of casseroles or sort through Ethan's belongings. Where would she put JuJu and his other eleven stuffed animal friends? Ted would handle everything just fine without her, in his efficient, business-like manner. He might convince his equally efficient mother, Olga, with her days-of-the-week dishtowels, to take time off work to come help him.

The "what ifs" came as they always did after the dream. In high school it was: What if Holly had gone to live with her father instead of her mother? The summer after the divorce, her father wanted Holly to live with him, but she chose to stay at her mom's house, near Alex. What if she hadn't gone over to Alex's that night? Now the questions were: What if Holly had decided not to go to the reunion? What if she had gotten the windshield wipers fixed?

Her dad's accident had happened the night she and Alex almost had sex in his kitchen pantry. Holly walked home from the Meyer's house, turned down her street, and jolted. The lights at her house were on at 2:30 in the morning, meaning that her mother knew Holly had snuck out. Even if Holly lied about where she'd been, there was no denying that she'd snuck out. She was busted.

Holly slumped onto the curb in front of Mrs. Bryan's yellow house. She put her head between her knees and made herself visit her Worst-Case Scenario Cave, which she'd invented in fourth grade after a field trip to Luray Caverns. The cave went from bad to worse to worst case, and it helped her disembowel her fears. Bad, the dimly lit entrance with slimy walls: her mom might suspend her phone privileges or allowance. Worse, the darker middle with spider webs and dripping water: her mom might restrict her from going out on weekends. Worst-case, the pitch black dead-end where creatures swooped and defecated from above: her mom might keep her from dating Alex. Any of these scenarios, even the worst, she knew she could survive.

Having bravely considered the worst, Holly was then able to go home. She rose from the curb and walked past two more yards until she got to her own. She didn't know that the cave went deeper still. When she opened her front door, she saw her mother balled up on the living room couch, her face swollen and red. The telephone in her hand repeated, "If you'd like to make a call, please hang up and try again."

"Mother, I'm so sorry. I snuck over to Alex's house. I'm sorry I made you worry. We didn't do anything bad. I just wanted to surprise him with some cookies."

"Your father is dead."

"What?"

"Your father was killed in a car crash tonight. I got a call a half an hour ago. He crashed into a tree, and the car burst into flames."

"No. That's impossible. I just talked to him yesterday. He was thinking about buying a black leather recliner. I was going to go with him to Haverty's, and then we were going to see a movie. We couldn't decide which ...he can't be."

"He was driving down Raymond Pike near the school. He veered off and hit that giant oak just past the old gas station."

The crash probably happened the same time she was braless in Alex's pantry.

Holly crawled onto the couch with her mom. They nestled as two spoons stacked sideways. They cried and slept, and later as the sun came up, cried some more. All the while, Holly held out hope that the police had identified the wrong man.

They hadn't. The next morning, Holly and her mom looked around her dad's apartment. The police had already done a standard search and found nothing out of the ordinary to make them believe his accident was anything but an accident. No suicide note, no alcohol, no drugs. But Holly and her mom did find in her dad's sock drawer a spiral notebook that haunted Holly forever after. In it, her dad had written about how much he missed Holly, how sad he was that she didn't want to live with him, and how melancholy her sixteenth birthday made him feel. In the same sock drawer they also found a small present with a card that read: "Happy 16th, Holly. Wishing you many rainbows to come." Inside was the crystal prism. Her dad knew how much Holly loved rainbows—every drawing she did as a kid had a rainbow in the background. And now he'd given her the gift of perpetual rainbows.

Holly longed for her crystal prism. She pictured it half covered in sand at the bottom of murky Lake Odell, where no light could ever get to it again. Its rainbow-making days were over.

The Holiday Inn room hummed. A cheap landscape print hung on the wall beside the bed. It was 8:08 am, and Peter would be late for school. Maybe Ted was letting him skip while they met with morticians. Or was it the weekend? Yes, she was pretty sure it was Sunday. Holly stared at the walls, covered in purple and tan rice paper that looked veiny and sickly like an old woman's legs. She reached for the remote and began channel-surfing through old sitcoms, cartoons, news shows, and church services (it was definitely Sunday). No single show held her attention for long, and except for a bathroom break, she stayed in bed all morning.

At noon she sat up slowly, her nightgown pulling against her neck. She hated nightgowns. She never wore them, although Ted must have never noticed since he'd packed this one. What else had he packed, her navy business suit? Slowly, she rose from the bed and staggered to her duffle bag on the desk. She reached in her bag for clothes but instead pulled out the get-well cards that jabbed at her hand. In the eggplant-colored desk chair she sat down to read.

Sue's card had a guy in a full body cast. On the inside it said, "You'd do anything to get out of work," only she had crossed out work and wrote "our reunion." She wrote: "This card is lame, but I was pressed for time. Hey, get better or else I'm going to develop a complex about jinxing my loved ones. I love you lots, Sue."

The front of Kate's card was embossed with a loopy cursive that said "My Sympathy Goes with You." Hallmark's rhyming poem about Courage oozed down the inside panel, followed by a curt "Love, Kate, Jim and Melody." Kate had probably pulled the card from her stash of twenty-five identical cards, all pre-signed and ready to send to anyone experiencing calamity. Sue probably received the same card after Jack died.

On the front of Alex's white card he'd drawn a mouse—he was always a decent artist—and on the inside he'd written, in his slanted uppercase print:

> To A Mouse by Robert Burns
> But Mousie, thou are no the lane,
> In proving foresight may be vain;
> The best-laid schemes o' mice an' men
> Gang aft agley

On the other inside panel he wrote:

Dear Holly,

I'm so sorry about your accident. I felt lost when I heard the news because I realized if I lost you, I would lose something in my life that gives me weight. Even after all these years, I've felt grounded by the relationship we used to have, which gives me hope in the possibility of knowing and being known.

I didn't come to the hospital because I didn't want to intrude on your family, but when you get well, I want to be the first one to buy you a cranberry spritzer. I'll drive up to Charlotte.

Love always,
Alex

Holly had a role in life she never knew she had—giving Alex Meyers weight. Unwittingly she'd succeeded in this role.

In tenth grade World Lit, before Holly had gotten to know him, Alex had chosen "To a Mouse" as his memory poem. He recited it before the class with a Scottish brogue, which Holly found preposterous. But when the class went on a field trip to see the movie *Les Miserables*, Holly saw a different side of Alex. Holly thought she was the only one crying when the bishop covered for Jean Val Jean's crime, until Alex tapped her shoulder. He handed her a napkin where he'd written, "Thought you could use this tissue. Okay, it's really a napkin. Great movie, huh?" Holly turned to thank him, and his mesmerizing blue eyes glistened with tears. She'd always thought he was handsome, as did the rest of the tenth grade girls, as did he himself, but she had never realized he was also compassionate. When the movie was over, Holly and Alex walked out of the theatre together and sat next to each other on the bus ride back to school. They discussed subjects ranging from Victor Hugo to Cyndi Lauper.

Holly put the greeting cards back in the zip pocket of her duffle. Alex needed her weight. She patted the roll of fat on her stomach—she might have more weight than he ever imagined.

The rest of the day and well past midnight, Holly binged on

TV, never changing out of her nightgown. Room service had brought her a turkey and cheese sandwich, and she drank water out of the tap.

The next morning when Holly awoke, she felt two strong aversions: She could no longer handle the veiny wallpaper of the Holiday Inn, and she could still not handle Ethan's tiny casket. She knew she should head back to her family. An Honor Student Mom would bravely return to choose a headstone, greet the funeral guests, and answer everyone's questions about the accident, but Holly could not. Ted and Peter were better off without her anyway. Peter didn't need a mother who yelled and grabbed his chin. The turquoise bra incident had come back to her the night before, during a racy scene of *Law and Order*.

Holly didn't want to be alone in an ugly hotel room any longer. Neither did she want to be with anyone who would pound her with questions. What she really wanted was to be with her soulmate. Alex would understand what she was going through, having known her when she grieved her dad's death. He would give her space and not judge her. If she could figure out how to get from Atlanta to Henrietta, she could stay with him until the funeral was over.

A long shower helped Holly's headache. Ted had done a good job packing her toiletries and make-up bag, but he hadn't packed any other clothes besides the khaki pants and navy t-shirt. For a second day in a row, she dressed in this uniform that smelled slightly of cigarettes. Holly added to her toiletries the Holiday Inn soap, shampoo/conditioner, and hydrating hand lotion.

The elevator ride down to the lobby made Holly feel dizzy again, but sitting down with a complimentary coffee helped, as did the bear claw, which was every bit as good as John the truck driver had said.

"Ma'am, are you alright?" the hotel manager asked from his desk adjacent to the breakfast room. "Can I help you?"

She hadn't realized how far down she'd slunk in her chair, and she straightened her back. "I'm fine. Just tired I guess. As a matter of fact, you can help me. I need to rent a car at the airport. Do you have some kind of shuttle service? I'm Holly Dover, I mean Reese, room 305, no 325."

The manager called the shuttle van, which drove her and an Asian couple to the Enterprise rental car office. The Enterprise clerk asked Holly two difficult questions: In what city would she be dropping off the car and how many days did she want it? She guessed Charlotte, five days, because surely the funeral could be over and done within five days.

In the Enterprise parking lot, Holly's hands shook as she tried to put the key into the ignition of the white Chevy Metro. A memory of screeching tires spooked her. She closed her eyes and rubbed her stitches, trying to rub away the car accident. No telling how long she sat like this before the Enterprise clerk tapped on the window, scaring her half to death. Through the glass he asked if everything was alright, and she nodded enthusiastically until he turned away.

Courageously she started up the ignition and slowly eased out of the parking lot. "Oh Father," she said, looking towards the rearview mirror, but her crystal wasn't there. On the highway her nerves settled, yet she stayed in the right lane with all the grandmas and trucks, never passing a single one. The right lane took her all the way to Huffton College.

2

Holly parked her rental car in the visitor's lot of Huffton's stately brick admissions building. Inside, the pretty coed at the desk gave her a campus map and told her that most English classes were held in Tucker, two buildings down. Holly didn't have Alex's home address, just his e-mail, so she was hoping to get lucky enough to catch him at work. When Holly stepped back outside, the sudden change from dark to light caused yellow spots to burst in front of her. She plopped down on a metal bike rack and closed her eyes.

Once the spots subsided, Holly pressed on towards the man who needed her weight. Inside Tucker a woman with a long grey braid pointed Holly in the direction of Professor Meyer's office. Dark, polished wainscoting and portraits lined the hallway. The nameplate on Alex's door, *Dr.* Alexander Meyers, impressed and intimidated her. Holly knocked. As she waited she tried to pull strands of hair over her stitches. Alex had never seen her with short hair or a giant head wound for that matter. Would the esteemed Dr. Meyers want to see this stray cat? When no one came to the door, Holly started thinking through schemes to find his home address. Then she noticed a class schedule among the various papers taped to the wall. Presently he was teaching Twentieth Century Poets upstairs in room 301.

The classroom door stood wide open, but Holly stopped shy of it and leaned against the wall. Alex's cute voice was reading, "soul something something door." Did he sense her presence at the door? Beneath her t-shirt she could actually see her heart beating.

Professor Meyers didn't need to get dragged into Holly's

problems. E-mail flirtations were one thing, but an unannounced visit was another, especially in her condition, especially at his place of work. Holly walked back down the hall and sat on a bench. Still, she'd come all this way, and if she left, where would she go? Before she could make a move, students began streaming from room 301, followed by Alex, who still moved lithely like an athlete. He spotted her right away.

"Holly? My lord, are you okay? Sue said you left the hospital. Where have you been?"

"I'm fine. I'm really just fine. I've been on a road trip." She grinned up at him. His black hair had thinned and gone gray at the temples, but it still aptly framed his handsome face. His blue eyes radiated from behind his glasses.

"You've been driving?" He sat next to her. "You have a *head* injury; you need to be in a hospital bed. I can't believe you're here."

"No!" she almost shouted and then corrected her volume. "Not the hospital. I needed to get out of the hospital. The hospital was my problem. I couldn't take it. I should leave. I'm sorry. I shouldn't have come. I'm really sorry." She started to stand up.

"It's okay, Hol. It's okay." He held her shoulder so gently and helped her sit down again. He cupped her chin. "I'm glad you came."

His blue eyes were so beautiful. "I loved the card you sent with Robert Redford," she said.

"Robert Redford?"

"The poem to a mousie."

"Robert Burns."

"I meant Burns," Holly said. "What did I say?"

"Holly, if something's wrong with your brain or something…"

"I'm fine. I don't need to go to a hospital. I heard the doctor tell Ted that I only have a concussion, no bruising or bleeding. Look, could I have made it this far if I were in stable condition? I mean, weren't in stable condition. I'm fine. I forgot to eat lunch is all. I'm just a little light-headed from hunger."

"Does your family know you're here?"

"Not specifically, but I left a message saying I was leaving town for a while. I told them I was okay. I know I'm terrible, but I just can't face them right now. I need to be away. I just really, really, really…" She choked down a sob.

"It's okay, Holly. We can go to my house and talk. I'm done for the day. I'll make something for you to eat and we can talk."

Alex made Holly rest on the steps outside the Tucker building while he got her car and returned to pick her up. They drove a few blocks to the two-bedroom house Alex had been renting. He parked her Metro behind his silver Camry in the dirt driveway that separated his lot from Chi Omega's.

Standing in Alex's front door, Holly could survey all the rooms, which surely took up less square footage than many apartments. Tan walls set off several black and white photos. Books were stacked everywhere. Her eyes circled the living room and stopped abruptly at the portrait she'd painted of Keisha Williams.

"You kept my painting of Keisha? I can't believe it." Holly had been in her African art phase at the time. "Geez, what a brooding teen I was."

"I think it's a fantastic painting. It'll be worth a fortune one day."

"Right," she said, though she couldn't help smiling at his praise. It was nice to have a fan. The colors were a bit muddy, but the painting wasn't half bad for a high schooler.

On a black futon in his living room underneath the painting, Alex built a nest for Holly with a pillow and quilt. He insisted that she lay down while he made them a snack. From the futon, Holly could simultaneously view the small kitchen and the home office. She imagined Alex sitting at his computer e-mailing her.

They ate imported Gouda cheese, sesame crackers, and grapes at the two-person café table in his small kitchen. The ochre plates, placemats and cloth napkins all matched. In between her famished bites they chatted about the food, the rental car, and the drive to Henrietta.

And then Alex asked the inevitable. "How are your boys doing?"

For a second she stared at him, shocked, and then she let loose a floodgate of grief. She covered her face with her hands. Alex scooted his chair to her side, pulled her gently into his arms, and stroked her hair. After several moments of sobbing, when her body had stilled, Alex broke the wordless silence.

"How badly were they injured?"

Holly said out loud for the first time, "Ethan is gone." She couldn't yet say "dead."

Alex pushed her out from his chest. "Ethan died? Oh my God, I didn't know. I'm so sorry. I must've completely misunderstood what Sue told me. I'm such an idiot."

Holly wiped her cheeks with the cloth napkin.

"I just can't believe it. I'm so sorry. How's your other son?"

"Peter's fine." Holly put her head on his shoulder and spoke towards his stomach. "Peter undid his booster seat and climbed out. I don't remember much. We started out for Northern Virginia. It was raining. I remember the tires screeching. The next thing I knew I woke up in the hospital and Ethan was..."

"Oh Holly, I'm so sorry. I didn't know."

"I couldn't take it. It was my dad all over again. I pictured the casket and the funeral, and I just couldn't take it. So I left the hospital. I'm a horrible mother."

"You're not a horrible mother. You're a grieving mother. Listen, stay as long as you want, and I'll take care of you. You need to call your family, though, to let them know where you are."

Holly pushed away from Ted's chest. "You want me to tell Ted I'm with you?"

Alex opened his mouth and closed it again.

"Tell me about the reunion," Holly said.

Alex walked over and picked up the phone above his kitchen counter. "What's your number? You don't have to tell him which friend you're staying with."

"Stop it!" Holly yelled. Then softer, "Not right now. I need more time."

"How about if we just call Sue? She hasn't been sleeping, she's been so worried about you."

"Not yet, Alex. Just please, tell me about the reunion."

Alex hung up the phone. "Why don't you lay back down on the futon." He led Holly by the hand back to her futon nest, where she lay down again. He sat down by her feet.

"I don't want to talk any more about the accident," Holly said. "I want to hear about the reunion."

Alex draped the throw blanket over her curled legs. "The reunion was boring actually. I was too worried about you to enjoy it. They made an announcement about your accident and had a moment of silence. I so wanted to come down with Sue to see you, but I didn't think Ted would want that. If I'd known about Ethan, I'd have come regardless. Oh God Holly, I'm so sorry."

"What else happened at the reunion? Who was there?"

"Holly, come on."

"What else?"

"They had a slide show. There was a good shot of you and Kate and one of me playing soccer. I left after the slides so I don't know about dinner."

"What else?"

"Holly."

"What else?"

"Billy Holton's wife is beautiful. Bruce Woodland is bald and pudgy. I don't know if you remember Chad Freeman."

"The red-haired punk who always cheated and smart-mouthed the teachers?"

"Yeah. He's now a pediatric oncologist, married to Jill what's-her-name, the field hockey player."

"How's Kate?" Holly asked.

Alex laughed. "Kate carried around a small photo album filled with baby pictures, insisting that *everyone* look at it."

"Jill Mileski," Holly interrupted. "That was the name of the field hockey player. I think I remember someone saying she and Chad started dating at UVA."

"That's right, Mileski." Alex began pumping his heel up and down. "Sue's been so afraid for you. She was sure you had amnesia and would wander around until you got yourself killed. She's so scared to lose another person in her life."

"I'll tell you what's scary," Holly said. "Chad Freeman working as a children's doctor—that's scary. Man, I'm stuffed. Thanks for lunch. I'm sort of tired." Holly turned onto her side and closed her eyes.

She didn't wake up until the next morning when two girls laughed right outside the window. They wore red and yellow Chi Omega shirts. According to Alex's microwave clock, she'd slept 18 hours. Her head no longer ached, and she welcomed the sunshine streaming through the windows. After the sorority girls passed, another lovely sound filled the little house. Actually it wasn't a sound at all but the absence of sound. It was the absence of children's voices, the absence of TV, the absence of Alex. Initially she basked in this rare silence, until she remembered that Ethan was gone and that his presence had been replaced with silence.

A young man walked by the window, wearing a straw cowboy hat, which triggered a new memory. Before the minivan crashed, she'd gotten stuck behind a green tractor, driven by a farmer wearing a rumpled straw hat. His hat, along with his rain slicker, kept him from getting completely soaked. He drove infuriatingly slow, and she started to pass him, nosing the minivan into the oncoming lane. Ethan screamed, and one of the boys threw something at her head. She swerved back into her lane, almost hitting the tractor's large back wheel. Overcorrecting, she jerked the steering wheel left. The minivan veered all the way onto the grassy shoulder of the oncoming lane. At that point they must have driven off the road into the lake.

But something was wrong. She didn't see the lake on her

left; she saw a white house with black shutters, flanked by large shade trees. There couldn't have been a house when there was supposed to be a lake. If she had driven off the road at that point, she would have crashed through a split rail fence and onto the grassy yard. Maybe she had seen the white house before she tried to pass the tractor. All along Odell School Road houses were either white clapboard or brick, and they all had big yards. But when she replayed Ethan screaming and the toy hitting her head, she saw the inexplicable white house. There must have been a segment of time between the white clapboard house and the lake. What had happened during the interval? She tried to press play: she swerved left, saw the white house, and then...But her mind could only fast forward to that last moment when the van was airborne: windshield wipers, screeching tires, lake, necklace.

Enough. Holly wanted to shower and go for a walk around campus. Rising from the futon and walking towards the bathroom didn't bring on the same dizziness of the past few days. Holly felt much more clear-headed.

Alex had left his bedroom door open, inviting Holly to follow the bedroom route instead of the hallway route to the only bathroom in the house. His bed was unmade, a tangle of light blue sheets, a gray t-shirt, and green boxer shorts. She held up the gray t-shirt and chuckled; the mock college seal touted a mock university, Catatonic State. Before replacing the t-shirt, she held it to her nose and breathed in Alex's scent; he still wore Polo cologne. Next to the bed, a book of Roethke poetry was splayed open on the nightstand next to three empty beer bottles. So much of Alex's high school persona had persisted: his preppy cologne, quirky sense of humor, love of literature, and taste for beer.

On a tall dresser a wedding photo of Emily and Alex sent a pang of guilt through her gut. The soft yellow lighting made Emily's red hair and ivory skin glow warmly as she gazed into Alex's eyes. Holly wished she'd been the one looking up at Alex from beaded white lace, instead of looking up at Ted from her taupe-colored dress, attire more appropriate for a shotgun wedding.

Just three weeks prior to Holly's wedding, at a fancy restaurant in uptown Charlotte, Holly had told Ted about her pregnancy.

He leaned back from the table. "I'm shocked. I thought you were using protection."

"I have," she said, "but not the first time." That first time had been a few weeks before. After many formal outings involving tickets, reservations and gentlemanly kisses at the door, Ted invited Holly over for a quiet evening of wine, laughter, approving smiles, steaks on the grill, garlic potatoes, spinach salad, and a roll... in the hay.

"I want to do the right thing," Ted responded and took a gulp of the restaurant's house red. "I'm not going to abandon you." He took another gulp. "I think we should get married. I want to get married. I know it's only been a few months, but I love you. I've already been looking at rings." Then Ted got down on one knee in front of the waiters and other diners and said, "Holly Dover, may I have the privilege of becoming your husband?"

Their marriage felt like a business transaction: this is the most efficient solution; here's the ring; sign the papers; it's a *privilege* doing business with you.

Her mother didn't even attend their wedding because she'd already planned a big office party that weekend and couldn't reschedule with only three week's notice. Of course the real reason was probably that she opposed their old-fashioned rush to the altar. "Best of luck," her mom had written in the note she sent with her $400 check. "You're going to need it." Kate and her husband Jimmy did attend Holly and Ted's little ceremony and gave a cross-stitched Bible verse as their wedding gift.

Holly carefully placed Alex and Emily's wedding photo back onto the corresponding dust markings on the dresser.

In Alex's bathroom Holly saw in the mirror a shocking bust of a sick person. Although she felt so much better, she didn't look it. The zit was mostly gone, drained of the reunion worries from which it had fed, but paleness and dark circles had taken over the duties of maintaining her unsightliness. Alex must have been appalled to look at her. Her stitches still flaunted themselves, and as she examined them, she became conscious of a small nagging ache at their locale. Fortunately, Alex had left a bottle of ibuprofen on the edge of the sink. She got two pills and went to the kitchen for a glass.

Alex's orange juice was the pulpy kind she didn't much like, but she was so thirsty after such a long sleep, she gulped down most of the glass before taking the ibuprofen. She also wolfed down two bananas. Then finally she noticed the note Alex had left on the café table next to the newspaper, weighted down by his silver-framed glasses. He had forgotten his glasses. In his note, he said he hadn't wanted to wake her, so he'd gone on to his 9:00 and 10:00 classes. He would be back by 11:30 to make her lunch and help her decide how to reach her family.

Maybe she could call Peter at school. Peter would be in Mrs. Jamison's class, working diligently at his little desk or sitting on the floor for story time. Tuesday mornings always brought a guest story reader. In the fall Holly had come in to read *Cloudy with a Chance of Meatballs* and afterwards had served meatballs with toothpicks. Had Ted thought to pack Peter's lunch? If she called the front office, they would page Mrs. Jamison, and she'd send Peter to the front office phone. Then Holly could tell him everything was alright. But everything wasn't alright. She'd have to lie, lie, lie.

Forget it. She had to get ready for her walk. And now she had a walking destination, Alex's 10:00 class, because certainly he needed his glasses.

In the shower, she borrowed Alex's soap and washcloth, aware that the very same soap and washcloth had just that morning glided over Alex's body. She pictured him standing there in the stream of water, pictured them both standing there. What had become of his hotel proposition? Surely it had shriveled now that she was a woozy hospital-escapee.

She wrapped herself in Alex's towel, determined to make herself presentable in this land of pretty young co-eds. In Alex's medicine chest she looked to see if Emily had left behind a bobby pin or barrette to secure her hair over the stitches. No hair clips presented themselves, but Alex did have some L.A. Looks hair gel that might assist her. When she removed the bottle of green gel, she inadvertently revealed a secret. It wasn't as though she were snooping. The package just happened to pop out at her, which was really the fault of the packaging designers who had set against a blaring yellow rectangle black letters that yelled to any passer-by: "Men's Rogaine. Clinically Proven to Regrow Hair." Thank goodness Alex had at least one physical insecurity.

In lieu of a hair clip, Holly found in Alex's home office a large paper clip, and with it and the L.A. Looks gel, she fastened a clump of hair over her stitches, giving her a girlish, slightly punk look. Holly's face required much more effort and ample amounts of eyeliner and foundation.

As a variation from the navy t-shirt she'd been wearing for three days, Holly borrowed Alex's Catatonic State shirt and then went in search of a belt. She crooked her finger into the belly button handle of Alex's sliding closet door. No belts could be seen in the jumble of packing boxes, books, Alex's size 13 shoes, and clothes that never made it onto hangers. The sight comforted Holly and confirmed her suspicion: Alex was the same pig he'd been in high school, a pig who definitely wouldn't harp on anyone else's housekeeping skills. Some digging turned up a black woven-leather belt, but it didn't fit right. Instead of tucking in her shirt with a belt, Holly knotted the shirt bottom.

When she tried to slide the closet shut, a woman's black flip flop fell in the path of the door, as if Emily had rigged it to remind Holly of her presence. Holly refused to feel guilty. If Emily hadn't run off to Hawaii with her fancy job, if she were at all dedicated to her marriage, Holly wouldn't have come to visit Alex in the first place. Holly rummaged through the closet floor until she found the flip flop's mate. The symbolism was not lost on her when she stepped into Emily's shoes.

Because Alex didn't have a full length mirror, Holly stood on the toilet to see how her khakis looked with the black flip flops. She rolled up the khaki bottoms, contriving a sassy pair of capris, and envisioned as the final touch a nice ankle tattoo.

What began as a simple butterfly tattoo drawn with a black ballpoint pen evolved into a garden, as elaborate as a 70's album cover.

At 9:55 Holly walked into Professor Meyer's Twentieth Century American Lit class. She tucked the campus map into her pocket and took a seat in the back row near the door. More lecture hall than classroom, the floor sloped and the desks were built-in. Most of the girls in the class wore pony tails and shorts. No one wore capris, and no one wore a paper clip. What a missed fashion opportunity for them. Down front Alex squinted at some papers and then wrote on the blackboard: "Watchdog of Society." Holly wanted to bring him his glasses, but she also wanted to remain a fly on the wall.

A cocky student whistled as he entered the room causing Alex to look up. His eyes darted from the student to Holly, and worry creased his expression.

Alex hurried up to Holly's desk. "Are you alright?"

Nearby students turned to look at Holly.

"Fine," she said. She lowered her voice. "I just wanted to see you teach."

"How's your head? Do you need anything?"

"I'm fine, I promise. I brought your glasses. I didn't know if you needed them." She pulled the glasses from where she'd hung them on the neck of her t-shirt

He put on the glasses and peered over them. "Nice shirt," he said, smiling.

As Alex glided back down the ramp, classroom chatter died. Holly bet that more than one of these pony-tailed girls pined after the handsome Professor Meyers, night after night in her lonely dorm room. He began his lecture with a commanding voice: "Steinbeck said that a writer's first duty is to serve as a watchdog of society—to satirize its silliness, to attack its injustices." He underlined the words "Watchdog of Society." "Tell me, what works from this semester have served as watchdogs for the twentieth century?"

The class remained silent. The clock on the wall ticked, and Alex tapped his finger on the lectern.

Holly blurted out, "Canary Row?"

Alex smiled, students snickered, and a guy on the front row turned and said, "See? It's a common mistake."

"Once again," Alex said, "it's *Cannery Row*, as Mr. Mclean here will attest. No birds, just cans. If anyone refers to it as 'Canary Row' on the final, I'll take five points and, I don't know, leave a dead canary on your pillow." The class chuckled obligingly. Some girls were probably thinking, "I'll take the dead canary if you'll just come by my dorm room."

Alex continued. "So, in what ways did *Cannery Row* serve as a watchdog to America in the 1940's?"

Class discussion finally got rolling, but Holly had trouble concentrating. She counted the number of blonde pony-tails in the room, twelve, and the number of times Alex said, "you see," seven. She admired her ankle tattoo from various angles. The boy beside her fell asleep, which allowed Holly to read the break-up note he was holding from his angry ex-girlfriend.

At 10:47 students began to close their notebooks and pack up their book bags. The sleeping boy startled awake and grinned sidelong at her. Professor Meyers dismissed everyone, reminding them of his office hours during reading period. The students dispersed quickly, all except a chubby brunette who wanted to chat with Professor Meyers about the final. Alex spoke with her patiently, looking up at Holly every so often. When they finished their discussion, the girl clopped up the stairs, and Holly tried to make herself look busy by searching for something in her purse.

With the classroom empty, Alex said, "You in the back there, do you have any questions?"

"What ya doing for lunch?"

Alex put a frozen lasagna in the oven and joined Holly on the futon. She was lying down with one leg on top of the other. He inspected her ankle.

"Nice tattoo." He scooted closer and lifted her ankles onto his lap. "I didn't think it was a real one. Have you been drawing on yourself? I do have paper."

"I need diversions."

"Such a beautiful design." He traced the design with his fingertip. "Such a beautiful ankle."

"Do you recognize the flip flops?"

"Of course. Emily won't take a shower without them." Alex didn't seem to care about the indelicacy of Holly wearing his wife's shoes or of Holly snooping around his closet.

"When will you see Emily next?" Holly moved her feet out towards his knees, a more respectable distance from his groin.

"Next Saturday, supposedly. She'll probably cancel. If something comes up at work, anything at all, I'm history. 'Oh, sorry honey, the Xerox machine broke down so I just won't be able to make it.'"

"Hey, I liked watching you teach this morning. You're really good. I can't imagine teaching a roomful of college students, or any other aged students for that matter. Is it hard to keep their attention?"

"Yeah, teaching Steinbeck to the Nintendo generation is always a challenge. But at the end of class I always wake the students and help them wipe the drool off their chins so they won't be embarrassed when they run along to their real college lives of dating and playing Frisbee."

"So teaching is frustrating?"

"Not the in-class part, not usually. I love to teach. What's frustrating is knowing that many of these young students will become nothing more than bill-paying television watchers. Anything they're learning now from the great writers will eventually move out of their lives, first to a high shelf, then to an attic, then to a Goodwill store, because they'll need to make room for bigger entertainment centers."

"I see you have a nice entertainment center."

"Yeah. Guilty as charged. Who cares about truth and beauty in real life if you can have it on TV just by tapping the remote. We'd all love to see Mount Everest, nice view and all, but after age thirty very few of us want to take the initiative or invite the sacrifice. Easier to just watch TV. Anyway, you probably got enough of my lecturing this morning."

"No, I know what you mean. Everyone's perfectly happy seeing Everest on the Discovery Channel. Who needs to really climb it?"

"Honestly Andy," Alex said using his Aunt Bee falsetto, "Why ever would you want to climb such a tall mountain?"

Holly laughed. In their senior year talent show Alex had done this Aunt Bee shtick with Billy, who played Andy, and John, who played Barney. Everyone loved them.

"So what keeps you teaching if all your students are just going to become couch potatoes?"

"Well, teaching allows me to pay the bills and buy my entertainment centers." Alex grinned. "Nah. I always have a handful of promising scholars—they motivate me. I also like to keep learning so I don't totally lose my idealism."

"I think I accidentally dropped my idealism in the Diaper Genie when Peter was a baby."

"That stinks."

"Yeah, pew." They laughed, and it felt so good, as if everything were fine.

When the laughter died, Alex said, "Holly, now that you're feeling better, what do you think about somehow letting your family know where you are? I'm not trying to bully you, but they must be worried sick."

"I'll call Sue, like you said, but not right now. Please Alex, I can't face it all yet. You have no idea what it's like to be a parent."

"Tell me."

"I shouldn't have tried to pass the tractor. It was raining. I didn't need to be in such a hurry. My most important responsibility is keeping my kids safe, and I failed."

"Holly, it wasn't your fault."

"I'm a terrible mom. I'm like a fish out of water. Motherhood is as alien to me as if Huffton's president were to hire me as a math professor, even though I quit understanding math in eleventh grade. I could fake it for a while, I suppose, but eventually they'd find me out, and I'd have to confess that I don't even like math, that I'm an *art* major.'"

Alex laughed. "I *know* you make a better mom than a math professor. You hated math. I bet you're a good mom. I bet you do all sorts of creative art projects with your kids." Only one kid, Holly thought. "I bet you give them cool tattoos."

"Anyway, what would you do if you weren't teaching?"

"Holly..."

"Okay, I'm a fabulous mom, you're right. So, what job would you like better than teaching?"

"Writing poetry," he answered without hesitation. "Problem is, I'd have to live in a cardboard box underneath a bridge. And where would I put my entertainment center?"

"I knew you liked to read poetry, but I didn't know you liked to write it. Read me one of your poems."

"Oh please. They're nothing."

"Really, I want to hear one."

Alex raised one eyebrow, challenging her sincerity. His brilliant blue eyes shone in the sunlight. Holly sat up and put her hand on his forearm. "Please?"

He stared at her hand on his arm. "Actually, there is one you'd like, but you can't laugh out loud. To yourself is fine, just not out loud."

Holly shamelessly watched the back pockets of his Levis as he walked into his little home office. The V stitching swayed back and forth.

Why did she ever let this back side keep walking? All because of a silly pillow-flipping incident on prom night. They'd sat on Kate's orange floral couch at two o'clock in the morning. Holly had gotten bored with Alex over the past few months and dreamed of some amazing boy awaiting her at college. Holly and Alex had decided on different colleges, and she was glad. Then Alex started spinning the orange pillow. He twirled it up a few inches and caught it. Twirled it up and caught it. Once or twice might have been fine, but after that, Holly wanted to grab the pillow with her teeth. How could anyone be so mindlessly repetitive? Had their relationship become so boring that Alex had to fill the time with pillow tossing? It seemed Alex had become uninspired by her. If he had even thrown the pillow *at* her, she might not have broken up with him, but as it happened, she broke things off that very night.

When Alex walked back towards the futon, thumbing through a green file folder, she tried to avert her eyes from the front of his Levis. He stood above her and looked down over his glasses. Ceremoniously he said, "To Holly, May, 1980. Violin music, please:

> Our rich,
> multi-layered times,
> when veins
> of emotion shine,
> when strata
> of words are mined—
> colorful,
> glimmering ore,
> that we excavate
> and hoard.

The end. Thank you so much."

Holly reached for his hand, moved that teenage-Alex had written her a poem, but even more moved that adult-Alex had kept it all these years, along with her painting of Keisha. "Thank you," she said.

Without letting go of her hand, Alex laid down the green folder and sat next to Holly, so close that their shoulders and calves touched.

"Do you have other poems about me?" Holly asked.

"I have lots of poems, but how could I ever surpass 'hoarded ore'? I peaked at age fifteen."

Alex turned and gently touched the hair at her temple.

"How's your head?" The freckle above his lip moved with his mouth.

"Fine."

"Let me take a look at your stitches."

"Playing doctor?" The sultry words snuck out from some velvety chaise inside her.

Alex reached across Holly for the pillow she'd been laying on and placed it in his lap. "Lay here, my little head wound girl."

He guided her head onto his lap and began smoothing her hair behind her ears. In high school he may have been a nervous pillow flipper, but his pillow usage had obviously matured.

"A paper clip?" Alex said, hunched over her hair. "You're very resourceful." Carefully he slid off the paper clip, freeing one small strand at a time, fingering each gel-hardened piece into the rest of her hair.

"One, two, three, four, five, six, seven. That's a lot of stitches. They look good, as far as I can tell." She could feel his breath on her wound.

His fingers weaved softly through her hair, which was now too short to braid like he used to do on the sofa in the Meyer's basement. Nobody had played with her hair in the longest time. Her eyes would not stay open and her heart continued racing. She was in Alex's lap, just a zipper away from the mystery. Languidly she moved her hand along the back of the futon until she found Alex's shoulder. His fingers moved from her hair, across her cheek, and over to her lips. With his other hand he lifted her head and kissed her, gently at first but when she reciprocated, his urgency increased. It was an urgency Ted hadn't shown her in years. Ted—his flaccid kisses made this kiss feel less like infidelity and more like vigilante justice. Besides, it was only a kiss. It was only a…his hand found her as it had in the Meyer's pantry. He undid a button that unfastened Holly's qualms and sadness and released her towards a journey they'd never before completed. This time, Mrs. Meyers was nowhere around. This time, on Alex's black futon, with teeth-grinding aggression, they journeyed uninterrupted until they reached completion.

"Geez," Alex said afterwards, smiling up at Holly. "You're way beyond my fantasies about you. You're, I mean, where are your whips and chains?"

Still interlocked, Holly closed her eyes and laid her head on his chest. Her head felt suddenly heavy and her heart, sad. All that she'd forgotten during their brief euphoria came rushing back: she still needed to call home. And now, in addition to the aftermath of Ethan's death, she would have to face the aftermath of what she'd just done. She let her body go slack, as if by not moving she could avoid the aftermath. Regardless of her body, her mind rushed ahead. In the immediate aftermath she and Alex would open their eyes and see each other's nakedness, which in the context of gathering pants and underwear would suddenly feel awkward. This immediate aftermath, a little snowball, would then begin rolling downward, growing and growing into the bigger aftermath, which she knew could get crowded and noisy with Ted, Emily, Peter, and possibly a bunch of lawyers. Better to stay put in the quiet here and now, with only Alex and the sound of his heartbeat and the caress of his fingertips on her shoulder blades.

They lay there for many minutes, until Holly began to worry that her dead weight might crush him, and she pulled away. As she stood, she quickly draped the quilt around her exposed plumpness. They sorted their clothes in silence, and Holly took hers into the bathroom. After she dressed, she removed her wedding ring and tucked it in a zippered pocket of her cosmetic bag. The ring left an indentation at the base of her ring finger.

When Holly re-emerged the smell of lasagna permeated the living room. The green poetry file was gone from the floor. Alex was in the kitchen opening and closing cupboards and clinking glassware. The domestic smells and sounds seemed incongruent with what had just happened on the futon just ten minutes before.

Across the living room Keisha Williams looked on knowingly. The painting followed a geometric rhythm similar to her "Home" sketch. Holly had tried many styles over the years, but this modified cubism must have defined her truest, default style. The planes in Keisha's face and the shapes in the background balanced each other with a harmony that her "Home" sketch lacked. Perhaps "Home" needed a wing to hint at the vantage point and balance out the two driveways. An urge swept over her to paint.

At his kitchen table, Alex served lasagna, toast, and beer. They ate in awkward silence. Alex rubbed his feet against hers as he used to do in the cafeteria, but it was different without shoes, all toenails and calluses. They watched a girl with an owl backpack walk along the sidewalk and a Brittany spaniel bound after a squirrel.

"What's your favorite meal?" Alex asked, his inane question shocking the silence.

She willed herself to converse, to act normal. "A Mexican soup with hominy and pork. My mother makes it, serves it with warm tortillas. It's called...I'm blanking; it starts with a P."

Holly's mind was cluttered with other P words. PAINTING: she really wanted to paint her "Home" picture. PERIOD: as in menstruation, not punctuation, as in, "I hope I have my period because I just had unprotected sex with Alex, and, even though I've been clipped, tissues can grow back together." PERIOD: as in punctuation, as in, "Who could blame me? Ted's a jerk, period." PETER: her pensive son who would wind up feeling the weight of all this. And, yes, yes, here it was, POSOLE: a soup made with hominy and pork.

"Posole," she said. "It's so simple but so good. It's a comfort food. I also love any kind of fresh pasta. What's your favorite meal?"

"I really love this one dish served at a little restaurant I go to with my parents in DC. It's an espresso encrusted beef tenderloin drizzled with béarnaise sauce and crushed pine nuts. And the asparagus side is fabulous, topped with..."

"Alex, I need to paint."

"Okay. Um, my bathroom could use a fresh coat."

"You were right when you said in your e-mail that I should figure out a way to paint. My excuses are flimsy. I know this sounds crazy and I know I need to call home, but I'd love to go right now to buy painting supplies. What if I set up in the corner of the living room? I'd just need a few hours to get the main composition mapped out. You probably have afternoon classes anyway. Or maybe I could ask to use space in the art building. Do you think they'd let me do that? Just for a couple hours. Then maybe tomorrow..."

"Tomorrow, what?"

Tomorrow swayed palpably between them. The mention of it shoved them further into the aftermath. It was a complicated word, one that she often spelled wrong—with an a, "tomarrow."

"Tomorrow, I don't know," she said. "Do you know any art professors?"

"I know one pretty well, Zoë Henley. We collaborated earlier this semester on a Transcendental Poetry and plein-air painting class. The students loved it."

"Can you call her, to see if I can use some studio space?"

"Holly, you keep avoiding your grief and now you're avoiding us."

She brushed her toes along the top of his hairy foot. "Please?"

"I guess I can call her."

Zoë had a class that afternoon until 5:00 and open studio until 10:00 that evening, but she said Holly was welcome anytime the following morning.

3

Officer Jack Sin asked Peter the very same questions as Officer Lewis. Was the van going faster than normal? Tell me about your fight with Ethan. Where do you think your mommy went? Peter guessed Atlanta. That's what his daddy told him, that his mommy used lots of money in Atlanta.

Peter asked Officer Jack Sin a question too, if he knew where his Obi Wan was. Officer Sin said to talk to Officer Lewis, who said Obi Wan wasn't on the list but that his daddy could fill out a form for the tow truck store. That's where they were keeping the minivan.

Daddy also needed to look for Ethan's favorite shirt with the racecar. Ethan had packed his racecar shirt for Grandmother Dover's house.

So Daddy and Officer Lewis were going to the tow truck store, but Peter had to go to Miss Judith's. Peter did NOT want to go to Miss Judith's. He wanted to see the van and the tow trucks. Besides, Miss Judith didn't even have any videos or toys, just some old stuffed animals. He could tell he should not argue because his daddy was not in the mood.

They walked across the street, but Peter did NOT hold his dad's hand.

"Hey there, Peter," Miss Judith said. "You're just in time to help me with Maxie." Maxie barked a lot, but she didn't scare Peter because if you just let her smell your hand, she stopped. Maxie smelled him and then he petted her white fur.

"Bye buddy," his dad said when he left. Peter kept on petting Maxie and watched his daddy walk back across the street and get into the police car.

"So," Miss Judith said to Peter, "come on to the kitchen. I have a very important job for you, if you don't mind. I want to give you this bowl of Maxie's dog food and I need you to leave her a few kibbles every couple feet, going from the kitchen to the upstairs bathroom."

"Why does she eat that way?" Peter asked.

"She usually doesn't. But tonight we need to lure her up to the bathroom so we can give her a bath. Maxie hates baths. So if you'll lead her this way." Miss Judith stepped out into the hallway and dropped some food on the floor. "Come here Maxie girl. Meanwhile I can run on ahead and get her bath things together. Okay?"

"Uh-huh. How many pieces each time?" Peter asked her.

"Oh, four or five should do the trick." She handed the bowl to Peter.

One, two, three, four, better stick to four. Maxie came to the stairs and then up and up. It worked every time. Peter had seven kibbles left when he and Maxie got to the bathroom. Peter backed into the bathroom and bent down with the seven kibbles in his hand. Maxie wasn't too sure and stopped in the doorway. Miss Judith was already in the bathroom with a towel.

"Here girl," Peter said nice and sweet. "Come on, girl." Maxie came right over to him, and Miss Judith shut the bathroom door. He did it!

"Gimme five," Miss Judith said. "Maxie doesn't come to just anyone, especially in the bathroom. Mr. Farrell can't get her to do anything. I'm afraid Maxie is a bit of a snob, but she must have decided she likes you. Now, if you'll turn on the water and get it warm—flip that lever for the drain—I'll take Maxie's collar off."

He and Miss Judith bathed Maxie and guess what she used to dry her long fur? A blow dryer. And guess who got to brush her? Peter did, that's who, while Miss Judith fixed macaroni and cheese. Yum.

At the kitchen table, Miss Judith said, "Peter, you'd be a great vet. You have a real knack with animals."

"When I'm seven, Mommy says I get a hamster."

"Really? Well that's not too far away. Less than a year. I'm sure you'll take great care of him."

Peter swallowed another bite of mac and cheese. "Miss Judith, if Mommy doesn't ever come back, do you think I'll still get a hamster?"

"You'll definitely get a hamster because your mommy will be back real soon."

"I don't think my mommy wants to come back. Ethan and me fight a lot. That's why we got in an accident."

Miss Judith took Peter's hand. Her hand was boney with brown spots. She said, "Honey," she liked to call him Honey, "now you look at me right this minute. That car accident was not your fault."

"Was it Ethan's fault? He was the one who took my Pikachu and threw it at Mommy."

"No, it wasn't Ethan's fault either. All brothers and all sisters fight. My sons and daughters fought all the time when they were little, and we never got in a car accident. It wasn't anyone's fault. See, the thing about accidents is they happen whenever they damn well please. Doesn't matter what you were doing at the time."

Peter thought that made sense, but he couldn't believe Miss Judith cussed.

4

After their lasagna lunch Alex needed to leave to hold his Tuesday office hours. He said he would have cancelled if final exams weren't approaching. Alex plucked several green hanging files from the file cabinet in his home office and gave Holly a seductive kiss goodbye.

Holly looked across the living room at Alex's file cabinet and back at the front door. Then she infiltrated his office. The Poems tab was easy to find among the alphabetized choices. Many titles intrigued her: "My Wife/ My Roommate," "Human Nature," "Song to Steinbeck," "Ode to My Can of Amstel Light," and six or seven more cryptic titles. Then Holly came to one written within the last month.

TO H.
MY GREATEST WHAT
IF
April 6, 1998
(An Unapologetic Rip Off
of Robert Frost)

"I shall be telling this with a sigh
Somewhere ages and ages hence:
Two roads diverged in a wood, and I"
I took the one *most* traveled by,
Because of my youthful ignorance.

A sultry woman was standing
On a road worn by footsteps of men,

Enticing me onward, demanding
I abandon my one truest thing,
In exchange for the thrill round the bend.

On my true path, the chickweed grew tall.
Rejection grew there with the weeds,
And muffled the sound of my soul's call.
Hence on worn path my footstep did fall;
To that path my cowed heart conceded.

Why I went, I cannot fully say.
More than courage, t'was candor I lacked
"Oh, I kept the first for another day!
Yet knowing how way leads on to way,
I doubted if I should ever come back."

At first read, Holly worried the she herself was the "sultry woman" who was "enticing" him away from his marriage. On second read, though, she knew Alex would never refer to his marriage as his "one truest thing," nor would he refer to Emily as his "soul's call." On April 6 when he wrote the poem, Emily was in Hawaii ignoring him, and on April 24, Alex was writing in Holly's get-well card that she was the one thing that gave him weight. No, Emily fit the profile of the sultry woman, who back during college "demanded he abandon his one truest thing." Holly had to be his "one truest thing" but also the source of so much "rejection."

That afternoon Alex and Holly had stepped onto a new path. If they continued down this path, Ted and Emily would get left behind, but if they didn't continue, Alex would end up feeling the same rejection he felt in high school. On either path Holly would hurt someone.

She placed the Poems file back in the drawer. Her heart could bear no more winless scenarios; plus, the snooping had to stop. She needed to get out of the house and go buy art supplies so she could paint in Professor Zoë's studio the following morning. Again she put on Emily's black flip flops and headed across campus, this time with her Ziploc baggie. On her campus map she located the Huffton Bookstore, across a big lawn from the Tucker English building.

"Do you all carry art supplies?" she asked the bookstore cashier, who wore a red shiny jacket from a bygone era.

"Yes indeedy. A ton," he said eagerly. "Back of the store, there's another room to the right."

The bookstore had a surprising range of colors and brushes, all very affordable. She chose small tubes of the six—Rhinestones Vitalize Boy George's Yellow Overcoat—and large tubes of black and white. As her shopping cart, she used a cheap canvas panel, on which she balanced her paints, synthetic brushes, and Ziploc baggie.

Sympathy from the bookstore cashier, his initial reaction to Holly as she fished out a Visa card from her pitiful baggie, quickly turned to embarrassment when her Visa was rejected.

"I'm sorry ma'am," he said. "My machine doesn't want to take your card. Sometimes it acts up. Would you like me to try a third time, or do you have cash?" He could see the crumpled bills in her see-through baggie.

Ted must have canceled her card sometime between now and when she was in Atlanta, where the card had successfully paid for her hotel and car rental. Had he found out about all the money she'd spent at Holiday Inn and Enterprise? She didn't want to think about it.

"I've got some cash," Holly said to the cashier. She counted up all her bills and quarters, but she only had $67.50. The art supplies came to $77.92. Holly relinquished the secondary colors—violet, green and orange—along with her smallest brush. Chartreuse and maroon she could approximate by mixing primaries, and she'd probably never get to the details that required the smallest brush. The new total, $62.03, left her with a five-dollar bill and some change.

The cashier put her art supplies in a Huffton College bag and said, "Thank you kindly, ma'am." When she reached for the bag, he put his hand over hers and looked straight into her pupils. "And God bless you," he added.

Holly reclaimed her hand from this boy who had no sense of personal space, and as she did, she noticed his wooden Jesus fish that hung on a black leather strap. Clearly he did not know what he was talking about. God was not going to bless her. She'd run from her family and cheated on her husband. If God did anything, he would more likely send plagues and boils. The cashier reminded Holly of a boy in Kate Arrington's high school youth group, Ronnie Finch. Both Ronnie and the bookstore cashier were religious, overly eager, and blissfully ignorant of social norms.

Not too long after her father died when Holly lacked the energy to argue, Kate convinced her to go on a youth group retreat, where she first met Ronnie. On the Friday they left, Holly's mom drove her to Kate's church, where teenagers, sleeping bags, parents, and an old blue school bus consumed one corner of the parking lot.

"Oh my, Holly," her mother said, "Are you sure you want to go on that rickety heap of metal?" She parked behind the bus. "Oh my, get a load of the Jesus freak bumper stickers. You don't have to go, you know."

"I promised Kate. Bye, Mom." Holly kissed her mom and grabbed her suitcase and sleeping bag from the backseat of the Plymouth.

Kate hadn't arrived at the church yet, and Holly stood there alone, thinking she'd made a huge mistake. Before she even finished reading the Christianese bumper stickers, Ronnie Finch walked over, stuck out his skinny hand, and introduced himself. Although she'd never met Ronnie, she knew who he was because everyone at school called him Bonnie Ronnie, due to his effeminate ways. He wore a blazer, a button-down broadcloth that he'd buttoned all the way up, and a large silver fish necklace. After he shook her hand, Holly asked if Ronnie was going to be her accountant for the weekend. Ronnie seemed not to get her sarcasm and answered that, no, he just wanted to be a friend if she needed one. Next to Ronnie stood a complexion-impaired girl holding an enormous teddy bear. Holly knew she'd arrived in the land of the bottom dwellers. Kate finally showed up just as

Holly started thinking about calling her mom to come get her, and Kate's presence reassured her, as did the vodka Holly had hidden in a Flex shampoo bottle.

Over the weekend Holly never needed the vodka. Kate, Holly, and the girls' counselor, who turned out to be Ronnie Finch's mother, stayed up way past curfew Friday night giggling, talking about God, and toilet-papering the boy's cabin. When Holly woke up the next morning, she stayed on the top bunk, staring at the splintery wood paneling and thinking about the things Mrs. Finch had told her. She started to cry. Mrs. Finch said God knew everything about her, which meant he knew that she and Alex had gone way too far and that she'd cheated on a math test. He knew what a top-of-the-food-chain bitch she could be to people like Ronnie Finch, even though Ronnie and his mom were nothing but nice to her. And God knew that right before her dad died Holly had broken his heart by choosing to live with her mom instead of him. Mrs. Finch said God would forgive anyone who asked, but Holly worried that there were just too many sins to forgive. Still, laying there in her red flowered sleeping bag, she decided to ask him for forgiveness anyway.

Right away a giant weight lifted. Thankfulness overwhelmed her. She thanked God for Jesus, for Kate, for Mrs. Finch, for Ronnie, for the sixteen years she'd had with her dad, for her mom, for the drafty retreat cabin. With the edge of her pillowcase she dried her cheeks and then jumped down from the bunk without using the ladder. She found Mrs. Finch outside the cabin and thanked her for their talk; she lent her gold add-a-bead necklace to Kate, who had commented on how great it would look with her outfit; and during breakfast, she offered Ronnie Finch her homemade cinnamon bun, even though each camper only got one apiece.

After the retreat, Holly said Hi to Ronnie at school, quit making fun of people, even got to know some theatre kids, quit drinking alcohol, quit cheating on tests, and broke up with Alex. Her friends never really noticed the change, which was gradual and unspoken, like Sue's shift from preppy to punk.

Only once, though, did Holly go back to Kate's youth

group. She never seemed to fit in with the fish-wearing crowd, not in Kate's youth group or in any of the various churches she tried over the years. Church people never became her people. On the one hand church people seemed too nice. She knew she could never be that kind or welcoming. On the other hand they seemed too easily offended. She never got the hang of which national policies and scientific theories and popular movies she was supposed to hate. Holly treated church like physical exercise, something she should do but ended up quitting each time she tried. Her longest church stint, 1 year, occurred at the church with the singles group where she had met Ted. Once Holly became pregnant, though, they quit going except on Christmas and Easter.

As Holly walked back from the campus bookstore to Alex's house, she searched for fish necklaces on the necks of the students who passed by her. She saw a couple of crosses but no fish.

All during his office hours, Alex's mind wandered from student discussions back to the ecstasy of the futon, which he had fantasized about for over 15 years but never expected in the wake of Holly's accident. The surprise of the futon made it all the more sweet. And the urgency of it, in the midst of Holly's pain, made it all the more meaningful.

When a student glanced at the photo of Emily on Alex's bookcase, a twang of guilt caused him to, in between students, move the photo to his desk drawer. He reassured himself that essentially Emily was having a kind of affair too. She made love to her drafting table every night, late into the evening. Alex wouldn't be surprised if there were also a man, some handsome Hawaiian architect. Almost a year of abstinence had to have left Emily with needs of her own.

On the way home from the English building, Alex walked to the supermarket to pick up wine, fresh pasta, chocolate cheesecake, and a red rose.

During dinner Holly stayed quiet, listening but not commenting while Alex talked about the students who had come by his office that afternoon. He had never had anyone to talk to about his students. Emily was always so preoccupied with her own work that when he said more than three sentences about his, her eyes glazed over.

When Alex got around to asking Holly about her afternoon, she blurted, "I don't want to call Sue."

Of course Alex didn't really want to call Sue either. What he really wanted was to get back to the futon, yet he knew they should call. Alex had only to remember his own worry when Sue first told him Holly had wandered from the hospital. Alex had imagined the amnesiac character, Penn, in Kipling's novel *Captains Courageous*. After losing his parents in the Johnstown flood, Penn "jest drifted around smilin' an' wonderin'." Alex had pictured Holly wandering around in a similar stupor. Sue and Ted must have dreamt up a bunch of horrifying scenarios by now.

"Holly," he said, "Sue and Ted still think you're lying in a ditch somewhere. You need to call them."

She rubbed her eyes. "I'm not ready yet. At lunchtime tomorrow, after I paint, I promise, promise, promise to call Sue and Ted and whoever else you want. If I don't, you can call them yourself. I know I sound like I'm going to forever put it off, I know I'm terrible for making everyone worry, but I just really, really, really need to paint. Painting used to always help me process. I need to process. I bought art supplies this afternoon and I desperately want to go to the studio in the morning. We'll call at lunchtime tomorrow, okay?"

Alex didn't answer at first. Instead he began clearing dishes. He wasn't a persuasive man; he was a poet not a lawyer, a moderate not an extremist. Recently Alex mentioned to his colleague Barney Hunter that he believed the Earl of Oxford ghost-authored all the Shakespearean works. Barney got all excited, arguing point by point about the stupidity of the Oxfordian theory. Alex quickly conceded, but then Barney seemed disappointed by the aborted fight. Alex could always see both sides, that was his problem. When Emily dug in her feet about taking the job in Hawaii, because it was the project of a lifetime and the best way to advance her career, Alex saw her point. And Alex could now easily see how painting might help Holly grieve. He understood that she was in a stage of denial, wanting to avoid her family and friends, just as in high school after her dad died she had wanted to avoid him. As an acquaintance in the Psych department once said, "There's no right or wrong way to grieve."

Not until Alex had put all the dishes in the dishwasher and stored all the leftovers in the refrigerator, did he respond. "Okay, Holly," he said. "I know I can't change your mind."

"I have a headache," Holly announced. "If I called tonight, I don't think I'd even be coherent. I shouldn't have drunk the wine. I need some ibuprofen. What if we just eat some chocolate cheesecake and watch TV?"

They snuggled into the futon, ate their dessert, and watched *The X Files*. Alex tried stroking Holly's stomach, but she didn't respond, and before Mulder and Scully solved the mystery of the inbred West Virginia family, she had fallen asleep.

Alex pulled the quilt over her and knelt by the futon. His greatest "what if" lay here on his couch, and the beauty of her frailty hurt him. He tried to memorize her—her pale face, her cheekbones, his old t-shirt, which couldn't begin to obscure her beautiful breasts. He needed to memorize her because he knew intuitively that tonight would probably be their final slumber party.

5

Wednesday morning Holly woke up not on the futon but in Alex's bed. In the middle of the night she'd gotten up from the futon and feeling alone in the world had found her way to Alex's bed. They'd made drowsy love, though love had little to do with it, but rather loneliness on Holly's part and knee-jerk reflexes on Alex's. He was gone now, and his bed looked depressing with its faded blue sheets and black metal headboard. In the morning light, his bed had taken on the cheapness and transience of a motor lodge. She rose quickly from it.

Alex's note that morning said that he could hardly stand leaving her to teach his morning classes because she was so beautiful lying in his bed. Also, he hoped they could call Sue when he got home. He included directions to Zoë's art studio. In a P.S. he quoted Langston Hughes—"If dreams die, life is a broken-winged bird that cannot fly." Holly wasn't quite sure why he chose this quote.

In the bathroom, Holly undressed and stepped into the shower. The tattoo scrubbed off and swirled down the drain. As she dried off, a pang for Peter's after-bath smell seized her. Nothing compared to a clean, naked boy wrapped in a plush towel, minutes away from bedtime. Who had been bathing Peter? Ted? Ted's mother, Olga? Peter liked to lie on his back to get the shampoo out of his hair, rather than have the water poured over his head. He threw a fit if someone tried to pour water over his head. And today was Wednesday. Peter needed to take a practice test Wednesday *and* Thursday in order to learn his spelling words for Friday. Peter needed her.

Though she didn't know her exact plans after painting in

100

Professor Zoë's studio, Holly's yearning for Peter drove her to pack her belongings and store her gray duffle on the front seat of the Chevy Metro. She left Alex's Catatonic State t-shirt neatly folded on his bed.

Holly walked to the art building, swinging the bag of painting supplies in one hand and rustling Alex's note in her pocket with the other. Today she appeared on campus as a tattooless housewife. In Zoë's studio, Holly sat on a stool with her bag of supplies in her lap and breathed in the fumes of paint and mineral spirits. For some, heaven would smell of gardenia or lilac; for her, though she never expected to make it there, heaven would smell of mineral spirits. The classroom was strewn with paint-splattered easels, floored with paint-splattered tiles, and junked with various paint-splattered works in progress. These works, whether on stretched canvas or brown paper, pulsed with freshness, unconfined by properly gilded frames or the expectations of the gilded frame owners. Quiet hovered over the room, the holy silence of color and shape.

From P. Goodwin's cubby, she borrowed mineral spirits and a plastic cup. Even if she had remembered to buy these things, she couldn't have afforded them. In the trashcan, she found a discarded glass palette with hardened paints on one side but a perfectly useable surface on the other side. She squeezed globs of color onto the glass from each of her five tubes. She dipped her finger into the cadmium red and finger-painted onto her canvas an oval, which she smeared with more red paint straight from the tube. With her other hand she squeezed the tube of black directly onto the canvas, enclosing the oval with a rectangular outline. The bottom of a large brush became an etching tool. A rag, another trashcan find, dipped in mineral spirits, became a blending tool. Adding and subtracting, a reddish face evolved with trusting green eyes, rubbery nose, and floating yellow hair. Bubbles came out of his mouth. Straight lines and gnarled ones in black and green framed the picture, along with red flames across the bottom. Yellow eyes looked out from the flames.

What emerged was not the "Home" picture. What emerged

was a boy, trapped underwater in a car. He tried to repeat her name—Mommy, Mommy, Mommy—but only bubbles came out. Ethan had probably died before he ever even reached the hospital, just like her father: crushed by metal, enveloped by flames, surrounded by demons. Holly stared at the boy. Her baby Ethan was dead.

A racking sob welled up, seeming to crack open her chest and suck the air from her lungs. The sound of it assaulted the quiet room. Rhythmic weeping followed and didn't cease until it drained her of all energy, even the energy to sit up. She dropped from the painting stool to the dirty floor, spent. She took a long, hard drag of air, held it, and let it out slowly. She looked again at Ethan's green eyes and long blue eyelashes. In and out Holly breathed. Although she thought she had no more tears, the painting soon went hazy and new tears trickled over her chin and down her neck. She kept wiping her chin on the shoulder of her navy t-shirt because her hands were covered in paint.

Ethan's cheeks in real life were not red but creamy and soft, spun from angora. But the red-cheeked painting was real life now, and the angora cheeks were not. They were gone, along with Ethan's baby lisp and questions and machine noises. His repeating had stopped forever. She craved the chance to touch his cheeks one last time, even if they were no longer creamy and soft, even if she had to lean over a casket and witness her baby in orange mortician's make-up. Only three full days had passed since Holly left the hospital, so Ted might not have held the funeral yet. She had to find out.

Holly cleaned the paint from her hands with P. Goodwin's mineral spirits and grabbed her Ziploc baggie, but left everything else she left behind. She jogged all the way to the payphone inside the campus bookstore. Into the coin slot she fed some of her last coins and dialed Judith's phone number.

"Hello?" It was Judith, thankfully, and not Judith's husband, Joe. Holly tried to catch her breath. "Hello?" Judith repeated. "Anyone there?"

"Judith?"

"Holly?"

"Yeah, it's me," Holly said. She wasn't sure how to begin. She watched a woman buy a Huffton College sweatshirt from the fish-wearing cashier. "I'm wondering, can you tell me, have they had Ethan's funeral yet?"

"Holly, are you okay? Where are you?"

"I'm fine. Please, Judith, tell me about Ethan."

"Oh sweetheart." Judith paused. "What do you mean his funeral? Master Ethan is going to be just fine. He'll probably come home from the hospital tomorrow."

"Fine? Alive?" Holly folded down to a squatting position on the floor in front of the payphone, and the stiff, metal cord jerked the handset out of her grip. The handset clanged against the side of the booth and dangled above the ground. Holly put her head on her knees.

"Holly?" Judith's muffled voice came from the dangling phone. The bookstore cashier was staring at Holly with his pitying look. She picked up the handset but remained squatting.

"Judith, Ethan was...the nurses said he was bagged and tagged, everyone got silent at the mention of his name, Ted said Ethan was downstairs in the morgue. How could he be alive? Are you sure?"

"Honey, I just visited Ethan this morning. He and I said we'd have us a game day in his bedroom once he gets home. He can't wait to be in his own room."

Holly asked again. "Ethan didn't drown in Lake Odell? He's coming home?"

"Ethan is fine and he's coming home tomorrow. His doctor says once he gets home he needs to take it real easy because he has pneumonia, and he has to take some medicine. But he's going to be just fine. He keeps asking for you."

Holly paused to take it all in. No casket. No casseroles. Alive, with cream-colored, baby fat flesh that wasn't gray or red or mortician orange. She could kiss his cheeks, and he could repeat his machine sounds all day long, and she would listen, over and over and over. Two boys, not one, both whole and full of life. "What about Peter? How's he doing? Has he been to school?"

103

"Peter's okay. He's right sad. He thinks you ran off because he and Ethan fight too much. He's been going on to school, and I think that's been good for him. Justin and Frank's moms have been carrying him to and from. Ted said Peter wet his pants yesterday, though. Holly honey, are you still there?"

"I'm here."

"Where are you?" Judith asked.

"It doesn't matter."

"Maybe so. The main thing is your boys need you to get on back home now."

"So Ethan's really okay?" Holly asked again.

"Absolutely. Come see for yourself."

"Thank you, Judith. Thank you for everything. Will you please call Ted and tell him and the boys that I'm coming home?"

Ted was mopping the kitchen when Judith phoned to tell him about Holly's call. Thank God Holly was all right, although Judith said she sounded confused and for some reason thought Ethan was dead. Holly didn't tell Judith where she was, and Ted imagined kidnappers next to the phone with a gun to Holly's head. After Ted hung up with Judith, he called Officer Jackson, who told Ted that he must quickly walk over to Judith's and have her dial star 69 because if no one else had called after Holly, they could find out Holly's location. Jackson reminded Ted not to call Judith but to walk over.

Barefoot, Ted sprinted across the cul-de-sac and repeatedly pressed the Farrell's doorbell. Joe, Judith and their silly barking dog all came to the door.

"I need you all to dial star 69 on your phone right now," Ted said. "Quickly, before anyone else calls. We might be able to find out where Holly called from." Ted followed them into the kitchen. "No one has called since Holly, have they?"

"No. Let me think. I mean, Judith called you, but no one's

called us since Holly. Here." Joe handed the phone to Ted.
Judith gave him a pen and paper.

Ted dialed *69. At first there was silence. Then the operator
came on: "This is your call return service. The number of your
last incoming call was 256-989-5506, 256-989-5509." Ted
scribbled quickly. "The call was received on April 29, 1998 at
10:06 a.m. To activate call return, press 1 now." Ted pressed 1.
The phone at the other end rang once. Ted could not place area
code 256. It rang again. 256 was nowhere near Charlotte, he
knew that much. It rang a third time. He pictured a metal
warehouse with Holly tied to a chair.

"Huffton College Bookstore, how can I help you?"

"This is Huffton College?"

"Yes sir, the college bookstore."

"Where are you located? I mean what town and state?"

"358 Carson Avenue, Henrietta, Alabama."

"Alabama?" Ted asked again.

"Yes sir."

Ted hung up. He looked over at Joe and Judith's
questioning faces. "She's in Alabama. I've got to go. Thanks."

"Let us know if we can do anything," Judith called from
behind as he darted out their front door.

It couldn't be the college where Alex Meyers taught. It was
just a coincidence that she'd called from a southern college town.
The kidnappers just happened to stop there for lunch or
something. He shouldn't let his mind speculate about anything
until he found out the facts.

He called Officer Jackson and gave him the number of the
bookstore. They talked about the possible connection with Alex
Meyers. Jackson said he'd check with the college and call right
back, which he did five minutes later.

"Mr. Reese?" Officer Jackson hesitated and Ted knew it was
bad news. "I called Huffton College in Henrietta, Alabama and
they confirmed that Alex Meyers is a professor of English there."

"But you thought Holly was in Atlanta, *Georgia*."

"We've contacted the Henrietta P.D. and they will go to the
Huffton College Bookstore and to Dr. Meyers' home

immediately."

Ted hung up without saying goodbye, and, as soon as he clicked the off button, he mumbled a word he probably hadn't used since he'd said it of Janie Johnson when he was fourteen and his mother slapped him across the cheek.

"Whore," he said out loud.

The "red lingerie" listed with items from the minivan now made sense. Ted hadn't remembered Holly having red lingerie but he assumed he just hadn't noticed. How long had it been going on?

"WHORE," he yelled. "I married a whore."

Ted flopped down on a kitchen chair. How could Holly do this to him? How could she do this to their family? He got up and walked out to the garage. Since the van no longer consumed half of the garage, thanks to his whoring wife, Ted now had work-space in front of the shelving and pegboard that held his tools and ropes. He took a rope down off its hook and the broom handle that leaned in the corner, and he began working on a mooring hitch knot. The mooring hitch was one of the simpler sailing knots. It helped him think.

Alex Meyers was just a punk from Holly's teenage years who was now some bi-focal-wearing, poetry-spouting professor. Associate professor probably. How could that boring punk entice Holly?

His father had failed to teach him the mooring hitch or any other knots during the times they went sailing, before he left them that is. His father had tied all the knots himself with the speed and agility of a magician. Ted learned the knots later from books and *Sailing* magazine. As he worked the rope he vowed to make the divorce proceedings as bloody as possible, fighting Holly for custody of the kids, the house, and every single fork and knife they owned. Holly would be lost without his income. What work could she possibly find after her six-year hiatus from advertising? He imagined Holly in some roach infested apartment, waking each morning to her job at K-mart, and he smiled. She'd find out what being a single mom was all about.

Ted threw the broom handle down on the garage floor. He

106

could not get the ridiculous mooring hitch tied. The whole thing kept slipping over the end of the broom handle. He stomped back inside and upstairs, the rope still in his hand.

But his footsteps got lighter as he entered his office and began thinking that it may not have been an affair at all. Perhaps Alex had arranged for Holly to do some freelance advertising work for his college, and in the back of Holly's delirious head she obsessed over this obligation. She stumbled out of the hospital with the one thought: I have work to do. Holly used to be quite obsessive about her work. The only problem with this theory was that 1) Holly never mentioned this freelance project and 2) Alex would have called the minute a delirious Holly arrived.

Holly would never choose Alex over him. After all, which man had she chosen to sleep with after only two months into their courtship and which had she never slept with? Which man did she marry and which did she break up with over and over again? Still, there was the time Ted had returned early from a trip and found Holly sitting in the hallway by the attic stairs hurriedly stuffing a band of letters into a shoebox. She said she was just taking a trip down memory lane, but when he asked if the letters were from Alex Meyers, she only replied, "Are you jealous?" Ted never found the shoebox either, even after nosing around the attic.

Ted walked from the office into their bedroom. He sprawled across their bed on his stomach, let go of his rope, and buried his head in Holly's pillow. When no tears came he raised himself onto his elbows. The Van Gogh book on Holly's nightstand caught his eye. He knew Alex had given her the book in high school, but he'd never bothered to open it, or else he would have read, before now, Alex's inscription:

Dear Hol,
    Here's the book you were eyeing at the National Gallery. I know we're young, but I feel as though we're destined to gaze upon beauty, together, for the rest of our lives. I hope when we're old and wrinkled, we'll still go to art exhibits. I'll say, "Put in your teeth, dear, and let's go."

I love you forever,
Alex

Destined. Ted slammed the book down onto Holly's nightstand. Her lamp toppled over but didn't break. With his rope he whipped the book, but he effected none of the paw-ripping damage he intended and so let the rope slither to the carpet. *Gaze upon beauty.* Alex might be able to take her to look at pretty paintings, but Ted was the one who had stuck with her after she got pregnant. He was the one who worked his tail off at a real job.

The phone on his nightstand rang, and Ted grabbed it. "Yes?"

"Ted?" It was his mother.

Ted messaged the back of his neck. "Hi Mother."

"Oh, it's you," she said. "I expected the answering machine."

Ted's mother usually called at times when she hoped no one was home, such as now when Ted would normally be at work and Holly would likely be running errands. That way Ted would have to call his mother back on his own nickel. Also, it was the end of April, and Ted's mother always called at the end of every month, right after she'd gotten paid and felt she could afford the long distance call. His mother was a tightwad. She'd been frugal before his dad left her, but afterwards when she had to support Ted and his brother as a high school biology teacher, she became miserly. They were just fine, his mother always said, with their fourteen-inch, black and white TV, their torn couch retrieved from a neighbor's front curb, and their wardrobes from Kmart. Yet his mom had sent Ted to Georgia Tech and Martin to University of Georgia, so Ted also had the greatest respect for her penny-pinching ways.

"I ran home on my lunch break," she continued. She didn't have time for a long conversation—not on her nickel. "I was thinking about you all and wanted to see how everyone was getting along."

Ted had not called his mother to tell her about the accident or Holly's disappearance. He respected her, but he rarely confided in her.

"We're all just fine. How are you?"

"I can't complain. How are my grandsons?"

"They're okay, except Holly and the boys got into a little car accident. The van is totaled but everyone's fine."

"What happened?"

"It was raining and the road was slick. How's school? When's your last day?"

"The kids get out June 5th and we're done on the 12th. Summer school starts the 19th. Are you going to get a new van? *Consumer Report* gives a high rating to the Honda Odyssey."

"I haven't thought about it yet. Hey Mother, I need to go. I'm expecting another call. Talk to you soon. Thanks for calling."

6

After popping inside Alex's house to leave him a note, Holly got in her white Chevy Metro and headed towards I-85, homeward bound. Between Atlanta and Greenville, she made her only stop to buy five dollars worth of gas and a banana—the Exxon attendant gave her the ice water for free—leaving her with nothing but a few coins. Hunger and thirst hardly mattered compared with her urgency to push home and hold her boys. Like a pregnant woman who was ten centimeters and fully effaced, this urgency overruled her fear of pain.

As she drove and drove, she remembered Ethan back into existence. The memories poured out as if she were grieving, which in a sense she was. She was grieving the near-loss of him, feeling the weight of what could have been.

Ethan's delivery, though only five hours long, was much more difficult than Peter's twelve hour delivery because the epidural didn't work. The pain required stamina she didn't know she had. Ted held the plastic vomit tray for her many times, but instead of being disgusted he kept saying, "You're doing great." He followed each of her screaming contractions with a cool, wet washcloth on her forehead. When Ted first held Ethan, slimy but perfect with all appendages present and accounted for, he wept, and Holly realized how worried he had been during the delivery. Then Ted laughed about Ethan's blonde hair. They couldn't get over the fact that their second baby had also gotten Holly's recessive genes.

As a baby, Ethan was always craning his neck back to look up at the ceiling or the sky. They joked that he would grow up to be a pilot. He wasn't a colicky baby, but he had plenty of fussy moments. So did Holly. Music calmed them both, especially Stevie Wonder's *Songs in the Key of Life*, especially when they took the time to dance. Peter would join in with his whirling dervish dance. Zoloft and the stroller helped too—what did women do before Zoloft and strollers? Basically Ethan liked to be held all the time. It was usually easier to hold him while she tended to Peter's demands instead of letting Ethan cry, because the crying was too much even for the Zoloft. Ethan enjoyed peek-a-boo more than any baby she'd ever seen. And he loved to laugh. Peter could make Ethan laugh by bashing Big Bear against his own head and falling down dead.

Trucks clogged the right lane of I-85. Holly crept slowly behind them for a while, allowing cars to speed by in the left lane. Only when she saw a generous break in the line of cars, with heart pounding, did she pass the trucks. Each time, she thought of the green tractor, but she still could not solve the mystery of the white house that stood where the lake should have been.

The interstate's boring, monotonous buzz contrasted with the momentous significance of this journey home.

"Dr. Meyers?"

The voice startled Alex who had been reading a student essay about the turtle in the *Grapes of Wrath* while he walked home from his Wednesday classes. He'd been trying to decide if the student had plagiarized because the thesis sounded vaguely familiar, maybe from Levant's. He would check when he got back to his campus office. The policeman stepped out of his patrol car, which was parked by the curb in front of Chi Omega.

"Are you Alex Meyers?"

"Yes."

"I am Officer Franks and this is Officer Benefield. We've just received a call from the Charlotte PD about a Missing Person by the name of Holly Reese. She made a phone call from the Huffton bookstore about fifteen minutes ago. The Charlotte police have reason to believe that you know Holly Reese, and we'd like to ask you a few questions."

"Sure." Alex wanted to invite the officers inside his house, before his neighbors, particularly any students, saw him talking to the cops, but he resisted the urge because he held the tiniest, unrealistic hope that Holly might still be in there, still sleeping as she had been that morning with her arm above her head and her nightgown scrunched up around her waist. Instead Alex planted himself where he was, on the sidewalk next to the patrol car.

"Have you seen Holly Reese in the last three days?"

"I have. Holly came here to…grieve. We're old friends. I had no idea the police were looking for her, and she had no idea either. She called her family to let them know she was okay."

"When did you last see her?"

"This morning."

"Where did you see her?"

"In my house."

"May we have a look around?"

The officers found no trace of Holly or her belongings in his house, except her note, which Officer Benefield read, folded, and gave to Alex. Before they left, the officers asked several more questions, including whether or not Alex was married, to which he wanted to reply, "Barely," but he made himself say, "Yes."

Alex closed the door behind the policemen and then sat on his unmade bed to read Holly's note. She said that Ethan was alive. What the hell? She said she'd jumped to the wrong conclusion after overhearing some conversations in the hospital. Holly never confirmed that Ethan was dead? Geez. Poor Holly. Poor concussion-addled Holly. If only she'd called home and avoided two and a half days of grief. At the end of the note she said she was returning home to see her kids, but she didn't say a word about Ted.

If she didn't go back with Ted, would she come back to Alex? And if she did come back, could he handle being a stepfather to her two boys? She didn't mention Ethan's current condition. Was he a vegetable? Could Alex handle being stepfather to a special needs kid? Alex and Emily had been quite content not to have children.

At the end of the note, Holly asked Alex to call Sue and closed with two loves—she *loved* their time together and *Love*, Holly. But love was one of the gargantuan unknowns, along with divorce, remarriage, and fatherhood. Did they love each other enough to rearrange their entire lives? All he knew was the tenderness he felt as he spotted a blonde hair on the pillow beside him.

Alex went to the kitchen to call Sue, who didn't pick up. In the message he left her, he stumbled over his words, not wanting to leave any scandalous details on her machine.

His own answering machine indicated two messages. The first message came from Emily. "Hey Alex, it's me. I have some really fun news. Give me a buzz as soon as you get a chance. I'll be in the office until 6:00 p.m. my time, 10:00 p.m. your time, *if* I can stay inside on this beautiful Hawaiian day. Love you. Bye."

The second message came from Zoë. "Alex. Zoë Henley here. Your friend trashed my studio. I came back for my office hours, and her stuff was spread all over the place. Palette left to harden, dirty brushes in the sink, paint tubes left uncapped. What's the deal? Is she going to come clean this stuff up? Her painting, by the way, is intense. Francis Bacon-ish. It left one of my freshman calling out for her mama. I'm here until 3:00. Give me a call."

Zoë took first priority since she'd only be in her office another 20 minutes and since Alex didn't want to deal with Emily. Alex changed into shorts and a t-shirt and walked across campus towards Andrews Art Complex. Huffton's massive shade trees and brick walkways had a way of calming him. In the middle of campus in what they called Central Park, Alex passed a couple making out on a blanket. He wanted to shout to the boy, "Hold on to this girlfriend of your youth, or you'll regret it for the rest of your life."

The minute Alex stepped into Zoë's studio classroom, he recognized Holly's hideous, beautiful painting and knew it was her youngest son trapped in a car.

Zoë walked out of her office partition in the back of the room. "I see you got my message. What gives?" She followed his gaze. "Powerful painting, huh?"

"Yes, it's really something." Alex turned towards Zoë. "My friend had to leave town in a hurry. She had an emergency at home. I'm sorry about the mess. Tell me how to clean it up."

"Here," Zoë said. "Take this can of mineral spirits and rag to clean the brushes and palette knife. The palette, just throw it away. Then lather up the brushes with this soap and let 'em sit."

"Once I'm done, I guess I should take the painting to my house."

"I'd leave it here while it dries, about four or five days. It's oil, and it's on there pretty thick. I like it. I really do. It's disturbing yet balanced; lots of nice movement. I may have my beginner class critique it just for fun."

Alex finished cleaning up Holly's painting supplies and brought them home in a grocery bag. He grabbed a beer and sat down to grade papers, but the image of Holly's painting haunted him. Holly's car had gone into water; it hadn't burned in a fire, as her father's car had. Yet she depicted flames. The painting had come from a dark, subconscious place that Holly never let anyone see. It was the same place where she kept her passion and her artistic temperament. She spent her life trying to disown this place, this wayward son who would unexpectedly barge in, loud and drunk, just as Holly was hosting important dinner guests. But she could never quite disown it, as evident by her painting. And the futon.

He sat down at his computer to write Holly a letter.

> Dear Holly,
>   I saw your painting. I am so sorry about your car accident. (Too bland.)

> Dear Holly,
>   I saw your painting. How the accident must

torment you. (Too British.)

Dear Holly,
  I loved having sex with you.

Forget it. Alex's lack of words made him feel...lacking. Anyway, Holly didn't need his words thrown into her bubbling brew. Dealing with Ted and the police and her children would be enough for right now.

That evening at 5:00 p.m. Central Standard Time, 1:00 p.m. Hawaiian Time, Alex called back Emily, hoping she'd still be at lunch so he could just leave a message and not actually have to talk to her.

"Good afternoon," her live voice said. "This is Emily Gregory." She'd kept her maiden name when they married because she thought it archaic for a woman to do otherwise. The Gregory sounded particularly detached from him at that moment.

"Emily. Hey. How are you?"

"Hey hon. Thanks for calling me back. Guess what? I've got awesome news. Bill just told me this morning that they want to promote me to team leader for the Hyatt project. Gary is having health issues again and can't continue to head up the team. I can't believe it."

The slightest hesitation passed before Alex forced himself to say, "Congratulations, Emily."

"You don't sound impressed."

"No," Alex said, "I'm very impressed. I'm always very impressed by your accomplishments. You must be doing excellent work. I'm just wondering what that means, if you'll no longer fly home or start sleeping at the office every night or quit sleeping altogether."

"It's only for three more months. I'm still planning on flying in on Saturday. Look, I know I'm working a lot, but this has been the opportunity of a lifetime. Can't you just be happy for me? This hotel is so extraordinary. After this, I'll get to pretty much name my projects."

"It's just…do you think our marriage is working?" Alex asked.

"I've been here for three months. Why all of a sudden is our marriage not working? I feel like you're pulling some trump card so I'll feel bad about my promotion."

"I'm sorry. I don't want you to feel bad about your promotion. I think it's a huge affirmation of you and your work, and I'm proud of you. But our marriage wasn't really working even before Hawaii. I haven't felt married for a long time, have you?"

"Of course I've felt married," she said and then lowered her voice. "We are married. It's not a question of feeling. Listen, can we talk about this tonight when I'm at my apartment? I've actually gotta run. I have a twelve-thirty with a hardware rep across town."

"By the time you get back to your apartment, it will be 2:00 a.m. Alabama time. I don't think I'll be very coherent then."

"I'll make sure to get home at 7:00 my time, 11:00 your time. Will that work?"

"Sure," Alex said, and they told each other goodbye.

He'd just been demoted, again, to a position beneath the hardware rep. With each of Emily's promotions, Alex got a demotion.

In college, Alex started out at the top of the ladder, as Emily's love addiction; the two were equally obsessed with finding ways and places to be together. But after college, when Alex was working on his masters and Emily started working at Barrett and Row Architects, Alex got his first demotion, to Emily's roommate. They'd talk late at night sometimes and occasionally have romantic interludes, but only if it were convenient to Emily's work schedule and only if she weren't too tired or preoccupied. She began binding up her pheromones in blazers and panty hose, and the desire for sex that had fueled their early relationship was replaced by her desire for a better career with better furniture, better restaurants and better vacations.

With Emily's first big promotion at Barrett and Row, when Alex was finishing up his doctorate, Alex got demoted again, to a business associate. He had to schedule lunch or dinner meetings with her days in advance.

Then, when his only decent teaching offer came from Henrietta, Alabama, and Emily refused to even talk about leaving her job in Atlanta, Alex got demoted once more to the status of an old friend who lived in another town. The Hawaii project cinched these relational terms. Alex felt as though he no longer had relevance in Emily's everyday life. Sure, she seemed to enjoy catching up over the phone now and again, but it seemed she could easily go for weeks without thinking about him.

With Emily's latest promotion to team leader, Alex envisioned her stumbling to remember his name: "Hi, um, um, hey you, how's it going?"

The phone woke Alex, and the book on his chest fell to the floor. He managed to pick up by the third ring. Holly must have made it home by now.

"Hey hon." It was Emily. "Sorry I'm a little late calling. There was a big accident on Kalakuaua Avenue."

"It's fine. No big deal," Alex said in a groggy voice. He walked into the kitchen to look at the clock. 11:45 was more than a little late—she'd said 11:00. "I fell asleep reading. Give me a second to wake up. Tell me about your latest Honolulu discoveries."

"Let's see," Emily said. "I ate at this amazing sushi bar today. It was a bit of a hole in the wall, but I think it was the freshest sushi I've ever had. Um, what else. I'm sort of getting interested in surfing. The other day a colleague and I brought our lunch to Gray's Beach and watched these two surfers that were pretty amazing. It'd be fun to take surfing lessons, but I know I don't have time. Are you awake yet?"

"Yeah, I think. I'm going to pour a soda here while we talk. That should wake me up. So you want to surf?" Alex grabbed a can of coke from the refrigerator and gulped some down while he listened to Emily chitchat about surfing.

When it seemed she had finished, Alex said, "So I'm thinking I could set up an appointment with a marriage counselor when you come home next weekend. There's a psych professor here who has a counseling practice on the side. He seems competent."

"A counselor?" Emily snorted. "So you think we're doing that badly? I think you're making a big deal out of nothing. I think you've been angry all along about me going hard after my career. What do you want me to do, work in Henrietta designing strip malls?"

"I want you to love your job. I want you to design the next Taj Mahal if that makes you happy. I just haven't played a part in your plans for a long time. I'm not even a consideration."

"I think we're just in a life stage where our work has taken us in two different directions," Emily said, "but I know eventually we'll figure out a way to work and live in the same place. This life stage will pass and we'll be fine."

"Yes, this life stage will pass, but what will be left of our relationship? The long distance has taken its toll on me, Em. I need someone to eat dinner with and sleep beside at night."

"We've been through this a billion times. Are you willing to give up teaching? No. Am I willing to give up my firm? No. A counselor can't solve our predicament. There's nothing we can do at this point."

"I've had an affair," he blurted out.

"What?"

"I've had an affair."

Emily hung up.

He hadn't planned on telling her, especially over the phone. He had hoped to tell her in a counseling session where a professional could help them talk it through, but he felt

118

compelled to shock her out of her indifference. He called her back, but she didn't answer, and he didn't know what to say on her answering machine, so he hung up.

Five minutes later Emily called back. "So who is she? Some 18-year old sorority girl?"

"It doesn't matter who she is," Alex said. "I think what matters is that our marriage is in trouble."

"Who is she?"

"Emily, I don't think that's going to help."

"Tell me who she is," she said in her intimidating boss-man voice.

"It was, she is. I didn't initiate it. It's a long story. She left the hospital, she thought her son was dead, and she ended up driving here. I didn't invite her; she just showed up. It was Holly Dover, Reese, from high school. She just showed up. I didn't mean for it to happen."

"You got together with Holly Dover? Your girlfriend from high school? Oh Alex, grow up. You make me completely sick." And with that, Emily hung up on him a second time.

Wide-awake now, Alex went to the refrigerator for a beer. He leaned against the counter as he drank it and thought about his two roads; they had diverged in college, intersected again over the past week, and now, needed to diverge once again. Two women, two roads. In Emily, he inspired disdain. Their relationship had been narrowing for many years leading up to this impasse. His relationship with Holly, on the other hand, closed for so many years, had burst open again.

Holly's neighborhood entrance sign did not welcome her. The stacked stone, up-lit and surrounded by the dusk's silhouettes, stood like a nightclub bouncer with hand on hips, demanding to know who she thought she was trying to enter The Cedars. Hadn't she heard? Fugitive mothers and philandering wives were not allowed in this idyllic subdivision.

Tentatively, she turned in. She pictured Ted's face, the one he would make when he found out about Alex. The scowl would be the same as when he spoke of his father leaving his mother. Holly's foot became weak against the accelerator, and she let the car coast down the hill and right onto Mackey Drive, where inertia slowed and then stopped it in front of a tan house.

8:25. The boys were asleep by now, Peter at home and Ethan in the hospital. She felt sleepy herself and settled her head against the driver's door. It was definitely too late in the evening to barrel back into Ted's life.

In front of the tan house, lush yellow pansies lined the garden bed to the right of the front door, which was green to match the shutters. And to the left side of the door—she saw the theme now—hung a green, nylon flag with a giant yellow pansy. The mom, dad and daughter stood near the bay window, watching the purple glow of a television. The dad had his arm around his daughter, and the two kept laughing Holly felt sure the family had a faithful Labrador and a fairy godmother right upstairs.

Just three streets over she knew Ted, Peter and Big Bear were hunkered down for the evening. She put the Metro into drive. When she got to their cul-de-sac, she saw just what she expected to see, Peter's lights out and Ted's lights on. Their house looked just as peaceful and respectable as the tan house on Mackey Drive. From the look of their meticulous lawn and shrubs, their perky aluminum siding, their tasteful white Clematis growing on the mailbox (Ted didn't want the purple variety), anyone might assume they lived as happily as any other family. Even though Holly was incognito in her white rental car, she worried that Ted might appear at the window and spot her. She turned off her headlights and rolled around the cul-de-sac. It was definitely too late for a scene with Ted. Peter was already asleep. At the hospital Ethan was probably asleep, too.

The blinds were up in Judith's living room, all the lights were blazing, and Judith was standing in her white satin robe talking on a cordless phone. Holly pulled into Judith's driveway. When she stepped out of the car, she glanced back across the cul-de-sac up at their bedroom windows. Nothing had changed, but she decided to run around to the Farrells' back door just in case Ted looked over. Before she even knocked on the sliding patio door, Maxie started barking wildly.

Judith yanked against the suction of the sliding door. Her bracelets jangled and one of her feathery high-heel slippers poked out from beneath her floor-length robe. Though Judith liked to slip into her robe early in the evening, she stayed in full make-up and jewelry, like a female Hugh Hefner.

"My heavens," she said. "Oh Holly, honey, welcome home." Judith stepped out onto the patio and hugged Holly tight. The bug zapper zapped sporadically. Judith kept on hugging past the socially acceptable limit, past Holly's attempts to pull away, until Holly let go of all inhibitions and began to sob on her neighbor's chest. She had barely even hugged Judith before and certainly had never cried in front of her, yet into the arms of this acquaintance, against the background of serial bug killing, Holly sobbed all the sobs that had been accumulating, not only over the past week but over a lifetime of longing for a nurturing bosom like this one. She sobbed until her nose became thick and snot threatened to glob down onto Judith's fancy robe. Holly raised her head, and Judith magically pulled a tissue from her sleeve.

Holly blew her nose. "Geez," she said in a nasally voice, "it's hard to have an emotional breakdown next to this zapper. And I think *my* life is macabre." Holly and Judith laughed and the bug zapper zapped again and they laughed some more.

"Come on inside," Judith said. "I was just about to get a soda. You want one?"

It seemed strange that Judith chose soda, not Scotch and soda. Holly asked for ice water and sat on a stool beside the island in Judith's kitchen.

"I think it's too late to surprise Ted tonight," Holly said. "I know Peter's already asleep. I was hoping you'd still be up."

"The night is young."

"Did you call Ted to tell him I was coming home?"

"I did. Then the police had him dial a code on my phone to

find out where you'd called from."

"The police? Ted called the police?"

"Ted thought something horrible had happened to you. He called the police the night you disappeared, and they put you on a Missing Person list." Judith swirled the Cheerwine in her glass. "Alabama, huh? A college?"

"Ted knows I was at a college in Alabama? He knows." Holly rubbed her swollen eyes. The chance of Ted remembering that Alex lived in Alabama was 50/50, but the chance of him remembering Alex worked at a college was 100%. Just last Friday, the day she left for the reunion, Ted had referred to Alex as "the absent-minded professor." He knew where she'd been, but did he know what she'd done? Surely he suspected. Holly had driven her little Chevy Metro right into the aftermath.

"I called your house several times this afternoon," Judith said, "to check on Ted and see if you'd made it back yet, but Ted never answered the phone. I spied on your house, too. Joe kept shooing me away from the window. The police came by at around two."

"Is Joe in bed already?" Holly asked.

"Heavens yes. He starts falling asleep during the 6:30 News."

Cracks in Holly's oblong ice cube fanned out from a central fissure and made the ice look like a fat, colorless leaf. "Thanks for the ice water."

"Well, it was an awful lot of trouble, what with having to get out the glass and turn on the faucet." Judith bent her head down to meet Holly's eyes. "Honey, if you want to tell me what's been going on, I'm a pretty good listener."

"I don't know what's been going on."

"You thought Ethan was dead?"

"Yes, all the conversations in the hospital pointed in that direction. The nurses said Ethan was bagged and tagged, but they must have been talking about some other boy in ICU. And then Ted and Sue said stuff that seemed to confirm it. I was positive Ethan was dead. I feel ridiculous now. I couldn't face his death, Judith. I was a coward, and I ran away."

"Did you blame yourself? Is that why you couldn't face it?"

"I tried to pass a tractor. I should've been more patient. It was raining."

"Everyone can be a bad driver at times. Everyone has accidents."

"I know, but..."

"I read in the paper about a woman who accidentally left her baby in the hot car all day. She thought her husband had taken the baby to the sitter, but the husband had put him in the back seat of her car. The child died and it was tragic, but no one despised the woman or her husband. Every parent has done stupid things. It's a miracle any of our children make it to adulthood."

"I know," Holly said, "but see, it's not just the accident I have to face now. I have to face what I did when I ran away. I went to Alabama to see my old boyfriend from high school."

"Oh."

"I didn't plan on seeing him, but I wound up there. What's worse is we really connected. The past few days with him have been amazing, as long as I could push the rest of my life out of my mind. But I have to be with my boys. And Alex is married and I'm married, obviously, at least for now. What am I going to do?"

"Have you and Ted been unhappy?"

Holly moved her glass so the ice cubes swirled around counter clockwise. "I've never put it in those words. I've never thought, 'Gee, I'm in an unhappy marriage.' We don't throw dishes at each other. We just don't connect any more. Our marriage is just background noise to raising the kids and keeping up the house."

"Background noise, sounds exciting," Judith said.

"Yeah, a Muzak marriage. Not entirely miserable, but insipid. Now that Ted knows about Alabama, I imagine our marriage will become overtly miserable. Lots of dish throwing to come. I can't imagine how it will ever survive. I have no idea what I'll say to Ted. 'Hi honey, I'm home! I had an affair, but now I'm back.'"

"Ethan's coming home tomorrow," Judith said.

"Well, there's a Norman Rockwell homecoming. Do you have any vodka?"

"Nope. I'm proud to say I don't have a drop of alcohol in this house."

"What? Have you quit?"

"Yes ma'am I have."

"Wow Judith, that's great. What made you decide?"

"Three Friday nights ago I drove drunk and threw up all over myself while I was driving. I smelled. The car smelled. I'm damn lucky I didn't kill anyone, and I felt really ashamed. I decided I'd had enough. I looked up AA in the phone book and went to a meeting the very next night. I finally admitted that I'm an alcoholic. It's not just that I enjoy my evening cocktail or that I'm a heavy drinker; I'm an alcoholic, plain and simple. I'm powerless over alcohol. I finally decided that I needed help. I needed this higher power thing. God helped me quit."

Holly looked at Judith's neck. There wasn't any fish necklace, but here was Judith Farrell talking about God, who kept popping up lately like some cosmic school marm, chasing Holly with a wagging finger.

"Anyway," Judith continued, "I came home after AA and threw out all our liquor. Joe was pretty miffed, seeing as our collection cost a small fortune and included some old, expensive booze, but he saw how serious I was. The next morning I stood in the garage in my robe and slippers looking at the boxes and trash bags full of liquor and I thought, 'It wouldn't hurt a soul to keep the two bottles of Lagavulin, for entertaining purposes.' Oh how I love that smooth as silk Scotch. But I knew what my sponsor would say, so I took everything, Lagavulin and all, to a dumpster. I prayed no one would throw a match in there. Don't you know, I went to bed every night thinking about that dumpster and about how I might sneak over there and crawl in like a bag lady to retrieve my liquor. On Monday I called the apartment complex that owns the dumpster to find out about trash pick-up. Thank the Lord, the trashmen had already come that morning."

124

"That's terrific, Judith. Congratulations. Now I can put you on my night time babysitter list."

Judith laughed. "I guess I've never really thought about the fact that you never called me at night. I babysat Peter the other night, though, while you were gone. I reckon Ted didn't check the list!" She laughed again. "I want to tell you that Peter is a delightful child. He and I bonded. He and Maxie bonded, too."

"Thank you for helping us. Peter and Ethan are going to be so messed up after all this. As if they weren't already messed up by my parenting. What do I tell them about where I've been?" Holly asked.

"Where you've been doesn't mean peanuts to them," Judith said. "It's where you're going to be from now on. They care about whether or not their mama is going to be around. They also care about *why* their mama left. Peter thinks you left because he and Ethan fight too much. Talking with your boys won't be about you; it'll be about them."

"You're a pretty smart lady."

"I tell you what, after all the booze I've consumed in my life, I'm just grateful to have any brain cells left."

A jaw-cracking yawn contorted Holly's face. "When I headed home today, I thought I would drive straight to the hospital to see Ethan, but it got too late. I'm exhausted. Do you know what time he's coming home tomorrow?"

"I don't know. Honey, my guest room has clean sheets on the beds; you're welcome to sleep here tonight. You can call Ted to let him know you're here and then go straight to bed." Judith handed her the phone.

"Will you call him?" Holly asked.

"Child..."

"Just tell him I want to have a good night sleep before I talk to him in the morning. I'm so wiped out from the drive."

SECTION III
PEREGRINE FALCON

Peregrine falcon, Falco peregrinus: High flying raptor. Slate blue above, spotted below. Speeds of over 200 mph. Cooperative hunting among mates. Lifelong monogamy.

1

"Ethan," she yelled as she woke up from her nightmare that combined her car accident and her father's. The demons had been clawing at Ethan's face.

Holly thought she might have yelled out loud, not just in the dream, but she wasn't sure. The last two years of high school, whenever she had the dream about her dad, she occasionally screamed out loud, and her mother would come in with a glass of water. One time when she was spending the night at Sue's, Holly screamed out loud and nearly scared Sue to death.

The white eyelet bedspread, which Holly pulled up to her chin, matched the ruffle curtains in Judith's guest room. Dust particles floated on the beams of morning sunshine. The room seemed to have been decorated with random items pulled from the attic—white eyelet, doll collection, pink and orange Mexican blanket, and chunky dark-wood boy furniture. While the room wasn't going to win any design awards, it made for a hospitable refuge, especially as the smell of bacon made its way up from the kitchen.

But the refuge was temporary. Slowly the reality of the day seeped into her consciousness: Today, Thursday, April 30th, she would face her husband Ted after betraying him so completely.

Holly willed herself to the Worst-Case Scenario Cave. In the Mouth of the Cave, she envisioned the easiest scenario: Ted shoots her, she dies, problem solved. In the Middle of the Cave, draped in spider webs, she saw a pretty-bad-but-bearable scenario: Ted leaves, she goes back to work, she has to figure out childcare. However, in the pitch-black, bat-infested Back of the Cave, the worst-case scenario lurked: Ted leaves, she goes back to work, but she also loses the boys in a nasty custody battle. This scenario Holly didn't know if she could survive. Ethan had just returned from the dead, and she couldn't bear losing him again.

Alex didn't even make it into the cave. Whether or not they stayed together didn't concern her at the moment. Her greatest fears centered on the boys.

For the last time Holly pulled on her well-worn khaki pants and navy shirt, which were now smeared with paint and would go straight to Goodwill after today. For the last time she picked up her duffle bag.

Downstairs in the kitchen Judith greeted her cheerily. "Good morning, honey. How'd you sleep? I hope you're hungry." She'd cooked up a feast of eggs, bacon, and chocolate chip muffins.

"I didn't sleep so well. The room was great, but my mind kept swirling. What did Ted say when you called last night?"

"Okay, Okay, and Thank you, Judith."

"That's not good."

"Probably not."

Holly fumbled with the knife as she buttered a warm muffin. "I thought I'd wait until Peter got off to school. As much as I want to hug him, I'd rather Peter not be there if Ted's going to go off."

"Listen, if you need to come back over, come on."

"I dread this," Holly said. She put down her muffin because her appetite was gone.

"Do you want me to come with you?"

"No. I need to go by myself and let Ted say everything he needs to say."

Holly rang her own doorbell with the formality of a salesman. Behind the boxwoods Ethan's beloved red bouncy ball gave her strength. Seeing Ethan alive was all that mattered, regardless of whatever Ted dished out.

Ted opened the door, crossed his arms, and stared icily.

"Where's Alex?" he spat.

She didn't respond, feeling instead like she might throw up.

"The police spent three days trying to find you." Ted shook three fingers at her as if he were flipping her off. "Cop cars were a regular sight in our driveway. I didn't sleep, didn't work, had to cancel our credit cards, had to juggle kids, grocery shop, buy car seats. Every other second Peter asked where you were. And the whole time you were with your old boyfriend from high school?"

"I was by myself in Atlanta the first day and a half."

"Yes, and you didn't bother to call."

"At the time, I thought the one phone message was enough. My head was messed-up. Can I come in?"

Ted didn't move from the doorway, and Holly had to maneuver around him. She dropped her duffle bag on the living room carpet, which had the indentations of recent vacuuming, and she slumped onto the couch. As she folded her hands on her knees, she realized her left hand was missing her wedding ring, which remained in the zippered pocket of her cosmetic bag. Quickly, Holly tucked her guilty hands underneath her legs.

Ted moved from his post at the front door and sat on the striped armchair, stiffly, with his hands on his knees like an Egyptian pharaoh.

"Did you sleep with him?" At first he was able to keep his face and voice emotionless, but his disgust rose with subsequent questions. "Were you having an affair before the accident? How long has it been going on?"

Holly stared at the fireplace, still full of ashes from winter. "Alex and I were e-mailing a little bit before the reunion. After the accident, I thought Ethan was dead, and I just couldn't face it."

"Judith said that. I don't understand how you could've possibly thought Ethan was dead. That doesn't make any sense."

"A nurse said to another nurse, when they thought I was asleep, that the boy in ICU had been bagged and tagged. I guess they were talking about another boy, but it sounded like they were talking about Ethan. And then everyone got silent at the mention of Ethan's name. And Sue compared the situation to Jack's death. And I swear you told her Ethan was down in the morgue."

"Wait a minute. You were awake when Sue visited?"

"I could hear, but I couldn't respond. My head wasn't right. Ethan's death was too much for me. Even though I couldn't remember everything about the accident, I felt like it was my fault; I felt responsible for Ethan's death. I couldn't take it, and I just walked away from the hospital and hitched a ride to Atlanta."

Ted raised his eyebrows.

"With a very nice truck driver. He dropped me at the Holiday Inn, but after a day I went stir crazy and decided to go to Alex's house until after Ethan's funeral. My head still wasn't right at this point."

"Did you sleep with him?"

Holly glanced at the staircase. "Are Peter and Ethan home?"

"Peter's at school and Ethan's at the hospital. Did you sleep with Alex?"

"Is Ethan being discharged from the hospital today?

"Yes. Answer me. Did you sleep with Alex Meyers?

"Yes."

"Disgusting," Ted snarled, contorting his face in the way she'd imagined he would.

"We didn't plan on it. Ethan was dead, and I was very messed up and very needy. I'm a pitiful, needy person, okay? You don't think anyone should be needy, but I am."

"So now I'm supposed to feel sorry for you?" Ted's voice edged higher. "You had an affair, and I'm supposed to feel sorry for you? What about me? I didn't know where you were for over three days. I worried that you'd been kidnapped or murdered. How could you do this to me? How could you do this to Peter and Ethan? I've been nothing but faithful to you. I did right by you after you got pregnant; I stuck by you through post-partum depression or whatever you call it. But you can't handle a difficult situation, so you run to the bed of your old high school sweetheart?"

"It was wrong of me. I wasn't myself."

Ted tapped his finger on the arm of the chair.

"Ted, you and I were having problems long before all this."

"That's a convenient excuse."

"I'm not trying to make up an excuse, but you have to admit, we've been on a sad plateau for a long time. Have you been happy with our marriage?"

Ted stood up. "Happy doesn't matter. The point is I stuck by you."

"Don't you want something more than I'm sticking by you because, by golly, I said I would?" Holly started to gesture with her hands but remembered her naked ring finger and returned her hands under her thighs. Ted didn't notice.

"I don't ever think about what I want," Ted responded. "I don't have time. I go to work, kiss my clients' feet, earn a paycheck and come home; then I do it all again the next day. It's not about what I want; it's about what needs to get done. It's called being a responsible, mature adult. Maybe you should try it sometime."

The insult achieved its intended goal, shaming her, but more than shame she felt sadness. To Ted, Holly's affair arose because of Holly's irresponsibility and immaturity, not because of any deficits in their marriage. Their marriage, therefore, along with any move toward reconciliation, seemed doomed. Further discussion also seemed futile, so Holly shifted focus.

"When does Ethan get home?"

Ted looked at his watch. "He gets discharged at 10:00. I need to go on. Someone has to take care of this family, right? We can't all just run off frolicking. I can't stand this. I need to go."

"I can drive my rental car and meet you at the hospital. Judith says Ethan has pneumonia. I'd like to hear what the doctor says."

"Suddenly you're interested in Ethan's condition? Don't even bother. You're about four days too late, Holly. I'm the one who's been dealing with the doctors. I'm the one who will pick up Ethan."

The door bell rang shortly after Ted left for the hospital, right after Holly had stripped off her khaki pants and navy t-shirt. In bra and underwear, Holly peeked through the mini-blinds of their walk-in closet. A police car was parked in the driveway and two policemen stood on the front stoop, dressed head-to-toe in navy polyester that twinkled in the sun with badges, buckles and weapons. She threw on a jean jumper, without a t-shirt underneath, and scrambled down the stairs.

Officers Jackson and Ramirez introduced themselves and told Holly how glad they were that she had gotten home safely. Holly offered them a seat and something to drink, as if she'd invited them over for tea. Their subsequent barrage of questions changed the tea party atmosphere and made her feel first like a mental patient who might not know what year it was and then like a criminal who might be running drugs across state lines. All the while the two men continued with their ma'am this and ma'am that, and they were polite enough to act reluctant, even embarrassed, when they got to the questions about Alex Meyers.

Holly heard the garage door. Her youngest son was alive and about to walk in the house! She interrupted Officer Ramirez and ran upstairs. She stood before the full-length mirror, tucked in her bra straps, and thankfully noticed that she needed to retrieve her wedding ring. It was easy to locate in her cosmetic case. As she scurried back downstairs, she wished she had bought Ethan a welcome home gift.

In the kitchen Ethan's creamy soft face peered around the door. "Mommy?"

He stepped inside, and Holy scooped up his tiny body and squeezed him.

"Ethan, I love you so much. I'm so glad you're okay. It's so good to hold you."

"Mommy, I can't breathe."

134

She loosened her grip. "Sorry baby."

"Mommy. I saw a real police car outside with a light on top."

"Would you like to see two real live police officers?"

"Really?"

Holly shifted Ethan to her hip, pulling her jumper to one side, exposing half her bra cup. She simply didn't care about propriety.

In the living room she introduced the men to Ethan. "This is Officer Jackson and this is Officer Ramirez."

Ethan twisted out of her arms onto his feet. "Is that a real gun?" he asked, staring at Officer Ramirez's hip. "Can I hold it?"

Ramirez laughed. "No, but I bet we could find you a police badge sticker. We have some in our car."

"Really?" Ethan said.

"Ma'am," Officer Jackson said, "I believe we have all the information we need to file our report. We'll call if we have any more questions. I'll see if I can find a sticker for this guy."

The policemen jangled and swished out the front door. Ted was waiting for the officers by their car.

Holly turned to Ethan. "Let's sit on the couch, baby boy."

Ethan lay in Holly's lap and held up his right arm to be scratched. Slowly, Holly ran her fingernails up the smooth inside of his arm and down the furry outside. He held up his other arm, and then each leg, one at a time. Ethan loved to be scratched on every inch of his skin. Some of his body parts carried hospital vestiges—a bruise at the bend of his arm, an I.D. bracelet, a pallid face. They scratched until Ted came in. In silence he laid Ethan's police sticker on the coffee table and walked upstairs with Ethan's overnight bag.

"Where do you want to put your police sticker?" Holly asked Ethan. "Here?" Holly stuck the silver sticker over the breast pocket of Ethan's t-shirt, but he moved it to the back of his hand. Then he flopped across Holly's lap, stomach down.

"My back now."

Holly lifted up his shirt and scratched every part of his back with both her hands.

"Are you glad to be home from the hospital?" she asked.

He lifted his head and said, "I liked the T.V. I missed my toys and swing. I get to have game day with Miss Judith now. I missed you scratching."

"I'm going to scratch you all day and all night. At midnight I'll still be here scratching you. I'm going to scratch you until you're thirteen years old."

He lifted his head again. "Fourteen."

"Fourteen? Are you sure? Okay, but at fourteen, we're going to quit cold turkey, no excuses."

Ted came downstairs with Ethan's bathroom cup and a white medicine bottle. "Ethan needs to take another dose of Clindamycin, then again at dinner and bedtime. Four times a day for ten more days." Ted used a dropper with a blue rubber tip.

"It tastes ookie," Ethan said.

"Shouldn't he take that with food?" Holly asked.

Ted handed Ethan the cup of water. "You wouldn't know, would you?"

"Hey Ethan," Holly said, "when you finish your water, why don't you go on upstairs and see your toys? We can scratch some more later."

Once Ethan reached the top of the stairs, Holly said to Ted, "We're both going to need to help him get better. I need to know about the medicine, and I need to know about his condition."

He folded his arms and spoke in a monotone. "He doesn't need to take the medicine with food. He got pneumonia from ingesting lake water. He should be fine after he finishes the medicine, but his lungs have taken a beating and he needs to take it easy. He was lucky. There was a man at the scene of the accident who rescued Ethan from under the water and got him breathing again."

"How long was he under the water not breathing?"

"They don't know. If this Milton Benson guy hadn't gotten to him when he did…"

"But he's going to be perfectly fine? No brain issues?"

"That's what the doctors say."

"Are you sure?"

"Look, if you don't believe me, then you should have stayed at the hospital to hear the diagnosis directly from the doctors, right? But I guess you had other *affairs* to attend to. Alex was more important than your son's condition, right? When you were in his bed you didn't give a flip about what the doctors…"

"Where's my red Ranger?" Ethan called from upstairs.

Before Holly could answer, Ted yelled, louder than necessary, "Bottom bin in your closet."

Holly stared at him. In less than a week Ted had become an expert on Ethan's medical condition and the whereabouts of his toys.

Ted sighed, "Now I need to get back in the car and pick up Peter from school. I promised him I'd get him once Ethan got home, and I would've gotten him on the way from the hospital, except Ethan begged to come straight home to see you."

"I could go get Peter if you'd like," she offered.

"No. He doesn't know you're back. I didn't tell him this morning because I didn't know your plans—if you would actually come home or take off again. Peter's been so worried about you. On Tuesday he wet his pants at school. He freaks out every time he gets in the car, especially before I bought him a new booster seat. He slept with me the first night."

"I hate that he's been so anxious."

"I gotta go. I called your mother to let her know you'd come home; apparently you hadn't thought to do that. She says she's going to call around 1:00 today." He sighed again at the burden of being the only responsible adult. "An Officer Lewis should be calling to ask you questions about the accident, and a State Farm adjustor, too. Do you even realize what a mess you've created? "

Peter liked activity centers at school. His favorite was games and puzzles. He got the easy-as-pie mouse puzzle because it was a real picture of real mice, not just a cartoon. He was the mouse puzzle king. He only got a few pieces together when he heard his daddy's voice at the door.

"Excuse me, Mrs. Jamison," Daddy said. "I forgot to tell you ahead of time that Peter has a doctor's appointment today. Hey buddy."

Peter left the mice and went to get his backpack and lunchbox from his cubby. Miss Kendrick was stapling at Mrs. Jamison's desk so Peter whispered in her ear if he could take home his grass baggie off the window ledge. She said yes, and he put the baggie in the outside pocket of his backpack where the grass could breathe.

When they got in the hall, Peter said to his daddy, "I don't want to see a doctor. I don't want to go to the hospital."

But his daddy told him a secret. "You actually aren't going to the doctor at all. I just wanted to take you out of school in order to see Ethan; he's home from the hospital!"

Peter would never fight with Ethan again. And he'd let Ethan borrow his Pikachu whenever he wanted.

"I also have other big news," his dad said, "but let's wait until we get in the car."

Peter waited. His daddy strapped him into his brand new booster. Peter waited until his daddy had put on his own seatbelt in the front. Then finally he asked, "Did they find Mommy?"

His daddy turned around to face Peter. "Yes, son, your mother came back this morning."

Peter just knew it. He felt like he might cry, but he also wanted to cheer. "She's back!" he said. "Is Mommy home or at the hospital?"

"At home. I'm taking you to see her now."

"Is she sick?"

"No, I don't think so. She didn't seem sick. I didn't really ask."

"Does Justin's mom know you're picking me up?" Peter asked.

"Ahh," his daddy said in a mad voice. "No, I didn't call Justin's mom. That's another thing I'll need to take care of when I get home."

His daddy started up the car, and Peter got his thumb ready on the orange button of the seatbelt that went through his booster, ready to press it at the first sign of trouble.

Holly waited for Peter on the stoop. The front lawn had thickened up while she'd been gone. When Ted's black Ford Focus rolled into the driveway, Holly scurried behind it and over to Peter's door. Her serious little man was busying himself with first things first. He undid his booster, pressed the lever to make the passenger seat flip forward, strapped his book bag onto both shoulders, picked up his Pokemon lunchbox, and then stepped out of the back seat. Holly picked up the entire schoolboy set and put him on the trunk of Ted's car. She put her hands on either side of his face, and said, "Peter Reese, I am so glad to see you. You are the best thing I've seen in days. I've missed you so much. I'd nearly forgotten how cute you are."

Peter patted the sides of her spiky head. He could no longer twirl her hair around his fingers the way he used to. "I'm glad you're home. I missed you. And Mommy, guess what! I got grass that I growed in a bag! We need to put it on a window ledge."

"That's fantastic. I can't wait to see it. Let's go inside and set it up."

At the kitchen table they pulled out the grass baggie, dulled by condensation from the wet paper towel inside. Holly oohed and ahhed and told Peter he was a great little farmer. Then she pulled out Peter's folder. For today, Thursday, he had no star since Ted picked him up early. For Monday, Tuesday and Wednesday, he had gold stars for good behavior, as usual. On Monday, though, there was a note about Peter crying at lunch, and on Tuesday, a note about Peter wetting his pants.

"Peter, I'm sorry that you've been sad while I was gone. I'm sorry I went away and didn't let you know where I was. I needed to get away by myself for a while, but I should have let you know where I was."

"I'm sorry I fight with Ethan so much," Peter said.

"It's okay, honey. It's normal for brothers to fight. Mommy just needs to learn to handle it better."

The phone rang and Holly realized that she wanted to pick it up and reenter her life again.

"Why don't you go up and say hi to Ethan. He's back from the hospital, playing up in his room." Peter grabbed his baggie of grass and ran upstairs.

The caller was Holly's mom, and Holly regretted picking up. After saying hello, Holly glanced at her watch out of habit because she usually tried to limit these phone conversations to five minutes. Past five minutes, the speeches began and there was no turning back.

"Honey, thank goodness you're alright," her mom said. "I was worried sick. So, Ted said you went down to Atlanta to clear your head. Why did you abandon Ethan and Peter and not tell anyone where you were?" Holly looked at her watch again. Fifteen seconds it took her mother to dish out her first spoonful of accusation. It wasn't a world record, but it was a respectable time. "Anyway, I'm glad you're home now," her mother said. "So you're all better, and everyone's back home again, including Ethan? How's your head?"

Her mother didn't really want to know why Holly left or how she was doing now; she only wanted to go on record for having asked. No real answers were expected and none were given.

"We're all fine, mother."

"What's wrong? You sound mad at me."

"I'm not mad." Just disappointed, as usual.

"Well, what is it?"

"Nothing. We're all fine, what could be wrong?"

"Kate Arrington called me," her mother said. "She wanted to know how you were feeling and if you'd gotten out of the hospital yet. I didn't want to tell her that you ran off, so I just said you'd be home from the hospital soon. You ought to call her as soon as you can. Sue Granger, too. Sue was very worried about you. You know, she missed the reunion to come visit you.

You're very lucky to have a friend like Sue."

Her mother's comments flowed with an undercurrent of criticism. "Yeah," Holly said, "I'm lucky to have any friends at all."

"I didn't say that, Holly. I just meant that Sue's a good friend. She's lucky to have you, too. Look, I know you're very sensitive now because you're probably exhausted from everything you've been through. I'll call back after you've had some time to rest. Love you."

Some misguided songwriters thought love was the answer, but Holly's mom knew the answer was rest.

Ethan's post-hospital request for dinner that evening was Domino's pizza, to which Holly would add a side of antibiotics.

"Ted?" Holly asked. "Where is Ethan's Clindo-whatever medicine? I'll give him his dose."

"Clindamycin. I left it on the coffee table, I think. But I need to be the one to give it to him. You have to shake it well and give it with water. You need to store it away from heat and moisture, not in the bathroom where you usually keep medicines. And you need to look for side effects like diarrhea."

"I think I might be able to handle it."

"I'll do it."

Holly could see his logic. After all, since she wasn't there for the doctor's instructions, she might wind up putting the medicine in Ethan's ear. Ted came into the kitchen and performed the complicated task. It was touch and go getting the dropper into the bottle, but Ted's surpassing medical knowledge got him through.

"Why don't we keep the bottle down here on the counter so we'll remember?" Holly suggested.

But medical expert, Ted Reese, did not concur. "I'm going to keep it on my chest of drawers so I'll remember." He took the medicine and his plate of pizza upstairs.

Holly and the boys talked during dinner about how Peter had grown grass from seeds, how Ethan had learned to use the remote control from his hospital bed, and how Mommy should get, in place of the tan minivan, a red, supersonic racecar with jet engines and machine guns. Ethan put his hands on an invisible steering wheel and made the sounds of a jet engine. Brmmm. Brmmm. Brmmm. As he turned an invisible corner, he knocked over his sippie cup of milk, which splattered droplets across the kitchen wall.

"Damn it, Ethan," she yelled. How quickly the joy turned to irritation. But she forced cheerfulness into her voice again, determined to no longer cry over spilled milk. "It's alright, sweetie. I'll get a washcloth."

Later, after she turned out the boys' lights, after lots of snuggling and sweet bedtime stories, Holly walked into Ted's office where he was clicking away on his computer. Holly sat Indian style on her grandmother's white wicker chair behind Ted's back. He kept typing.

"They're good boys, aren't they?" Holly said.

Ted swiveled the desk chair around to face her. "Abandonment can make the heart grow fonder."

Holly stared back at his meanness, not ready to argue but not ready to grovel either. How silly of her to think they could talk about the boys in a civilized manner. She'd always known Ted had the potential to be just as nasty as his father.

"I didn't mean to abandon anyone. I thought Ethan was dead, and I freaked out."

"You knew Peter wasn't dead. You knew I wasn't dead."

"I feel horrible, believe me."

"I guess you had some whoring to attend to in Alabama."

Her tears gathered quickly.

"What kind of mother abandons her children?" he asked. "You don't deserve them. You don't deserve me."

"I'm sorry." Talking hurt her throat, guilt being such a large pill to swallow.

"You're not sorry. Why don't you just go back to Alex?"

"I planned to come home even before Judith told me Ethan

was alive. That's why I called her, to find out about his funeral. I had to see him one last time before they buried him. And even though I thought you all were better off without me, I knew I had to see Peter, and you, too. My mind's been really screwed up. I shouldn't have gone to Alex's. I'm sorry"

"I don't know if I can ever accept your apologies, ever live with you, ever even look at you." He turned back towards the computer.

"I'll sleep downstairs on the couch," Holly said.

"You're certainly not sleeping with me."

She found a pillow and blanket in the hallway linen closet and went downstairs to her latest living room nest. On the couch, staring past an *Art World* in the magazine rack, Holly wondered how she could survive a divorce. She thought about Sue and wondered how she had survived Jack's sickness and death.

When Jack died, Holly had felt awkward writing a note to Sue because they'd been out of touch for so long, but Sue wrote back quickly, with an amicable willingness to resume their friendship. "I'm doing alright," she wrote, "but I never know when or where I'll have a bad public cry and embarrass myself." She wrote of a time when she went to a restaurant and the waitress asked if she wanted a table for one, and Sue began blubbering, so much so that the waitress took her by the arm into the ladies room and sat her down on a chair. After Sue told the waitress why she was crying, the waitress left and returned a few minutes later with the restaurant manager, a man, who brought her a free daiquiri right there in the ladies' restroom. Sue's life happened like that; she always had a story to tell.

Holly found her number and dialed it. Sue answered after one ring.

"Hi Sue. It's Holly. Did Alex let you know I was okay?"

"Yes, but I can't tell you how relieved I feel to actually hear your voice. Oh Holly, are you home? I was so worried."

"I'm home, but I feel as though I'm in a stranger's house. I'm sleeping on the couch tonight."

"How's Ethan?"

"Ethan came home from the hospital today, and he's pretty much back to normal, except he has pneumonia from almost drowning. He's on an antibiotic and needs to take it easy for a couple of weeks. I was…just a second." Holly walked with the portable phone out onto the patio where Ted couldn't hear. The night air was pleasantly cool. She spoke softly, "Did Alex tell you about us?"

"He told me you stayed with him, but he didn't mention that you two were an 'us.'"

"I hadn't planned it."

"Wow."

"Yeah," Holly said.

"Alex said you thought Ethan was dead?"

Holly briefly described the overheard conversations at the hospital, the need to get away, the hitchhiking, the Holiday Inn, and her decision to see Alex.

"Why Alex? It's been years."

"Not exactly," Holly said. "We'd been e-mailing lately, flirting, planning to spend time at the reunion. You know the card he wrote me in the hospital? He talked about how much our relationship still meant to him. So I drove to Huffton College and slept on his futon. Alex fed me and nursed me, and we talked and talked the way we used to."

"You did more than talk, though, right?"

"It was incredible."

Sue screamed. "Get out! You and Alex?"

"But when I found out Ethan was alive, I came straight home. Ted and the police—I had no idea the police were involved—traced me to Alex's so Ted knows we were together. Now of course, Ted can't stand the sight of me. He called me a whore. I'm sleeping on the couch tonight, as I told you, but," and she lowered her voice, "part of me still wishes I were back on Alex's futon. How am I going to figure all this out? How did you make it through when Jack was dying?"

"It's a moment by moment thing," she said. "Tomorrow you'll wake up and deal with the things going on tomorrow—you'll get the kids off to school, clean the dishes, cook your dinner. When Jack was sick, I told myself I just had to make it through that day. Just had to make it through whatever horrible procedure was happening that day. If I looked ahead—at the medical bills, insurance, funeral, future of my job, life as a widow—God, I just wanted to crawl back in bed.

"You can't make any decisions right now, either. That's for sure. Time really does change things. Three months after Jack's death, a co-worker and I were sneaking this plastic hotdog-man onto the antennae of my boss' new convertible—it began a whole series of hotdog-man pranks in our office—and I remember thinking, 'Wow, I can't believe I'm able to act normal again.'"

"Well Sue, what you would call normal, the rest of us would call..."

"Abby Normal," they both said simultaneously in the British accents reserved for this one-liner.

"Shut up," Sue said.

"I don't know," Holly said. "I can't imagine things will ever feel normal again. Don't know if I want normal. Normal around here wasn't so hot, to tell you the truth. I can't imagine any resolution with Ted; he's really furious and hateful."

"I don't know. Maybe things don't ever feel normal exactly. Maybe it's more like scar tissue over a wound. Why don't you start seeing a counselor, someone who could help you sort through everything? That's what I did for a while."

"Oh geez, Ted will never agree to pay for it."

"Then I'll pay for it. Send me the bills. I'm serious."

"Thanks, but I can't even think about that right now. I'm exhausted. I'd better let you go so we can both get some sleep."

"You scum. I won't push the counseling thing, okay? It was just an idea."

"Sorry, I'm just really tired." Energy had been draining from her body as they spoke.

"Promise me you'll give yourself time, at least a couple of weeks, before you make any decisions about Ted or Alex."

"I don't know how long I can camp out on this couch."

"I'm serious."

"I'll try," Holly said.

"Listen Holly, I'm pretty sure I'm flying through Charlotte on Tuesday or Wednesday of next week on my way to Tampa. I'll call you. Maybe we can have coffee at the airport, sit in those cool rocking chairs."

"That'd be great."

"I think I have a crush on the project manager in Tampa. His name is Carlton. I've only spoken with him on the phone, but he's really funny, dry-funny the way Jack was. He'll probably look like a manatee, though, or a Chihuahua, and I'm sure he'll be wearing a wedding ring."

"Oh geez, even you wouldn't pursue a man with a wedding ring, and here I've gone and…Hey, don't tell Kate, okay?"

"Even me? Great, you think I'm a slut *and* a tattletale."

"Sorry. I love you. Call me from the airport. Good night."

Holly turned out the lights, and as she lay sideways on the couch, bending her knees to fit, her wound grazed the upholstered arm and burned slightly. Her stitches felt strange to the touch, rougher than before, and when she went to the bathroom to check them, she saw that they'd already begun to dissolve, just as the doctor said they would.

Back on the couch, she struggled to get comfortable. After the one side of her neck and shoulders stiffened, she turned on the other side, her face two inches from the backrest. Laying on her back and putting her feet up on the sofa arm worked for a while, until it didn't. She tried her stomach with the tops of her feet resting on the arm.

The night stretched on.

2

The sound of a boy's footsteps on the stairs made Holly bolt upright. She began folding up her blanket, trying to hide the evidence of her couch banishment, but Peter reached the living room too quickly.

"Hi Mommy," he said, locking in on her blanket and pillow.

"Good morning, Peter. Happy Friday." Holly could hear Ted's electric razor upstairs.

"Mrs. Jamison said today is the first of May!"

"Well, Happy First of May. You almost ready for school?"

"Why were you sleeping on the couch?" he asked.

"Oh, it's just that I couldn't fall asleep, and I wanted to read, but I didn't want to wake your dad, so I came down here. Have you eaten breakfast?"

"No. I want Lucky Charms. Dad bought us Lucky Charms."

"How about eggs? Or pancakes? I can make you a real breakfast."

"But mo-om," Peter said, "Dad showed me how to make Lucky Charms, and I can do it all by myself, even the milk. While Dad shaves, I come down to make my cereal."

Proudly, Peter performed his new-found skill while Holly began making his lunch. The pantry overflowed with all the packaged food Ted had bought. From the cornucopia, Holly pulled a Twinkie and the fixings for peanut butter and jelly. Who knew they still made Twinkies? With knife and chunky peanut butter she mutilated the white bread, which was softer and doughier than the whole wheat she normally bought. She hoped that somewhere in the back of the fridge a few carrots or an applesauce lingered to carry the nutritional load of Peter's lunch.

Holly never heard Ted's footsteps before he swept into the kitchen. "Peanut butter and jelly?" he asked in the accusing tone of a trial lawyer. "He had peanut butter and jelly yesterday. I didn't ask you to make his lunch. Today he gets ham and cheese. Right, Peter?"

"But I've already made it." Holly held up a deformed sandwich triangle. "What am I supposed to do with it?"

"It's okay," Peter offered, trying to ease the tension. "I don't mind peanut butter and jelly again. It's my favorite!"

"Fine with me," Ted said. "Peter, we've got five minutes. Put your bowl in the sink and go brush your teeth."

Peter exited the kitchen, leaving Ted and Holly to clank around in dour silence, each giving the other wide berth as Ted made coffee and toast and Holly finished packing Peter's lunch. Ted's dress pants, dress shirt and untied tie aroused Holly's curiosity, but she resisted the urge to ask him about his plans, knowing that Ted would turn anything she said—the sky is blue, the earth is round—back to her whoring ways. And instead of asking him if he'd bought any fruit or vegetables, a question that could be construed as criticism from a whore who had no right to be critical, she dug around the entire fridge on her own until she found two Del Monte fruit cups hidden inside the vegetable drawer. The coffee maker beeped. Ted poured himself a cup but didn't offer one to Holly.

"Are you going to be around this morning?" he finally asked. "I need to run by the office after I drop off Peter, and I'd rather not have to wake up Ethan and drag him along, but I will if I have to. After my four-day hiatus from work—due to my Missing Person wife who wasn't missing, it turns out, just unfaithful—I owe Pierson some serious face-time. I told him you were in the hospital this whole time, but he never sent a note or anything. He had his secretary call yesterday to ask when I was coming in."

"I'll be here with Ethan," Holly said.

"Okay, good. I already gave Ethan his morning medicine, and he went right back to sleep." Ted reached for the door to the garage. "I'll transfer his car seat to your rental car. For goodness sake, Holly, how much is that rental costing per day?" He slammed the door before she could answer.

Moment by moment, Sue had said. Holly wrote a note to put in Peter's lunchbox, avoiding contractions and big words in hopes that he could read it without Mrs. Jamison's help.

> I love you, Peter. You are a kind, smart, and brave boy. I am glad you are mine. I cannot wait to see you after school.—Love, Mom

After Ted and Peter left, Holly carefully opened Ethan's door and found him among his bed of stuffed animals sleeping soundly, safe and beautiful and perfect. He rarely slept through Peter's school preparations, but his poor little recuperating body must have needed it.

Holly made herself a cup of coffee and thought about Alex's café table, where he fed her and let her cry on his shoulder. Two days had passed since she'd seen him. What was he thinking about their relationship? Probably that he'd had a nice little fling, end of story, or that he'd made a huge mistake, which now needed rectifying. Had he written Holly an e-mail?

Indeed, after Judy Garland welcomed Holly home, an e-mail from profmeyers@huffton.edu awaited her.

> Dear Holly,
>
> I miss you so much I can hardly stand it. I want to be with you. I need to talk to you about so many things.
>
> I went to Zoë's studio yesterday and saw your sad, tortured painting. I'm sorry you went so long thinking Ethan was dead. Your painting speaks to me so clearly about your dark, artistic side, which I've always loved and you've always covered up.
>
> I talked to Emily tonight. I told her about you and me. It was the only way to get her to

realize that our marriage is in deep trouble. She
hung up on me. She disdains me. Any chance
our marriage had of survival is now gone.

I need to talk to you, Holly. I hesitate to say
this because I know you're dealing with so
much, but I feel rudderless without you.
Yours,
Alex

A swamp of emotions sucked at Holly's tired body. Guilt
that she could so easily go back to the futon, betraying Ted all
over again. Guilt that she could so easily abandon the futon,
rejecting Alex all over again, for the fourth time. Guilt that she
had left Zoë's studio a mess. Giddiness that the boy she had a
crush on liked her back. Lust for the thrill of the futon. Love for
Alex that was deeper than lust or giddiness. Shame that she
might have broken up two marriages. Her conflicting emotions
mixed together in a muddy swirl, like all the paints mixed
together. What color does that make, Mommy? A yucky brown,
honey, just a yucky brown.

Ethan, she could hear, was now awake and making his
animals go through their morning ritual. Good morning, JuJu.
And in a higher pitched voice, Good morning, Ethan. All eleven
of them had to exchange greetings with Ethan before he got out
of bed. Holly printed off Alex's e-mail, deleted it from her
mailbox, and signed off. The hard copy she folded and put into
the pocket of her pajamas, tucking away these emotions for now.

Moment by moment.

Holly and Ethan watched *Barney* while she got him fed and
dressed. Barney and the big-toothed older boy led the gang on an
island adventure after finding a portal in the back of his closet.
Everything about Barney depressed her: the derivative story
lines, the artificial lighting, the one-instrument songs, and the
mindless enthusiasm of these child-actors who were destined to
become drug addicts. She turned off the show before the "I
Love You" song, that vapid dirge, which depressed her most of
all. Holly told Ethan they needed to go across the street to

schedule his game day.

When the Farrells' door opened, Judith's fuchsia pantsuit blazed out like a backdraft.

"Wow," Holly said, "You look ready to conquer the world. Where'd you find fuchsia sandals the exact color of your outfit?"

"T.J. Maxx, honey. I'm meeting my daughter, Verna, for lunch today. Come on in. How ya doing? How was the homecoming? I see Ted didn't s-h-o-o-t you."

"I can spell," Ethan protested. "Peter taught me. Cat, c-a-t."

"Why you sure can, Master Ethan, I should have known." Judith winked at Holly. "You want to go out back and throw Maxie's ball?"

"Okay. That's spelled o-k."

Judith led Ethan and Maxie out the sliding door, and Holly and Judith sat on kitchen stools where they could watch boy and dog through the window. Joe was hammering in the garage.

"Well," Holly began, "Ted didn't shoot me, but he's furious, called me a whore, said he didn't think he could ever accept my apologies or ever live with me again. I can't see that there's much hope for us."

"It hasn't even been twenty-four hours," Judith said. "You can't decide if there's hope yet. You can't resolve anything that fast. Give it some time. My goodness, you kids want everything now."

"I got an e-mail from Alex this morning." Holly took the letter from her pocket and handed it to Judith, who pulled out tortoise-shell glasses from her straw fuchsia handbag. She read the letter slowly.

When she finished, she laid it against her chest and lowered her glasses. "You're not going to see him, are you?"

"No, but a part of me wants to. He knows a side of me that no one else knows. I feel so bad that I'm leaving him hanging."

"I know this is really hard, but I wouldn't talk to him if I were you. You have big decisions to make about your marriage and your family. For these decisions, I think you already know everything you need to know about Alex right now, without calling or writing him."

"His wife is probably going to leave him. He sounds so lonely."

"Talking to him will only muddy the waters."

"Oh my gosh. Yes. Like mixing all the paints. It makes muddy brown."

"That's right. Nothing will look clear. Yellow can never look yellow."

Outside Ethan threw the red ball towards the back fence, much to Maxie's bounding delight. "Well, what should I do?" Holly asked.

"Nothing." Judith took off her glasses and patted the skin around her eyes.

"What do you mean nothing?"

"Nothing. Not a damn thing. Don't write him. Don't call him. Let some time pass."

"But Judith, he sounds so miserable. I'm miserable, too."

"You'll both be just as miserable if you talk or meet. Maybe I should tell you about my scandalous affair."

"Recently? Does Joe know?"

Judith looked toward the garage. "No, it happened long before I met Joe, but I never have told him about it. I just never thought he could handle the fact that my second marriage came from an affair during my first marriage, which had lost its pizzazz. My first husband Jerry took me for granted. 'We're having pork chops *again*?' he might say, or, 'Honey, I believe that dress makes your hips look big.' See, other men look mighty fine when you're being taken for granted. Bobby, my second husband, was that way. Bobby was alright, but I doubt I'd ever have picked him if I was just a single gal out looking. I picked Bobby to advertise to Jerry (and myself) that I was still able to reel 'em in. Don't get me wrong, I'm not saying that's what you're doing with Alex. All I'm saying is that you have all sorts of emotions playing against each other and you need to be away from him to see what you're really feeling."

"I'm sure you're right." Holly picked up the letter from the counter and re-folded it. "Well, we'd better let you go so you can get ready for your lunch date."

"You're going to call him, aren't you?"

"No. No. I just have a thousand things to do, and I know you do too."

"Ethan seem to be doing well," Judith said as they walked toward the sliding door. "Can I come over after lunch to play Cooties with him?"

"That'd be great. Ethan's in good spirits, except that he gets out of breath when he goes up the stairs. He seems to be doing alright out there with Maxie."

"And Peter?"

"Good, really good." Holly and Judith stepped onto the patio. "Ethan, time to go. Judith's coming over this afternoon for Cooties."

Judith was absolutely right about not calling Alex, but Holly couldn't just ignore his e-mail. She replied with two quick lines asking him to please not write or call for the next two weeks.

When Alex received Holly's e-mail on Friday night, he theorized that Holly's dutiful alter ego, the repressed Mrs. Reese, had done the writing after having tied up in the basement the other Holly, Futon Holly, the one with the ankle tattoo. Somehow he needed to free Futon Holly while also honoring the requests of Mrs. Reese. So he did not write her or call her, as per request. Instead, he got in his car and drove six and a half hours to Charlotte, where, in the wee hours of the morning, he stopped by a Walmart and bought two cheap wine goblets, Cranberry 7 Up, and a Charlotte street atlas.

Eventually he found Holly's cul-de-sac, Gilead Knob Court, parked at the entrance of the street, and walked by several houses until he got to 4316. Her house was much more traditional and symmetrical than he had imagined, with perfectly round boxwoods marching along the front and hunter green shutters. No wonder Holly felt trapped. The purse-lipped Mrs. Reese ran the show.

Alex tiptoed up the front steps and tried to quietly pull his offerings out of the blue Walmart bag, but the plastic crinkled out of control. Surely Ted would wake up and load his shotgun. Nervousness made Alex want to laugh, just like the time he and Holly snuck up to his parents' kitchen in the middle of the night. On the left side of the stoop, Alex placed the Cranberry 7 Up and two wine goblets on top of his Catatonic State t-shirt, hoping that Holly, not Ted, would be the one to discover his offering.

Alex drove out of the cul-de-sac and toured the neighborhood until he found the parking lot of The Cedars' swimming pool. There he parked his Camry, reclined his seat, and fell into a fitful sleep.

In the morning he awoke with the sun. He ran his fingers through his disheveled hair and wet it down with melted ice from his McDonald's cup. From that same water source, he brushed his teeth, spitting into a well-groomed flowerbed. For his other bathroom duties, he walked around the pool house to a cluster of trees that hid him from the surrounding homes. The Cedars pool was not a bad place to be homeless.

He drove back to Holly's cul-de-sac, parking one house down from her, with an unobstructed view of her front door where he could just make out the top of the Cranberry 7 Up bottle. A newspaper lay in Holly's driveway. Who would retrieve it, Ted or Holly? Either one, Alex planned to slink down and spy. For half an hour he kept watch on Holly's hunter green door, until a neighbor lady came out on her front porch and eyed him suspiciously. He drove off, deciding to go in search of coffee.

An unusual quietness greeted Holly on Saturday morning. Peter and Ethan had stayed asleep, and Ted had left a terse note saying that he had gone to Lowe's to service the lawnmower. Saturday was lawn day for this lawn man who took pride in his perfect criss-crossing mow pattern on his weedless fescue. With no husband, no kids, and good coffee, Holly hoped to get past A-1 in the newspaper, glad to immerse herself in the problems of other people.

Holly had never settled her opinion about newspaper etiquette in the suburbs and whether or not it allowed for walking to the end of the driveway in pajamas. Her pajamas, after all, were modest. Obviously, changing into clothes and bra was the most respectable option, but Holly believed that reading the newspaper while fully dressed was a completely different activity than reading the newspaper in pajamas. A robe was another option, but her terry cloth robe transformed her into a pudgy pink penguin. So Holly chose that morning, as she usually did, the pajama option. She dashed for the newspaper, averting her eyes from the neighbors' houses.

Midway down the front steps, a pink bottle caught her eye, then wine glasses, then the Catatonic State t-shirt. She jerked her head up, scanning for Alex in the cul-de-sac, the yard, and even behind the boxwoods. She walked to the edge of the lawn, neighbors be damned, and looked down the street, but it appeared that the Enola Gay of spritzers had come and gone, driving thirteen hours round trip to deliver his payload. How did Judith expect her to ignore this?

Inside Holly took off her pajama top and put on Alex's t-shirt, which smelled freshly laundered. The cranberry 7Up sizzled as she unscrewed the cap. She filled one of the glasses and held it up to the window, watching bubbles pop into the air.

The crunching of loose asphalt startled Holly. She reached for the neck of her Catatonic State t-shirt, ready to whip it off if the car was Ted's, but the car that inched into the cul-de-sac was silver not black. Her heart raced. It was Alex's silver Camry. His car didn't stop in front of her house but kept on creeping past her. Did he think she wasn't home? Had he changed his mind? She flung open the front door, still holding her glass of cranberry spritzer.

Alex set the gas station coffee in the cupholder of his Camry and stared at Holly's front stoop. The goodies were now gone. Slowly he drove around the cul-de-sac, concentrating on the brass handle of Holly's front door, willing it to open. When the door did swing open he was so surprised he slammed the brake and the car lurched forward. Holly barreled into the doorframe, and her breasts swayed freely underneath her shirt— his shirt with the Catatonic State seal. He thought of the balcony scene in *Romeo and Juliet*: "*See how she leans her cheek upon her hand! O that I were a glove upon that hand, that I might touch that cheek!*" Alex wished he were the t-shirt upon that body.

When their eyes met, she smiled, so adorable with messy hair and no make-up. Soon their smiles dissipated, though, and the two stared at one another, immobilized by the complexities of their relationship. Gone was the freedom they'd enjoyed at his house in Henrietta. Alex didn't know exactly what he'd driven almost 400 miles to say, but he had to say something, even if he had to yell it across the street. For the briefest moment he looked down to press the button that lowered his window. When he looked up again, as his window lowered, Holly was walking back inside.

"Wait," he yelled. And then more quietly, to himself, "Come back to me."

He kept his foot on the brake, hoping against the odds that Futon Holly had just stepped inside for a second to get a jacket or scold a kid.

Initially Alex's flirtatious smile dazzled Holly, but then it disturbed her. In the context of her own home, Alex was awry. His leering eyes didn't belong in her G-rated cul-de-sac, so near her kids, with Ted just miles away. Alex belonged in Henrietta, compartmentalized to his remote bachelor pad.

Holly feared Alex would step from his car into her cul-de-sac, penetrating her suburbia before she was ready, so she retreated back inside, slamming the door and slapping a palm against it as if she'd made it to home base before getting tagged. Her breathing steadied and she listened for Alex's car, but he hadn't moved yet. She felt bad that he'd driven six and a half hours.

Holly crept into the corner of the dining room, ten feet back from the mini-blinds, where she could spy on Alex's Camry still idling across the street. He ran his hand through his hair and looked one last time in the direction of her front door. Then he turned his head, and his tires began to rotate.

And then he was gone. Gone was the man bearing romantic gifts; soon to return was the man bearing a serviced lawnmower.

Alex drove out of the cul-de-sac and headed home. During his long drive, he swung back and forth between feelings of rejection and hope. True, Holly didn't jump into his car or beckon him inside, and she did shut the door on him. But on the other hand, she was in fact wearing his t-shirt and holding the spritzer he'd left her. The dutiful Mrs. Reese may have eventually turned back to her duties inside the house, but at least for a moment Futon Holly had enjoyed Alex's gifts and just maybe had considered running out to his car. The two different Hollies inspired a poem that evolved during the six and a half hour trip. When Alex stopped for gas, he wrote down the words on his yellow notepad:

> Two Poles
> One pole is made of metal,
> cold, gray matter.
> What's the matter?
> It's tough
> and ram rod straight
> and born of only reason.

The other pole is made of wood,
raw and pliant.
Would it bend?
It would
if pressed upon
by all the weight of love.

Just one question:
reason or love?

With only one stop for gas and poetry, Alex arrived at his house by 4:00 in the afternoon. He gathered up his toiletry bag, old coffee cup, yellow pad and atlas and wrangled this armful as he tried to unlock his door, only to discover that he'd left his front door unlocked. He smiled at how absent-minded and impetuous he'd been on Friday night when he left on his road trip.

Once Alex stepped over his threshold, he saw the actual reason for the unlocked door: Ms. Emily Gregory was sitting on his futon. His atlas and yellow pad flounced to the floor. What a different futon denizen Emily was, her back rigid and her one leg primly crossed over the other, pumping impatiently. In her lap she held a thick file folder. She looked more like Alex's real estate agent than his wife, except her face conveyed too much contempt to ever sell a house.

Alex was speechless. He knew Emily had planned to book a Saturday flight, but after their phone conversation about Holly, after Emily had hung up on him and wouldn't return his calls, Alex assumed the visit was off.

"Where've you been?" Emily asked.

"I didn't think you'd be coming," Alex said and bent down to pick up the Charlotte atlas and the Holly poem, which he placed face down underneath his toiletries bag. He looked up at Emily who stared at the items in his hands.

"Have you been with your little friend from high school?"

"Do you really care where I've been? You haven't cared

where I've been for a long time. You wouldn't even return my phone calls."

"There was nothing to talk about over the phone. The only reason I'm here is to serve you with these papers from my lawyer. I want a divorce. You seem to want one too."

"Just like that, without further discussion?"

"What's there to discuss?"

"How my affair didn't arise out of thin air. How you've had your head so far up your drafting table that you couldn't see the state of our marriage. How we haven't had sex in over six months. How you've never wanted me to visit you in Hawaii. How you've had an affair too, at least with your career, and I wouldn't be shocked if also with another man."

"How dare you. I may be a lot of things, but unfaithful is not one of them. That apparently is your forte."

Though she sat on the futon looking up at him, she seemed to tower above him with her self-righteous shoulders and superior eyes.

Alex replied, "So you can't see anything you've done to damage our marriage? Anything at all?"

"Puh-lease. Working a lot is different than cheating."

"Not to me."

She tapped her manicured fingernails on the folder. "Let's just sign the papers and call it a marriage. Time of death—" she looked at her watch, "4:06 p.m."

"I'm not signing papers I didn't know about until five minutes ago."

"Of course. I'll leave them with you to read over."

"Fine."

He went to put his toiletries away in the bathroom and closed the door. Emily never waffled once she'd made a decision. Once she slammed down her gavel, she never went back to explore the shades of truth. There was nothing Alex could do. His marriage was over, whether he wanted it to be or not. He probably wanted it to be over, but not without analysis, discussion and understanding. He wished he had someone to talk to about everything. Although he had plenty of wonderful colleagues to philosophize with, he had no one besides Holly to talk to about his personal life.

He heard the front door close. It didn't exactly slam, but Emily shut it hard enough to make a statement. Out in the living room, the file folder with the divorce documents lay open on the futon; otherwise, no evidence of Emily remained. Alex didn't know if she'd gone to a nearby hotel or back to Atlanta, so he spent the rest of the afternoon and evening trying to do things that Emily might approve of if she happened to come back. He cleaned. He graded papers. He made veal Parmesan for dinner. But Emily never returned.

Before he went to bed, Alex sat on the futon with the divorce documents in his lap. He hadn't necessarily meant for his relationship with Holly to lead to a divorce with Emily. It had all happened so fast. If he hadn't told Emily right away, he might have had time to figure things out.

The divorce proposal, in compliance with the laws of the State of Georgia, mentioned equitable distribution of property, alimony (there would be none since Emily made more money than him), and something that was pure retaliation, pure Emily, something that he knew immediately he would never sign his name to: adultery as the stated grounds.

Several years ago, a friend of Alex's in Atlanta, Chase Peterson, had gone through a divorce, and Alex knew that Emily could have chosen, as Chase had, "no fault" as the grounds. The term was "irretrievably broken," which so aptly described Alex and Emily's relationship. Chase Peterson could have chosen "substance abuse" as his grounds, but he didn't want to waste time proving that his wife was a methadone addict. He just wanted out as fast as possible. For Emily, though, speed was apparently not as important as self-absolution.

Alex closed the file folder and cast it aside on the futon. An Amstel Light called his name. After a few swallows he called their house in Atlanta. He left a message on the answering machine telling Emily that he'd read the papers and wanted to talk. The taut cords of restraint kept his upper and lower jaws together and his words spare.

Fifteen minutes later Emily called, not from Atlanta but from the Henrietta Marriott.

"Alex, I don't want to talk. I just wanted to see if you've read the papers and if you'll sign them before I fly back."

"I will not sign the papers," he yelled. "You know adultery is not the only grounds for divorce. You are so full of self-righteousness. You know I am not the only reason our marriage is falling apart. I'm not about to take all the blame. You can just plan on a lengthy, expensive trial if you're going to insist on it, and then I'll be glad to tell the judge about Chicago."

Emily was silent.

Five months ago in a moment of largess, Emily had invited Alex to come along with her to a weekend conference in Chicago. Although she was to be in meetings most of the time, she told Alex she thought he'd enjoy sight-seeing or grading papers in the luxury of her posh hotel. On Friday night, Emily returned to the room after cocktails with her boss and a few others from her firm. She came into the room, took off her heels and panty hose, and sat on the edge of the king sized bed.

"I bet you could use a good shoulder rub after such a long day," Alex said.

"I guess," she said without commitment.

Alex sat on the bed behind her and began to massage her shoulders and neck. Emily rolled her neck from side to side, seeming to enjoy Alex's ministrations. From her neck muscles, Alex moved his fingers up onto her head. His massaging turned into stroking, first her hair in the back, then her hair in the front, then the sides of her face, then her clavicles, then her....

Emily stood, whipped her body around and kicked Alex squarely in his chest. His back slammed against the mattress, bounced up, and slammed down again. Alex clutched his chest and struggled to catch his breath.

"Oh my gosh," Emily said, "I didn't mean to. It's just..." and her voice changed, "I wish you could just give me a massage without demanding more. I'm so tired of this."

For almost two weeks afterwards, Alex had a grisly bruise between his pectoral muscles. Emily never apologized, but for the next few weeks she called him more than usual and sent him a blue grass CD he'd been wanting. They never talked about Chicago, and thereafter, barely kissed each other on the cheek.

After her silence Emily said, "So, you're saying that if I change the grounds to 'no fault' that you'd be willing to sign the settlement without going to court?"

"I guess so," he replied. "I don't know. This is all so sudden."

"I'll talk to my lawyer. He'll give you a call Monday. I'm going back to Atlanta tomorrow morning to check on the house and make sure Carla's taken care of the leak in the guest room. My flight leaves at 6:00 tomorrow evening."

"You're not changing your mind, are you?"

"No."

"How is it being project manager?" Alex wanted to back away from a dogfight.

"Fine, but it's only been three days. I'll probably stay in Hawaii longer than six months."

"Maybe you'll have time to learn surfing."

"I don't think we'll have any trouble selling the house," Emily said. "We'll probably make $50,000. I might see if I can find a real estate agent tomorrow, even though it's Sunday. Do you think the Suters will consider letting you buy your Huffton house?"

"No, they're so attached to the college. I think they'll always want to hold onto it."

"I need to go, Alex."

"Bye."

3

Holly dialed the police department from the patio because she didn't want to disturb Ted who was working from home again, as he had the day before, to supervise the tricky administration of Ethan's medicine in addition to the other parenting and household duties for which Holly could no longer be trusted. In front of Holly's chaise lounge chair, Ethan and Peter played on the swings, dangling over the seats and stirring the mulch around with their hands and feet. They played together on the swing set almost every day after Peter got home from school.

"Good afternoon," Holly said to the police receptionist. "This is Holly Reese. May I speak to Officer Lewis?" After their brief meeting on Friday, Officer Lewis had filed the van wreck as a "no fault accident, no fatalities," and Holly was grateful he chose not write her up for traveling too fast under rainy conditions. "I need to ask Officer Lewis about the recovered items from my minivan. I was in an accident a couple weeks ago."

Holly wanted to find her crystal pendant. Three days had passed since Holly turned from Alex's romantic overtures towards an angry husband and two demanding kids. She was trying, as Sue advised, to navigate her days on a moment by moment basis, but she wasn't so sure she could endure much longer, not without her pendant.

"Officer Lewis isn't working today," the receptionist said. "He'll be in tomorrow morning. Would you like his voice mail?"

"Is there someone else who could help me? It's really, really important that I find this particular item: it's a crystal teardrop that hangs on a nylon string." Ethan started kicking mulch into the grass. Holly clapped her hands and shook her head at him. "See, my dad gave me the necklace right before he died, and it's like he…Anyway, it has a lot of sentimental value, and I just really need it back. It was on the rearview mirror of the minivan, so I know it must have been recovered. I mean, where could it have gone, right?"

The receptionist put Holly on hold.

Holly hadn't heard from Alex since he'd driven away from her cul-de-sac. He may have written her, but she had vigorously resisted the urge to check e-mail, a feat made easier by Ted's near-constant presence on the computer. Also resisted had been the urge to wear, touch, or smell the Catatonic State t-shirt, which she'd hidden in the back of her lingerie drawer, although each morning when she got a fresh bra and underwear, the mere presence of the grey cotton keepsake pulled her like a vortex into the memories of the previous week when she'd worn it to Professor Meyer's lecture and been stripped of it after class.

For three days Holly tried to rebuff her thoughts of Alex, concentrating instead on her penance as the polite, tentative houseguest who tried to stay out of Ted's way and not ask questions. If Ted were upstairs, she and the kids tried to stay downstairs. If he were downstairs, they went outside. Holly cooked inventively from the odd food assortment Ted had bought, until Sunday afternoon when she could no longer avoid a grocery run. Then she dropped off the kids at Judith's, shopped for the bare essentials, and paid for them from an account she wasn't sure had sufficient funds or hadn't been cancelled. Ted didn't even join them for meals. Instead, Holly made him a plate, left it outside his office door, and knocked lightly to let him know it was there.

This limbo, she knew, she could only sustain for so long, in the same way a nude model in an art class could only sustain a dramatic twist of torso or lift of elbow for the five-minute short pose, not the 60-minute long pose. That morning, as she'd woken up sore again from sleeping on the couch, she thought the only way to endure the long pose would be to find her crystal pendant.

The receptionist connected Holly to an officer who was able to track down the list of recovered items. He said that no necklace or pendant had been included on the list but that Mr. Reese had picked up all the items the previous week.

"Mr. Reese picked up the items?"

"Yes, that was Tuesday of last week."

Ted hadn't mentioned the van contents, but of course, the mention of it might have taken up more than his allotted 20 words per day. "Thanks a lot," Holly said.

"No problem, Mrs. Reese. I sure am glad you and your boys are okay. Next time y'all need to pay attention to those recalls."

"Recalls?" Holly said.

"Tire recalls. You know, your van had bum tires."

Holly acted like she knew about the tires and thanked the officer for his help. She told the boys, now digging in the sandbox, that she needed to run inside to talk to their dad.

At Ted's closed door she listened to see if he were on the phone and then tapped lightly with her fingernails. "Sorry to bother you, Ted, but can I come in for a minute? I just need to ask you a couple questions."

He unclicked the lock but did not open the door. She waited, but apparently unlocking the door was the closest she would get to an invitation. Slowly she pressed the door open.

"I just called the police department," Holly said. "I asked about the recovered items from the minivan because I'd really like to find my crystal prism. They said you picked up the items last week. You didn't by any chance find my necklace tucked in with all the other stuff, did you?"

"No. I never saw it, and it wasn't on the print-out of the recovered items. I imagine your necklace is lying on the bottom of Lake Odell."

Holly's heart sank.

"But," Ted said, "if you want to look through it, I put the box of recovered items at the top of the attic stairs, next to the suitcases."

Holly brightened. "Great, I'll look there. Also the officer mentioned something about the minivan's recalled…"

"I already cleared out your suitcase, I hope you know." His voice had sharpened to a steely point. "I washed all the clothes. All of them. Every last piece. Maybe your necklace got caught up in some of the laundry I did." He stood up. "I know. Why don't we go take a look in your drawers? Huh? Come on. Let's you and me go see what's in your drawers."

Holly froze, thinking that Ted had probably discovered the Catatonic State t-shirt in her underwear drawer, though she couldn't imagine her unobservant husband noticing the inconspicuous item in the first place, and then recognizing it as anything other than a shirt she'd owned for years, and then figuring out it belonged to Alex. In the past, for Ted to have clued in to its suspicious origins, the shirt would have needed high-contrast block letters that spelled out Huffton College on the front and Alex Meyers on the back, and even then Holly would have needed to leave it on Ted's chair. Yet Holly also knew that betrayal may have evoked in Ted new detective tendencies toward suspicion, snooping, and putting two and two together.

Ted stormed into their bedroom and Holly scurried behind.

"Let's start here," Ted said as he opened Holly's underwear drawer. He stirred the garments around, swirling the gray t-shirt from the back to the front. Holly stared in horror and waited for him to lift it up.

"Not there," he said through clenched teeth. He slammed the drawer shut.

Now Holly was really confused. If Ted hadn't discovered Alex's t-shirt, what in her drawers was making him so angry? Ted proceeded to the second drawer, full of little-used exercise clothes, but he slammed that drawer shut, too. When he got to the third drawer, her pajama drawer, he said he'd found what he was looking for. He pulled the drawer completely out of the chest, dumped its contents onto the floor, then shoved the wooden drawer into Holly's arms. From the pile on the floor, Ted plucked out what he'd been looking for: the maroon teddy she'd bought at Victoria's Secret.

"Let's see," he said, "maybe your necklace got caught up in

this little red negligee you bought for your rendezvous with Alex. It's been through the wash, but you never know." Ted stretched the snap crotch an inch in front of Holly's face. "Did your necklace get caught here, on this microscopic piece of lace?"

Holly's eyes watered, and her arms trembled from the weight of the drawer, but she held herself to this humiliating tableau, knowing that both she and Ted needed her to be punished for this newly revealed crime that indicted her not just of adultery, but of premeditated adultery. The scanty piece, bought before the accident and packed in her suitcase as part of her reunion trousseau, revealed her intention of hooking up with Alex. The sheer lacy fabric exposed the deceit of her previous claim that the unplanned affair just happened as the result of a grieving heart and a concussed brain.

As their frozen state wore on, Ted's anger morphed into awkwardness until he dropped the teddy at Holly's feet. "Please throw this thing away," he said and walked back to his office.

Once she set down the drawer, Holly inspected the two red scrapes that had flared on the inside of each forearm, but the sting felt appropriate as she picked up the teddy. Quietly she walked downstairs, dropped the blood-red evidence in a plastic grocery bag, and dumped it directly in the garbage can out back. The offending item was physically gone, but she knew that, psychologically, Ted would continue to hold the teddy in front of her face for a long time to come. All over again, she longed for her crystal.

Holly called to the boys, who were still digging in the sandbox. "Hey Ethan and Peter? I need to pull some stuff down from the attic, and I need you to help, okay?"

"The fold-up ladder!" Peter said.

Ethan chimed in, "Ladder, ladder, ladder."

"You'll have to be super quiet because Daddy is working. Okay? But if you stay absolutely silent, I'll let you climb the ladder."

"Weeee," Peter said.

Puffs of pink insulation wafted down from the hot attic as Holly unfolded the much anticipated ladder. Holly gave Ethan the important job of collecting the pink floaters while she and Peter carefully climbed up, just high enough to clear the attic floor and survey by flashlight the mysteries there. Peter maintained his promised silence until his flashlight lit upon the foil-wrapped box where the gray HVAC ducts converged.

"It's a giant alien spider!" he squealed.

Holly shushed him and waited for a rebuke from Ted's office, but none came. During Ethan's turn she kept one hand over his mouth. Holly brought down the box of minivan items, which smelled like wet leaves, followed by the two empty suitcases. The boys rode the suitcases like ponies, and at the doorway of Holly's bedroom, Peter reared back his suitcase and whinnied.

"Whoa there," he said. "How come your dresser exploded all over the floor?"

Holly had forgotten about the mess Ted had made. She set down the cardboard box, put all her pajamas back in the drawer, and slid the drawer into the dresser. If only her other messes could be cleaned up so easily.

"Daddy was looking for something," she explained.

One by one Holly pulled out the minivan items from the cardboard box. Methodically she arranged the items on the carpet in front of her: 1 set of car keys, 7 small plastic toys, a pulpy map, jumper cables, a warped Dodge manual, 3 wavy junk mail envelopes, a container of baby wipes, 2 sippie cups, 3 pieces of candy, and 4 ruined cassette tapes. On second sweep, she looked inside the plastic container of baby wipes, unscrewed the lids of the sippie cups, unfolded the map, and fanned through the Dodge manual. She un-taped the bottom of the cardboard box and looked under the flaps. But she could not find her crystal.

She and the boys scoured every pocket in each empty suitcase, though of course it made no sense that the pendant would have flown off the rearview mirror and landed inside the closed suitcases. Still, hope had a way of defying logic.

Leaving the dead-end pile in her bedroom, Holly and the boys returned to the back yard, where Holly once again called the police department to get the name of the company that had towed her minivan. The crystal had to have settled in some odd nook or cranny of the minivan, and if she could just scour the van, she felt sure she'd find it. The owner of Action Towing of Concord told her that her insurance company had already transferred the vehicle to a salvage yard, and before that, the police had thoroughly inspected the vehicle and removed all the items, which they should have returned to her. The owner said they'd never even touched the inside of the Caravan, and his defensive tone made Holly wonder if he often got accused of theft.

Holly's State Farm agent informed her that the salvage yard had already auctioned off the Caravan and a check for the Actual Cash Value had been mailed to her and Mr. Reese the day before. When Holly asked who had bought the car at auction, her State Farm agent said to call Tony's Salvage. When she eventually tracked down Tony, he said to call State Farm. She hung up on him.

Forty-five minutes later she was driving her white Chevy Metro to Lake Odell in hopes of finding the crystal on her own, without the help of the powers-that-be. Her crystal, she realized, could have washed up on shore.

She'd left her house in the name of "errands" and dropped off the kids at Judith's. Underneath her shorts and t-shirt, she wore her old brown bathing suit, and beside her in her Happy Mother's Day tote bag, underneath her coupon pouch placed as decoy, she'd packed a small towel.

Past the business park, the mega-church, and two swanky neighborhoods, the land along Odell Road opened up, spreading out the ranch-style houses onto many-acred lots, with newly plowed gardens and weathered barns. Holly slowed from 55 miles an hour to 40 and then 30 as she approached the scene of her accident.

She scanned the left side of the road for the white house with black shutters. She pictured the pounding rain and the green tractor driven by the farmer in rain slicker and straw cowboy hat. Why had Dodge never sent her notification about the recalled tires, so clearly ill-equipped for sudden braking on a slick road? Two houses gave Holly pause, the white clapboard house with Williamsburg blue shutters and a white two-story with double porches, but a third white house made her pull over on the shoulder. All the details matched her memory: 4 sets of black shutters, large pin oaks on either end, sprawling front yard, and a split rail fence that had clearly not been damaged or recently repaired. She pictured her van veering towards this fence, yet she knew this house was not the place where she nearly killed herself and her kids.

She pressed in the mile tracker and drove on, past another house and another, past a horse farm and a large forested tract, past a cow pasture and five or six more houses, until she finally came to the lake. Nothing seemed familiar along the 2.4 mile stretch of road that separated the white house from the lake. She wondered if she had actually gotten her concussion when the toy hit her head, causing her to swerve toward the white clapboard house, correct back onto the road, then lose control a few miles later. Or maybe when she swerved towards the house, she'd hit her head then. Whatever the case, she couldn't remember anything that had happened during that 2.4 mile stretch, not anything Ethan or Peter had said, not anything she had said, nothing, until the necklace flew off the rearview mirror and her van nosed towards the lake.

The sight of Lake Odell made Holly nauseous, her stomach remembering her flight into the water. Once she passed the lake, she found a driveway to turn around in and headed back towards the lake, where she pulled off on the grassy shoulder. The sun flickered on the water's metallic surface. Holly walked along the shoulder beside the guardrail, but the guardrail stopped once it reached a patch of trees. Construction engineers must have tried to save money on guardrail since the trees would just as readily stop a lakebound car. What the engineers didn't count on, though, was the death of some trees on one side of the cluster. There, a perfect gap had opened, allowing the briefest lake access for her minivan. There, highway officials had recently placed 6 sand-filled barrels. There, she found black tire marks that trailed from the road and across the white line. Nine days ago she and her boys had skidded across this impossible path. Today she marveled that she was observing the scene from this side of death.

Down the grassy embankment she slid onto a mixture of red clay and sand that found its way inside her sneakers. She walked back and forth along the small shore, kicking at the sand, finding only a bottle cap, a plastic pen and some knotted fishing line. The fisherman Milton Benson must have been standing at this same spot when the unidentified flying minivan landed in front of him. Holly felt for the crystal along the edge of the grassy bank, though, short of a hurricane, the bank was too high for flotsam.

After a group of three cars passed on the road, Holly stripped down to her bathing suit and waded into the water. Robot-style, she dragged her feet over a swath of slime, moving parallel to the shoreline and venturing a little deeper with each pass. A part of her truly believed her feet would eventually slide over the crystal, so when her foot skimmed a suspicious rock, she would pick it up hopefully and then slam it down. Back and forth she tacked until the water reached her neck and she began to dive madly, exploring the bottom with her hands. The more she came up empty-handed, the angrier she became and the sloppier her diving form, with arms and legs flailing, sand swirling, and lungs heaving. Finally, shaky with fatigue and unable to dive again, she sputtered, "Father, where are you?" But there was no answer except the call of a Bob White.

No longer able to tread water, Holly began floating on her back, like a wooden stick, broken-off and aimless. The brightness of the sun forced her eyes shut, and under her eyelids the sun went purple, its color wheel opposite; then the purple circle faded to red-brown nothingness, blank like the 2.4 mile stretch of her memory. She thought of Virginia Woolf the day she walked into the drowning waters of Ouse. On her second time trying, that time with heavy stones in her pockets and more resolve in her heart, had Woolf seen brown nothingness as the oxygen drained from her body?

Holly didn't want to drown, but she wasn't ready to go home either. For a long time, she simply floated, unmoored from her family, from Alex, and from her crystal prism.

When Holly arrived at Judith's door to pick up her boys, she didn't try to fix her lake-inspired hair or change into dry clothes because she wanted to tell Judith about Lake Odell.

"Thanks so much for watching the boys," Holly said, "but I want you to know that I didn't really run errands like I told you. I actually went to Lake Odell to try to find my crystal prism."

"Your what? Come on in honey. The kids are out back."

Holly sat on Judith's living room floor to spare the furniture from her wet shorts, and through the sliding door they watched the boys chase Maxie while Holly told Judith the history of her crystal necklace: about her father's death, her sixteenth birthday, the rainbows, the rearview mirror, and all the late-night conversations she'd had with this inanimate object.

"Does that sound crazy?" Holly asked.

"At least it wasn't fuzzy dice." Judith cackled and then apologized for laughing. "No, it's not too crazy to talk to an object that reminds you of your father."

"The last time I saw it," Holly said, "the necklace was flying off the rearview mirror right before the minivan crashed into the lake. I've looked everywhere I can think of—the recovered items from the van, the suitcases. I called the police department, towing company, salvage yard, insurance agent. And I just scoured the bottom of Lake Odell with my feet at the spot where the van went in."

"Lord have mercy."

"I think it's really gone. I don't know what I'm going to do without my necklace." Tears came. "Ted is so angry, he acts like he's going to do something violent. And last Saturday Alex showed up at my house. We didn't talk. He just cased the cul-de-sac in his car and left a gift on my doorstep."

"He drove all the way from Alabama?"

"Six and a half hours." Holly sniffled. "He's backed off, it seems, though I haven't checked e-mail."

Judith left the room and returned with a box of generic facial tissues.

Holly blew her nose. "I can't believe you're not sick of my continuing saga."

"No, I've been praying, and I'm glad to know the specifics."

"Pray for me to find my crystal. I need it so much. And pray that Ted quits acting so mean. And pray for my parenting because even though I'm so incredibly thankful that Ethan and Peter survived the wreck, the boys still get on my last nerve. Ethan hasn't been home from the hospital a week, and I've already yelled at him more than once. I accidentally made Peter bang his head." Holly's voice cracked. "I just, I opened the bathroom door too fast, and he fell."

"If I had a nickel for all the times I wanted to kill someone in my family, especially my husbands." Somehow Judith's genteel drawl made murder sound quaint, like an event followed by sweet tea on the veranda. "I've wanted to click the "Undo" button on every person in my family at one time or another. Except I've never come across an Undo button. You can divorce your husband, but then you find yourself at your daughter's wedding sitting down the pew from him and his new wife, who has great legs and a beautiful smile, and you realize you never really "undid" him. I'm saying that after three divorces and enough booze to keep a small distillery in business.

"And surely you realize you're not the only mother in the world who's yelled at her children or opened a door in a huff. All mothers do these sorts of things. It's our dirty little secret. But you can't undo being a mom, even if you do something crazy that ought to disqualify you from the job. I kicked out my son Kip when he was seventeen because I found out he was doing drugs. Kip is my youngest son from my first husband, Jerry, but Bobby was my husband at the time, and neither Jerry nor Bobby agreed with my decision. I was adamant, though. Kip was stirring up a hornet's nest in our house—wrecking cars, getting DUI's, knocking holes in the drywall. So I kicked him out and told myself he could rot on the street for all I cared. I thought I was through with him. Out of sight, out of mind. But it doesn't work that way. I thought about him obsessively. Replayed every conversation we'd had since he was two. Watched the local news every night. Finally, after three weeks, I tracked him down. Do you know where he was sleeping? On the floor of a roach-infested apartment with a crack dealer. He had lice in his hair and had dropped 20 pounds. Oh Lord, I should never have kicked him out. I felt so guilty. But I had to dust off my fanny, regroup, and press on. I brought him home, cleaned him up, paid his debts, and forced him into rehab."

"I don't know what to do with all the guilt," Holly said. "I feel guilty about the wreck. I feel guilty about the affair. I feel guilty for living in my own house. I wake up with the guilt and go to bed with the guilt. I just really, really need my crystal."

"First of all, the wreck wasn't your fault. The road was rainy and you had to deal with a slow tractor."

"I also found out my tires had been recalled."

"See? Anyone could have lost control in those conditions."

"But I can't remember anything during the period between when I first veered off the road and when the van flew into the lake. I think I must have done something stupid during that time. Something doesn't add up. When I try to remember, I feel this overwhelming sense of remorse. I really need my crystal."

"You don't need that little crystal. Oh, it's been a great way for you to talk through your thoughts and feel a connection to your dad, but it can't help you. Only one thing can help you."

"What?"

"I think all these years when you've talked to your father/necklace thing-a-ma-jig, what you've really wanted is to talk to is your heavenly father." She pointed up towards the ceiling.

"I don't know about that. I used to pray when I was a teenager, but I never got any answers."

"Maybe you weren't ready for answers. For me, God answered questions I didn't even know I was asking. I prayed I

174

could hold on 'til happy hour, prayed Joe wouldn't discover my hidden liquor bottles. What I thought I wanted was to protect my drunken evenings when my failures and responsibilities went mute and I could escape my daytime reality, but that's not what I really wanted, see. I didn't want to be a drunk escapist; no one does. What I really wanted was to find peace in my daytime reality. But with my daytime reality being such a pain in the neck, what with wayward children and emotionless husband #3, the only way for peace was to turn to God. Don't you know, God is the real Southern Comfort." Judith laughed at her liquor allusion.

"Do you really think this God of yours wants to talk to a wife and mother like me? I mean seriously. I'm not exactly the family values girl."

"Sure enough, honey."

4

Tilting back in his swivel-tilt Execu-chair, Ted clicked and unclicked his black ball point pen—always a black pen, never a blue. He was tweaking the spreadsheet for Clearwater, whose account he had miraculously won, even though the final negotiations took place via portable phone in his back yard while two policemen in his living room filled out a Missing Person report. Fortunately he had already done all the groundwork on the Clearwater account, so when he spoke that wild morning to the CEO Junior, the obnoxious 26-year old heir apparent, Ted only needed lucidity enough to regurgitate information they'd already been over a million times. Meanwhile, the Missing Person had not been missing at all but was, it turns out, off in Alabama screwing her old boyfriend

Ted threw his pen at the wall of his home office, leaving a black mark on the white wall. Over the past week his rage rose up at unexpected times. While transferring Ethan's car seat, he had suddenly hurled the awkward contraption out onto the driveway, scraping up the plastic on one side.

Much worse, yesterday afternoon he had shoved a drawer into Holly's stomach and a negligee at her face. Never before had he gotten rough with Holly or any other woman for that matter. Ted wasn't the violent type. His high school basketball coach used to ride him for not being aggressive enough. Ted was never good at drawing a foul. But Holly's red negligee set him off. Not only did it prove that Holly had planned her tryst with Alex, not only did it expose her contempt towards Ted—while he'd been slaving away at the Nashville IT Expo, she'd been spending his hard-earned money on lingerie for another man—but more than anything, the negligee represented a sexual enthusiasm Holly hadn't shown toward Ted in years. For Alex, Holly planned red lace and snaps; for Ted, sweatpants and reluctance.

He wasn't proud of these lapses in control. No matter how much Ted could justify them, he couldn't suppress his fear that he was turning into his father. His father never hit or even yelled much, but he had a way of acting so perturbed, so disgusted, so on the brink of hitting and yelling, that everyone backed away from conflict with him. When Ted was eight years old, a year before his parents' divorce, his father had railed against his mother in an incident eerily like the drawer incident, only instead of a red negligee it was navy-blue Mary Janes.

The girlish-looking shoe with the strap across the front was probably the only style of ladies' shoes Ted could identify by name because his mother wore them all the time.

"What are you thinking?" his father yelled at his mother, shaking the shoe in her face. "You can't wear Mary Janes to the firm's Christmas party."

"My ankle," his mother said, looking down at her foot, which she'd twisted the day before when she tripped over his brother's racecar. Ted and Martin had been her happy gophers trying to help her stay off her feet.

"Good God, Olga, there'll be tuxedos and evening gowns. You think I'll be caught dead with you shuffling around in these hideous, old-lady shoes?" He shook the shoe closer to her face. "Do you want to look like you just came off the boat?"

At the time, Ted didn't know what "just came off the boat" meant; he thought Mary Janes must be a kind of boat shoe, but when he grew older he realized this phrase, which his father threw out whenever he was especially angry, referred to his mother's Russian immigrant status. The phrase implied that his mother was an unsophisticated indigent, taken in by the charity of America and his father, a gift for which she should remain in a perpetual state of thankfulness and humble submission.

Like Holly, Ted's mother didn't move or bat away the shoe or cry, even though she suffered the added humiliation of her son's witness. No, his mother simply gazed down at the floor, her hazel eyes the picture of longsuffering. Of course, unlike Holly, his mother had done nothing to deserve this treatment except shun the frivolity of fashion in order to coddle her twisted ankle. Ted didn't remember whether his father or his mother turned away first, but he did remember a little later standing at the front door with Martin and the babysitter, watching his mother hobble to the car in her sparkly blue high heels.

Peter yelled up from the bottom of the stairs. "Daddy, come quick." Ted rolled his eyes—working from home was impossible. "Daddy, something's wrong with Ethan."

In that instant Ted realized he'd forgotten to give Ethan his medicine, not just at lunchtime but at breakfast as well. The Clearwater work had engrossed him—he'd won the account but now he had to help set up the new system. That morning he'd gotten up at 5:00 and, still in pajamas, gone straight to his computer, pounding out flowcharts before the sunrise. He'd intended to wait until Ethan got up to give him his medicine.

On the way downstairs Ted grabbed the Clindamycin bottle from where he'd been guarding it in his top dresser drawer. In the kitchen he filled a plastic cup with water and tried not to spill it as he power-walked out back, dodging plastic lawnmowers and red bouncy balls. Ethan lay sprawled out in the grass with his head on Holly's legs. He looked pale and heated but fully conscious. Holly stroked his sweaty head, and Ted squatted down to put his hand on Ethan's pounding chest.

"I think he just got short of breath," Holly said. "His heart was about to burst through his chest a second ago, but it's slowing down now. The boys were running all over the place, chasing Maxie—she got out of the fence again. It was too much for his lungs. I should have made him stop running."

"I hate that yippie dog," Ted said.

"Ethan just sort of squatted down and couldn't catch his breath. Thank goodness I happened to be watching from the kitchen window."

"He's been feeling so much better lately; it's hard to make him take it easy," Ted said, almost kindly. He held up the bottle of Clindamycin. "But I also think his airway may have been extra constricted because I forgot to give him his medicine this morning and at lunchtime too. Here, let me give it to him now."

"I just assumed you'd given it to him," Holly said, "even though I never saw you come out of your office. I didn't want to interrupt your work to double check. I should've checked."

"It's my fault, okay?" Ted snapped, embarrassed that he'd been hiding the medicine in his drawer and annoyed that she'd been too skittish to knock on his office door, as if he were a volatile man.

"Ethan buddy," Ted said, "I'm so sorry I forgot to give you your pneumonia medicine. I'm going to give it to you now. I brought some water to wash down the taste."

Ted knelt beside Holly and put the dropper in Ethan's mouth, squeezing just a little at a time, letting Ethan breath in between swallows. Ethan made the same face when they forced him to eat broccoli. Ted's folded leg pressed against Holly's thigh and their faces hovered inches apart, none of which felt awkward until Ethan finished drinking his water, and then Ted inched self-consciously away.

"I got it!" Peter said as he ran outside from the house. He had a wet washcloth that he carefully folded and draped across Ethan's forehead. "I learned this on TV!" he said.

Holly smiled at Ted, and Ted couldn't help but smile back. Peter was such a great kid, so serious, and dramatic, and unintentionally hilarious.

"Peter," Ted said. "You're a good helper. Thank you. Maybe you can help me remember to give Ethan his medicine. Can you help me do that?"

"Yes!" he said.

"I think he's fine," Ted said to Holly, "but let me bring him inside and call Dr. Rudolph."

Ted cradled Ethan's hot little body. Holly walked ahead of them, carrying the medicine bottle and cup. She opened the door for them and kissed Ethan on his head as he passed. Gently Ted laid Ethan on the couch.

Holly said, "I'll put this on the...where would you like me put the medicine, Ted?"

"Wherever, I don't care," he said roughly. Why did she have to act so skittish? "Peter can rest here. I'll call the doctor from my office."

Back in his tilting chair, Ted paged Dr. Rudolph and waited for him to call back. Ted closed his eyes and felt more convinced than ever that he had indeed turned into his father. His anger inspired in Holly the same walking-on-eggshells manner his father inspired in his mother. Ted had so wanted to make a statement about Holly's untrustworthiness that he'd hidden Ethan's medicine, a retaliation unfitting to the crime and wrought with collateral damage. His father had done the same thing with Ted's science award, which he'd won in the third grade for his baking soda/baking powder project. One night Ted forgot to take out the trash, so his father took away the award. He said Ted could have it back when he'd learned proper responsibility and respect, but Ted never saw his first-place blue ribbon again. His mother called it "your papa's retaliatory streak," a phrase which almost gentrified the ugliness.

When his father divorced his mother and left her with nothing, it was his father's ultimate retaliation. His mother had to work and go back to school, and Ted had to become the man of the house, taking care of Martin, making meals, and vacuuming their sorry little apartment. Ted and Martin couldn't play sports when they were younger because their mother didn't have time to get them to and from practice, and in high school when they could ride the late bus, his mother could rarely attend their games or bring the orange slices.

God, please don't let me turn into my father.

Dr. Rudolph called back and instructed Ted to time Ethan's heart-beats for one minute. Ted walked downstairs to where Ethan lay on the couch. One hundred beats. Dr. Rudolph said it was within the normal range.

That evening, Ted sat with Holly and the boys at the dinner table, something he hadn't done since before the accident, and after halting conversation over fish sticks and French fries, Ted walked over to the Clindamycin bottle on the counter by the coffee maker.

"This is a much better place to keep Ethan's medicine," he said. "I'll make a dosage chart for the two remaining days and put it here too. And maybe Peter can keep his cold compress handy just in case." Ted smiled. "I've got a truckload of work to do before I fly to Knoxville next week." He walked over to Holly and handed her the Clindamycin. "Would you start giving it to him?"

On Monday morning Delta announced the delay of Ted's plane to Knoxville after he'd already waited 20 minutes in the black plastic seats at gate 32. The announcer claimed that boarding would begin in ten minutes, probably not enough time to get more coffee.

Peter had cried when Ted left for the airport, and he asked *if*, not when, he was coming back. Ethan called Peter a baby for crying. Peter pushed him, etcetera, etcetera, and the usual morning drama unfolded. Ted had to admit he would thoroughly enjoy the peace and quiet of his hotel room, but he felt bad about leaving town so soon after the accident. He would make sure to bring home presents.

Right or wrong, he simply couldn't hold off Clearwater any longer. It had been over two weeks since they'd signed on the dotted line, and the young heir apparent was chomping at the bit. Ted opened his presentation folder and stared blankly at the three cost analysis graphs. Two seats away an older couple sat down with two Tourister carry-ons and several handbags spread around them. The wife pulled a magazine from one of the handbags, which also held a large wrapped gift, and she drummed her red fingernails on the magazine cover.

She looked over at her husband. "Did you remember to adjust the thermostat?"

"Yes," he said.

"And the doors? Did you remember to lock the door into the garage?"

"Yes. I checked all the doors and the stove and the timer light. Don't worry—*Grandma*. I'm sure Jessica's doing great." The silver-haired man looked at his watch. "She couldn't have had it yet, not with her first. We'll get there in time, I know we will. Everything's going to be fine."

"It feels like yesterday I was picking her up from Green Farm Elementary," the wife said, "and in five years, she'll be picking up *her* baby from elementary school. It just doesn't seem possible."

"I can't wait to see what it looks like. I hope it has your green eyes."

The grandmom-to-be smacked her husband's knee. "He or she is not an *it*," she said. "I can't wait to know the sex so you'll stop saying that."

Growing old together—this was all Ted ever really wanted. The same comfortable family. The same comfortable chair, reupholstered every decade or so and a 50th anniversary bash with kids and grandkids flying in from all over the country.

He never wanted his father's life—the partnership in the law firm, the condo at the beach, the white leather furniture, the loneliness that came from a life of retaliation. Holly called his father Oyster Shell, O.S. for short, because he was so hard, rough, and closed and because the only time they ever saw him was when they visited him at the beach. "O.S. sent the cash," Holly would say when they got his check tucked inside his annual Christmas card; inside, the card would begin, "Dear Theodore and family." His father referred to his daughter-in-law and only grandchildren as "and family."

Ted didn't want to abandon his family as his father had for some ditsy legal secretary with fake boobs and red fingernails, and then after he grew bored of her, a string of other ditsy women with fake boobs and red fingernails. He didn't want to leave Holly without financial support, forcing her to raise the boys on her own the way his mother did.

Yet if he stayed with Holly, a 50th anniversary bash would be tainted by her betrayal. They'd be celebrating 50 years of marriage but not 50 years of fidelity.

Ted was willing to bet that this nice grandmom-to-be had never betrayed her husband. Then again, he was willing to bet that her husband had never thrown drawers. But he also supposed the two probably had their own batch of hurtful memories, which never went away but lessened in importance when compared with events like the birth of their first grandchild.

Ted stared out the window at the tarmac. Where was his plane? The grandmom-to-be accidentally kicked one of her handbags, and the wrapped present slid over towards Ted. He picked up the lightweight box and handed it back to her.

"Thank you," she said. "Gosh, I'm glad it wasn't something breakable. It's a baby blanket. I knitted it myself. Our daughter is going to have a…" She choked up, and her husband put his arm around her.

"Congratulations," Ted said.

Once Ted had gone to Knoxville the computer became available again, and Holly could no longer resist checking to see if Alex had written. After lunch, she assigned Ethan "quiet time" in his room, locking his door from the outside, due to her ingenious reversing of the doorknobs. She prayed against all odds he might actually fall asleep. Peter was off at school, Ted was off in Knoxville, and when Holly sat down at the computer, she closed her eyes for a few minutes to enjoy the solitude.

Among all the Viagra spam and group forwards from Kate Arrington, with photos of puppies and quotes about motherhood, there were three e-mails from profmeyers @huffton.edu; she read them in chronological order.

> On Saturday:
> Dear Hol,
> I know you've asked that I not write, but I have to. I have so much to tell you. First of all,

you looked adorable this morning, standing at your front door, wearing my Catatonic State t-shirt. I hope you enjoyed the spritzers. Second, I need to know if Ted was home and if he was the reason you wouldn't come talk to me. Third, when I got home from Charlotte, I found Emily waiting for me with divorce papers.

I want to see you so badly. Please, Holly, just consider meeting me any time or place that you can manage. I can drive to Charlotte again, for lunch or whatever. Let me know.
I love you,
Alex

On Monday:
Dear Hol,

Don't tell me you're really going to ignore me, after the intense time we shared together at my house. Did that time mean so little to you?

I don't think the real you is the one who shut the front door on me and won't write me back. I think the one who shut the door is the you who always has to perform your duty and always has to live up to everyone else's standards. I think the real you is the artist who isn't afraid to follow her heart. The real you wanted to run to my car and drive off with me into the sunset. But then the dutiful Mrs. Reese scolded the real you and made you come inside.
Your forever soulmate,
Alex

On Friday:
Dear Holly,

I am now the proud new retainer of a divorce lawyer named Michael E. Sullivan, III. He calls me Alexander and I haven't corrected

him. He says Emily and I should be divorced in two months tops, as if that's grand. I guess expediency is alright by me because time is not going to change Emily's mind. She never bends once she's made up her mind.
Alex

Waiting nine days and reading all Alex's e-mails in a cluster allowed Holly to see what she'd been unable to see before: yellow looked yellow. Alex's words gnawed at her with an old familiar annoyance similar to her feelings on prom night when Alex kept tossing Mrs. Atkinson's pillow. Alex was accepting divorce with the same shrug of his shoulders that he accepted Emily's workaholism and their separate residences. "Emily never bends once she's made up her mind," he wrote lamely. Maybe Emily never bended because Alex never cared enough to try to bend her. The lady definitely needed some bending. Why didn't Alex take a leave of absence and insist on going with Emily to Hawaii? He had a fatalistic lack of initiative, and much worse, perhaps a lack of conviction.

Back on prom night, Alex began tossing Mrs. Atkinson's floral chintz pillow because he and Holly had gotten bored once the after-party reached a 2 a.m. lull. Alex could have said, "Let's go for a drive," or "Let's go short sheet Kate's bed," but instead he just sat there, tossing the pillow and catching it, tossing and catching, over and over, accepting their boredom.

When Holly had visited him in Henrietta, he never insisted she go see a doctor, never missed a class on her behalf, never insisted they talk about the future, never tried too hard to get her to stay. And though he tried to get her to call Sue and Ted, when she refused, he let it go. Now the spritzers on her doorstep showed some verve, but still, when she opened her front door Alex just sat in his car, willing to let the moment pass however it would. Maybe he was respecting for her request to be left alone or maybe he thought Ted was just inside the house, but mostly he cowered to the tenuousness of their relationship.

It's not that Alex didn't love Holly, just that his love

185

suffered from inertia. He was still pillow tossing.

And yet, Alex was her soulmate who understood her two sides, the tentative artist and the big bully, Mrs. Reese, and he had driven six hours in the middle of the night to see her and would willingly drive back again for lunch.

She clicked onto a Reply screen and poised her hands over the keyboard. Of course their time together had meant something to her, she just didn't know what.

> Dear Alex,
>
> I'm sorry about the divorce. Our time together did mean a great deal to me, but I need more time to sort things out with Ted and the boys. My life is in limbo. I'll be in touch again soon.
> Holly

For the first time, Holly wondered what the limbo must be like for Ted. How could he possibly concentrate on work after all they'd gone through? Or deal with Paul Nye at Clearwater Distribution? Paul Nye, at the age of 26, prepared only by a bachelor's degree in business from UT, had taken the reins of his daddy's company and had promptly begun condescending to grown men with twice his experience. Ted had told her about young Master Nye, as he called him, when he first started courting the Clearwater account several months back.

Holly opened a new e-mail to Ted@networkone.org.

> Dear Ted,
>
> I hope you got to Knoxville okay. How is young Master N? Did he need your help going potty?
>
> I thought I'd let you know that Peter seemed perfectly calm in the car this morning when I took him to school. He chattered the whole way and never even noticed when a car pulled in front of us. I think he's getting back to

normal.

On Thursday the form is due for Ethan's preschool next year. I thought I'd go ahead and sign him up for two days again, and we can always cancel later. Is that cool?
Take care,
Holly

He replied that evening:

Dear Holly,

Nashville is going pretty well. No, young Master N didn't need my help going to the bathroom today because his daddy was there to help him.

I'm glad Peter seems less anxious about the car. Yes, I agree about Ethan. Go ahead and sign him up for two days next year. See you Friday.
Ted

5

Peter lay on his belly and pulled his yellow choo-choo train along the wooden track. Ethan and Mommy had all the other trains hooked together in a long line. They made the track while he was still at school. Ethan said it was the best track ever, but Peter didn't think so. Ethan liked to make crazy tracks that went all over the place—under Ethan's table, in and out of his closet, out into the hall. But Ethan's tracks never joined. Peter didn't like a track that dumped you onto the carpet.

"Choo, choooo," Peter said to himself.

Before the van crashed into the lake, they heard a "choo-choooo." But they couldn't see the train or the tracks. He wondered how far the train tracks were from the lake.

"Mommy, will you help me make a blue lake?" he asked.

While his Mommy got the blue construction paper and scissors, Peter went to his room to find his Hot Wheels jeep. He made sure to take his yellow train with him so Ethan wouldn't steal it. Of all his cars in his bin, the jeep looked most like the minivan. Now all he needed was his black dress-up belt to use for the road.

Back in Ethan's room he set up Mommy's nice blue lake beside the track, not too close and not too far, and he set up the belt-road beside the lake. He put the jeep-van on the belt-road and set the yellow train back on the tracks.

The van went along the black road, and Peter sang the sneezing rhyme, "Ahhh-choo, God bless you."

"What ya doing?" his mommy asked. "Our little train whistle tradition?"

"Except you forgot," Peter said. "But I remembered. I

never, ever forget."

"When did I forget?" his mommy asked.

"Before the van crashed."

His mommy's eyes got so big he could see white around her eyeballs, like she'd seen a ghost. "Peter, when did you hear a train whistle? Was it before or after we almost hit the green tractor?"

"After that."

"Wait a minute," his mommy said, "there was a train whistle after we almost hit the green tractor? I don't remember a train whistle. I don't remember you saying our rhyme. I don't remember anything after the green tractor."

"I'll show you," Peter said. "Hey Ethan, we need your Old MacDonald tractor and one more Hot Wheel."

His mommy lifted his chin and asked, "Are you sure you're ready to do this?"

Peter said, "As soon as Ethan brings me the tractor and Hot Wheel."

"I guess I'm ready, too," his mommy said.

In the closet Ethan dug out his favorite purple racecar and tossed it to Peter. Then on his lowest closet shelf he opened up Old MacDonald's red barn, and all the animals and farm stuff fell through the wire shelf into the bottom bin, like always. You had to put the barn on the ground, before you opened it, but Ethan never did. Ethan picked up the green tractor and put Old MacDonald's one round leg into the hole of the tractor seat.

"His hat, his hat, his hat," Ethan said. Old Mac Donald always lost his yellow cowboy hat. Ethan looked around the bottom bin and closet floor. His mommy said maybe it was still in the barn, and she was right.

Peter set Old MacDonald and his green tractor ahead of the jeep-van on the black belt. The tractor's back tires were fatter than the belt and rolled along the carpet on either side of the belt. Further up the belt facing the tractor, Peter set the purple racecar. He began moving the tractor and the minivan.

"The green tractor went slow," he said to his mommy. "Putt, putt, putt. Then Ethan took my Pikachu so I throwed Obi-Wan at him and he throwed Pikachu at you. You got m-a-d

189

mad and turned the wheel all crazy and went off the road like this. Urrr." Peter drove the van off the belt. "Another car came on this side of the road." Peter pulled the purple Hot Wheels towards the van.

"Yes," his mommy said, "I remember. I was going to pass the tractor. I had plenty of time before the purple car got to us. But then one of you yelled and threw the toy at me. I swerved onto the shoulder on the other side of the road. There was a white house with black shutters."

"You got mad, mad, mad," Ethan said. He was sitting on his bed watching.

"I'm so sorry I got mad, honey."

"You're welcome," Ethan said. Sometimes he mixed up his manner words.

Peter pushed the jeep-van back onto the black belt. "But quick, you got back behind the tractor just before the purple racecar came past us. Whoosh. Then you yelled something bad."

"What did I yell?" Mommy asked.

Peter kept driving the purple car on the carpet. He wondered where the purple car was going that day. To the store to buy an umbrella?

"Peter," his mommy said, "what did I yell? Show me what happened to the minivan after it got back behind the tractor?"

Peter left the purple car on the carpet and began driving the tractor and minivan along the belt-road. "You called us a name I can't say."

"It's okay to say it, honey. I need to know."

"I can't," Peter said.

"Mommy can't remember so I need you to help me. What name did I call you? It's okay."

"You won't get mad?"

His mommy promised.

Peter closed his eyes. "You said we were...horrible craps. You said 'I hate you.'"

190

Horrible pieces of crap—that was the exact phrase Holly had used. She remembered now.

"You horrible pieces of crap," she'd yelled after she swerved back to her side of the road, just avoiding a head-on collision with the oncoming car and nearly bumping the tractor with the passenger side of the van. Her heart pounded and her left ear stung where the projectile toy had hit her. "You horrible pieces of crap. You almost made me wreck this car."

"Ethan did it," Peter yelled. "He threw my Pikachu."

"It's my Pikachu," Ethan said.

"Is not."

"Is too."

"SHUT UP," Holly screamed and spit flew from her mouth. "I'm trying to DRIVE. It's mine. No, it's mine. No, it's mine. Who cares? You're going to get us killed over some stupid piece of plastic made in Taiwan."

The tractor finally pulled off Odell School Road and Holly sped up around the next curve. The crystal swung wildly. "Why, father, why?" She yelled out loud. "I can't take it. I'm sick of these kids. I HATE THEM."

Hate. She always told the boys never to say it, but she had said it that day.

A thick, stifling silence descended on the minivan. No one said a word. The only sounds were the sniffle of Peter's crying, the patter of the raindrops, and the pumping of blood against Holly's temples. She'd gotten the silence she demanded, but this stolen treasure brought more turbulence than the initial fighting she'd tried to end. To turn down the silence, she opened the driver and passenger windows and let the wind flap loudly and mercifully through the open windows. Rain grazed her arm and face. Holly saw Lake Odell up ahead, and she smashed down on the accelerator. The road ahead would soon veer right, but her focus stayed left, in a bee line towards the lake. For that moment, she felt so hopeless to ever control her boys and to ever accomplish anything outside of her boys. For that moment, she thought they would all be better off letting this watery portal take them from misery to peace. For that moment, their future dimmed to lake-brown.

Off in the distance a train whistle blew two smoky beeps, and Peter yelled their conditioned train whistle response, birthed from Dr. Seuss-like silliness and reinforced through years of repetition.

"Ahhh-chooo. God bless youuu!"

Peter's train whistle rhyme snapped Holly out of her insanity. They had only just begun such family traditions, with many new ones to come during elementary school, then middle school, then high school. The years of trains, bedtime stories, practice spelling tests, blanket forts, and plastic figures would give way to years of sports, clubs, rock bands, acne, GPA's, and girlfriends, all with traditions and catch-phrases of their own, which would, along with the fighting and screaming and interruptions, form the weave of their unique family lore. The train whistle rhyme snapped Holly back to sanity, where she instantly knew that of course she wanted to see their family story unfold over time. She took her foot off the accelerator and stomped on the brakes with all her force, forcing life, but the van continued barreling across the white line, over the grassy shoulder, and into Lake Odell.

The tractor hadn't caused the wreck. The rain hadn't caused the wreck. The recalled tires hadn't caused the wreck. She herself had caused her minivan to fly headlong into Lake Odell, almost killing herself and her two boys. Oh Father, God. Holly drew her legs into her chest and rested her forehead against her knees. She dug her fingernails into her scalp until it burned.

Peter tapped at her arm. "What's wrong, Mommy?" Tap, tap, tap. "Mommy?"

Holly rose to her knees and pulled Peter into her arms, clamping his head against her cheek. She rubbed his soft hair as if trying to erase his traumatic memories. His neck smelled alive with dirt and grass. This brave boy had survived her malicious intents, and she held to him like he'd been resurrected from the dead. Peter tried to pull back, but Holly kept her arms vise-like around him. The jeep-van, which he still held in his hand, dug into her thigh.

From his perch on the bed Ethan sang, "Old MacDonald had a farm, e-i ,e-i, oh."

"Ethan, come over here, will you?"

Holly pulled Ethan into a three-way hug.

"I'm so sorry I yelled at you before the accident. I love you both so much, no matter what." No matter whether she went to jail like Susan Smith. No matter whether she and Ted divorced.

"Mommy, scratch me." Ethan kicked his leg a few times. "Come on, Mommy." She continued to hug Peter with one hand and began scratching Ethan's legs with the other, up one and down the other.

"Mommy, do I need to take some medicine?"

Holly stopped scratching. She stared at his needy green eyes. "Ethan, I'm so sorry you got pneumonia from the lake and had to go to the hospital. You almost died. What if that man hadn't been there to rescue you? And Peter. You got out of your seatbelt and saved yourself. I'm so sorry you had to save yourself. You were so brave, and I'm so glad you're okay. Did I tell you both that I love you?"

That night, once she'd put the boys to bed, Holly went into the garage and sat in the driver's seat of the white Chevy Metro. The gas gauge registered less than an eighth of a tank, anathema to Ted who never liked it to get below a quarter. The orange needle pointed to one of the many ways Holly failed to measure up, but this infraction was minor compared to her colossal failure at Lake Odell.

For a brief moment she'd meant to drive into the lake.

Her guilt welled, yet her garage retreat offered no relief, no confession booth, because her crystal no longer waited for her there. Holly could think of only one other outlet: a nice slow cigarette. She could pull into Judith's, ask her to babysit for 10 minutes while she drove to the Circle K, and then sit on the patio with her Marlboros and sedate her nerves with nicotine. She started the engine, put the car in reverse, and let her foot off the brake. The Metro rolled back a few inches before Holly caught a terrible sight in the rearview mirror—Garage Door. She punched the brake. The back bumper tapped the garage door, and her heart crashed through her chest. Her hands shook as she pulled forward and parked.

She sat for a moment with the motor running and went into her worst-case scenario cave: front of cave—they'd have to fix the garage door for a couple hundred dollars; middle—they'd have to replace the entire garage door for a couple thousand; back—they'd have to replace the garage door, pay for major body work on the rental car, and pay all the legal fees for the divorce that was sure to follow this last straw.

On the driver's side armrest an inch from her fingertips, the four automatic window buttons arrested Holly's attention. One press and a welcome brew of carbon monoxide would saturate her lungs and carry her away from all her failures, leaving Ted and the boys in peace. This time Ted would surely enlist the help of his mother Olga. Eventually Ted would hire an efficient and patient nanny. Maybe he would end up marrying the nanny.

Holly snickered. This old logic of escape seemed ludicrous, pure 8th grade melodrama. Holly turned off the ignition and pressed the garage door opener. To her amazement the door opened easily, up and over her head, making its normal creaky sounds. She walked around and squatted to inspect her back bumper, which also looked unscathed.

"Thank you," she said and realized she was not addressing some vague universal force but Judith's God, the God Holly first met when she was 16. "Thank you, Father God."

Holly knelt. "God, I've done a horrible thing, but I need to face it—in jail, in divorce court, wherever. I'm the only mother Peter and Ethan have. Forgive me for the lake. I'm so sorry. I did a horrible thing, but you saved us anyway. Thank you for giving me back my boys. I want a second chance. Show me what I need to do. Please give me a second chance."

Holly laid her forehead on the grimy bumper and wept. She

wept for the lake and the affair. She wept for all the times she'd yelled at her boys and seen them as intrusions. And she wept for the fact that in spite of everything, she still had these two healthy, happy kids, whom she didn't at all deserve.

When she was spent, she stood, and a calmness spread over her body, the same as she'd felt in the drafty retreat cabin when she was 16. It was a feeling that God knew all her offenses but wasn't shoving a maroon teddy in her face.

Calmness, however, did not mean Easy Street ahead.

"God, I need to tell Ted about the lake, so he can make his decisions." She pictured Ted's hateful, red face as he came at her with the pajama drawer. Bile surged in her throat. "Oh God, how will I ever tell Ted?"

The following evening when Ted returned from Knoxville Holly had made his favorite meal, Russian potato cakes and meatballs, which she'd first learned to make when they were dating. That first time, she'd had to ask Ted's mother Olga for the recipe, even though they'd never met, had to sneak Olga's phone number from Ted's Rolodex, had to call her two more times with questions; but Olga had been delighted to share her old family tradition. In recent years, all the pots, pans, bowls, graters, and knives, had only been worth it on Ted's birthday, until tonight. Tonight Holly believed she was serving a last supper because afterwards she planned to tell Ted her lake epiphany.

With the aid of ketchup, the boys gobbled up every bit of food on their plates, and Ted stayed at the table through the entire feast, patiently listening to Peter's scene by scene recap of that afternoon's *Pokemon* show. For most of the meal Holly stared at their marked-up kitchen table, embedded with the archeological traces of Peter and Ethan's development—from rubber-tipped utensils to gash-inducing stainless steel, fat crayons to markers, bouncy seats to Sassy seats. She wondered who would get the kitchen table when Ted divorced her.

Holly collected the dirty plates. "If you'll wait a sec, I'll get dessert."

"Brownies!" Ethan yelled. He'd gotten to lick the beaters that morning and had been begging for the brownies ever since.

"I need to get something, too," Ted said. "A surprise." He walked upstairs and returned with a yellow plastic bag from the McGhee Tyson Airport. For Peter he pulled out a foamy, bright-orange University of Tennesee football and for Ethan, an orange and white hacky sack.

"Thank you, Daddy," Peter said as he cocked his arm back for a pretend pass.

"You're welcome," Ethan said, and they all laughed.

Holly passed out brownies and napkins.

"Everything in Knoxville is bright orange," Ted said. He ate half his brownie in one bite. "The UT fans are rabid. Master Nye wore a different orange tie every day, and every writing utensil I ever saw in his hand was orange. Every other cubicle at Clearwater had an orange Volunteer pennant or coffee mug or decal. I think it's going to be a while before I can eat an orange."

"I like oranges," Ethan said.

"Who cares," Peter said.

"Hey guys," Ted said, "why don't you all go outside with your football and hacky. I'll be out in a sec. You can take the rest of your brownies with you."

A wake of crumbs followed them out the kitchen and into the garage on their way to the front yard. Holly groaned.

Ted stood at the counter beside Holly. "I got you a little something that's actually not orange but tasteful beige." He pulled from the airport bag a soy candle in a small tin canister, made by the Knoxville Mountain Soap Company. "Its handmade and you can use the candle wax as lotion."

Not since Ethan was a baby could Holly remember Ted bringing her a business-trip present. The last she remembered was the beautiful pottery mug from Charleston with dripping brown glaze and white slab daisy. She'd unwrapped it on the table next to Ethan's bouncy seat and then threw her arms around Ted. Symbolically, she had broken this mug a few weeks before the reunion. The soy candle was also symbolic, a peace offering, which Holly greatly appreciated but which was based on incomplete information. Perhaps Ted wanted peace with the Holly who accidentally drove into the lake, but not with the Holly who meant to drive in the lake.

"Thank you so much, Ted." Holly took a deep breath, readying herself for her confession, wanting to get it over with…

But before she got a word out, Ted said, "It's pure soybean wax, all natural. I thought it sounded kind of interesting. You let the wax melt and then scoop some out and rub it on your skin. Here, I'll get some matches."

Holly didn't have the heart to short-circuit Ted's gesture of reconciliation with her confession. This was his moment, and she would let him have it.

In ritual-like silence, Ted lit the soy candle and Holly leaned down to smell it. "Mmmm," she said, "I love the lemon ginger. This is great."

"Here." Ted dipped his finger in the wax and daubed it on the back of Holly's hand. "Rub it in."

"Boy, it's like silk." She rubbed her hands together. "Thank you, Ted. It means a lot to me."

"It's just a little something. Well, I better go check on those rascals. Dinner was superb."

After Holly finished the dinner dishes, she pulled up a folding chair next to Ted just inside the garage, and together they admired their boys. Peter circled the cul-de-sac on his bike, dinging his bell, his blonde hair glowing in the sunlight. Ethan vroom-vroomed his tricycle in between a driveway obstacle course of two muddy boots, a paint can, and one bright orange UT football. The setting sun cast chiaroscuro shadows on their clothes and faces.

"Peter's riding his bike like a pro," Ted said. "He's using the foot brake now."

"He's a quick study."

"A child progeny," Ted said.

The first time Holly had told the child progeny joke, when

Peter had dumped a bowl of spaghetti on his head, Ted hadn't gotten it. She had to explain to her non-liberal-arts husband the difference between progeny and prodigy. But since then, he was the one who repeated the phrase straight into family vernacular. That Ted would presently want to enter this realm of familiarity was another gesture of reconciliation.

"That's right," Holly said, "a progeny, though I wouldn't want to brag."

They got silent again, and Holly recognized another opportunity to tell him about the lake. She turned her chin slightly in his direction. But Ted rarely seemed so content, legs stretched in front of him, hands on his full stomach, angelic children playing before him. She hated to so quickly undo the potato cakes and soy candle. Now.

But Ted again spoke first. "Hey, what did State Farm say about the minivan?"

Her stomach turned. Holly hadn't called State Farm as Ted had requested. Initially she just forgot, but earlier that day when she ran across her reminder note, she purposefully didn't call. She worried the insurance woman would discover her secret and not cover the accident.

Holly lied. "I left a message with the receptionist, but she hasn't called back. I'll keep trying."

"That's weird. Their office is usually so responsive. I guess I should start looking for minivans anyway. I'll check out the ads in tomorrow's paper."

Holly wrinkled her nose. Another minivan felt like a return to her old life of trying to keep up with the Annes and Sharons of the world. A minivan had taken her from a dead end cul-de-sac to an ugly brown lake. She couldn't face another minivan, but after she told Ted the truth about the "accident" she'd be lucky to have any car at all.

"Well," Holly said, "I'd better herd the cats inside for baths."

"Peter," Holly called out, "come on to Ethan's bed for a bedtime story."

After bathing the boys together, Holly usually separated them for bedtime stories, but tonight she wanted Ethan and Peter to hear the same story. Ethan and Holly shifted and moved stuffed animals to accommodate Peter. Ethan in red footy pajamas and Peter in Superman ensemble both smelled of Milk and Honey bubble bath.

"Can we do Mrs. Jamison's magical chalk dancers?" Peter asked.

Holly had invented the chalk dancers the week Peter started kindergarten. At night Mrs. Jamison's chalk came alive and danced over the desks of any children who were scared or missed their mommies, and the next day those children felt not just two times braver, not just five times braver, but—and Holly and the boys would repeat the line together—ten times braver. The chalk dancers accomplished other feats, such as dancing over the gold behavior stars Peter hoped to earn the next day or dancing over the classroom doorway, chanting Peter's name for line leader.

"No," Holly said, "No chalk dancers. Tonight I'm going to tell you a story about a farmer named Milton Benson."

Of all people, Holly's high school friend Kate had gotten Holly thinking about Milton Benson. Kate had waited over two weeks post-wreck to finally call, this after not visiting the hospital and after sending the generic get-well card. Their conversation had annoyed Holly because Kate barely asked any questions about Holly's near-catastrophic event, focusing more on her baby girl, Melody, who was now pulling up on furniture and using her stellar fine motor skills to feed herself Cheerios. And because Kate didn't seem interested in Holly's problems, Holly didn't tell her about her fling with Alex. The only way she'd ever tell Kate about Alex was if one day Kate called with news of some equivalent disgrace, say Melody's drug arrest. But annoying as their conversation was, an offhand comment about the accident had resonated with Holly. Kate said, "What a miracle. God sent that Milton Benson guy to save you and your precious

199

boys. Who fishes in the rain in the middle of a weekday morning? And why did Milton Benson happen to pick a fishing spot not 20 feet from where you crashed?"

Holly had told Sue about Kate's miracle theory when Sue called from the airport. Her flight had been delayed and she didn't have a long enough layover to meet.

"If God cares so much to send a miracle," Sue said, "why not send it 5 minutes earlier and save you from crashing your car in the first place? Then Milton Benson would've been unnecessary. I mean, sure, maybe God used Milton Benson to save you from drowning, but why not save you from driving into the lake? If you're going to bother sending a miracle, why not send it on time? It was a half-assed miracle, if you want my opinion." When Holly stayed quiet, Sue apologized. "Sorry, Hol. I'm just a bitter old widow, begrudging everyone else their miracles."

Ever since these conversations, Holly kept thinking about this man who had saved their lives. She started sketching the Milton Benson of her imagination on the side of grocery lists and the back of junk mail. Some sketches took on an Asian simplicity with bold lines and minimal shading. Some took on a comic book flair with bulging, superhero muscles. And some used a softer, more realistic approach that seemed to best capture what she imagined was a gentle and unassuming heroism.

"Once upon a time," Holly began, boys snuggled on either side of her, "there was a farmer named Mr. Milton Benson. Mr. Benson lived in a shabby old house, down a shabby old road, just a short walk from Lake Odell. Now Mr. Benson looked like a normal old farmer, who spent his days plowing his fields, planting his seeds, and harvesting his vegetables…"

"You forgot watering his seeds," said Peter.

"Right. So even though Mr. Benson looked like a normal old farmer, who spent his days plowing his fields, planting his seeds, *watering his seeds*, and harvesting his vegetables, he was really a part-time secret agent for X, a mysterious superpower. Every now and then, in the middle of Mr. Benson's farm chores, the silver button on the front pocket of his overalls would glow bright red. Whenever it glowed bright red, Mr. Benson would immediately stop what he was doing, press the button, and listen. Through the button, which was like a telephone, X would tell Mr. Benson about his next top-secret assignment.

"One day, on April 24, 1998…"

"That's last month," Peter noted.

"That's right. Last month, just three weeks ago, on a very rainy day that kept him from working outside in the fields, Milton Benson was in his barn repairing a tractor when all of a sudden his silver button began to glow. He put down his screwdriver and waited until the wind stopped rustling through the slats of the barn. Then he pressed the red button and heard the voice he knew so well. 'Go,' X said. 'Go right now to your regular fishing spot on Lake Odell.'

"Well, Mr. Benson thought that was a very odd assignment, especially in the rain, but since Milton was a secret agent and X was his boss, he had no choice but to put on his rain slicker and rubber boots, grab his favorite fishing rod, dig up some worms, and walk down the muddy road to Lake Odell. By the time he arrived, he was wet and cold. With shivering hands, he pulled out a fat, wriggling worm, baited his hook, and cast his line out into the lake. 'Plop!' went the red and white bobber.

"Milton Benson waited and waited and waited, and not a single fish so much as looked at his worm. He started to wonder if maybe he had heard wrong—maybe X had said a different lake or a different time. Old Mr. Benson didn't hear as well as he used to. But then a blur of tan metal flashed in the corner of his eye. It took Mr. Benson a few seconds before he realized that the blur of tan metal was a minivan, which crashed into the lake just 20 feet away.

"Being a secret agent, Mr. Benson knew exactly what to do. He threw down his fishing rod, took off his rain slicker and boots, and dove into the water towards the van. When he got there, a six-year old boy named…let's see, Gonzales…"

"Nooo," Peter protested.

"Okay. When he got there, a six-year old boy name Vladimir…"

"Nooo. A boy named Peter!"

"Oh alright. Peter. So, when Mr. Benson got to the tan minivan, *Peter*, a very strong, very brave, and, I might add, very intelligent boy, had already managed to escape from the van. He said to Mr. Benson, 'Help me save my mommy and brother.' 'What's your brother's name?' the man asked. And Peter replied that his brother's name was…" Holly looked down at Ethan. "What do you think the brother's name should be?"

"Ethan!"

"Good enough, I guess. Together Peter and Milton Benson freed *Ethan* and the mommy from their seatbelts. When Mr. Benson got Ethan out of the van, he could tell that Ethan wasn't breathing, so he breathed his very own breath into Ethan's mouth while he carried him to shore. Then Mr. Benson got the mommy out of the van."

"Nuh-uh," Peter corrected. "He got you out first, and brought you to me. I held your shirt while you floated on the water. *Then* Mr. Benson got Ethan."

Holly kissed Peter's head.

"Then what?" Ethan asked.

"Peter and Milton Benson got everyone to shore and waited until the ambulances came. Then Peter went with his family to the hospital, and Mr. Benson walked back home. And there on Mr. Benson's front porch, next to his old Labrador named Emma Sue, lay his secret agent's payment, which was always the same after each and every mission: a sparkling red ruby the size of an acorn. Mr. Benson put this newest ruby in his coffee can with all the other rubies and put the coffee can back underneath the work bench in his barn. Then, he went back to working on his tractor.

"Now the rumor up in heaven, I mean at the secret agency, is that X decided that very day to enroll Peter and Ethan in the training program for junior secret agents. But I don't know, that may just be a rumor."

Ethan made his fingers into a gun. "Pow, pow, pow."

"So," Holly continued, "Milton Benson, Peter, Ethan and the mommy all lived happily ever after. The end."

Peter asked, "Can we go see Mr. Benson on his farm some time?"

"Maybe we will sometime. I don't know where he lives. Okay guys, time for bed."

"Can we do us-the-guys?" Peter asked. In us-the-guys the boys acted out the story as opposed to using action figures. "I'll be Milton Benson. Ethan can be everyone else. Please?"

At Holly's hesitation and slightest smile, Peter ran out of the room to grab costumes. If nothing else, the spontaneous drama would postpone her having to tell Ted about the lake.

Peter returned in Ethan's jean overalls, which were skin tight and shin high. He carried a plastic light saber as his fishing pole. In addition to his plum role as lead actor, Peter assumed the role of director, telling Holly and Ethan to sit single-file on the bed, facing the headboard with Holly in front. They were to close their eyes and hang their heads as if unconscious. The play unfolded in a linear though rambunctious manner until Peter tried to give Ethan mouth-to-mouth resuscitation and bedtime unraveled into a wrestling free-for-all.

"Boys!" Ted yelled from out in the hallway.

They all felt scolded. Quickly, Holly rallied her rowdy thespians to strike the set, change out of costumes, and crawl into bed.

Both tuck-ins complete, Holly froze in the darkened hallway. She stared at the yellow triangle of light that fanned out from Ted and Holly's bedroom. Ted, she could hear, was flipping through the newspaper. So many evenings in the past, Holly had paused in the hallway to brace herself for Ted's sexual advances. Tonight she braced herself for a confession that might end their marriage.

"Father?" she prayed without speaking. "You were with me when Milton Benson showed up. I need you to be with me now."

She walked into the light of their bedroom, breathing in and out through her nose. Ted glanced up casually from his newspaper and yawned, exhaling with an exaggerated huh-ho-ho that acknowledged the official end of a long but satisfying day.

Holly sat down on her side of the bed and looked at him.

"What?" he asked with pre-tsunami oblivion.

Holly hadn't rehearsed a lead-in. She couldn't jump straight into such explosive news without a lead-in. She looked into his unaware eyes then down at his *Charlotte Observer.* "What's going on in the world today?" she asked.

"Oh, I was just reading about the riots in Indonesia, but I keep reading the same sentence over and over. I'm tired. You tired?"

"Oh no. I mean, I wasn't coming to bed. I stayed here while you were out of town, but tonight I was just planning to grab my pillow and go down to the couch." Holly pulled the pillow onto her lap, mortified that Ted might think she was trying to sleep beside him in their bed, misinterpreting the soy candle, acting as though everything were back to normal. Although she dreaded the shoulder-crimping couch, she would return there after they talked.

Ted looked at her until she could no longer avoid eye contact. "You can sleep here if you want."

His eyes and voice were soft but not imploring. It was not a sexual proposition. It was an olive branch in the form of a Sealy posturepedic. Maybe she should accept his offer and save the confession for another time. And yet, and yet, and yet.

"Thanks, Ted. Thanks. Um, there's something…Hang on."

She bolted into their bathroom, still clutching her pillow, squeezing into their coffin-sized toilet closet. "Father?" she whispered in the darkness. She turned on the bathroom fan so Ted couldn't hear. "Can you hear me, Father? I don't know if I should tell him. I don't know if I can. He seems so hopeful. Tell me what I should do." Holly listened. She half expected an audible response. On the wall behind the toilet, hung the cross-stitch Kate had made for their wedding, a vestige of Holly's mint-green and mauve days: "What therefore God hath joined together let not man put asunder." Leave it to Kate to use a Bible translation with "hath" and "asunder."

"Is that your answer?" Holly asked. "A 'thou shalt' command? What does that even mean, 'let not man put asunder?'

Would telling Ted about the lake put things 'asunder,' or would *not* telling him put things 'asunder?' Which is it?" Holly tried to listen for an answer but only heard the whir of the bathroom fan. She pictured the toilet lid flapping like God's lips. Knocking on the lid, she asked, "*Can*st thou heareth me? *Arse* thou home?"

A surge of fear humbled her. "I'm sorry God. I'm a bitch to everyone, even you. Sorry for saying bitch."

She pivoted around, slumped onto the toilet lid, and buried her head in her pillow. Asunder or not asunder, Holly knew she couldn't keep pretending the lake was an accident. Pretending had gotten her to the lake in the first place. She had pretended to be satisfied with her Dodge Caravan life. Maybe Alex had been a form of pretend, too, a vacation from reality.

"I know you're here, God. I know what I have to do. I already knew it yesterday in the garage. Oh God, Ted's probably out there lining up his yard clothes for what he thinks will be just another Saturday. Oh God, help."

Inhale, exhale. Lamaze breathing got Holly out of the bathroom and into the bedroom, where Ted was now absorbed in the Sports section. Another Lamaze technique, the focus object, got Holly across the room and back to her side of the bed. She chose to focus on the Grand Canyon poster above their headboard, a Clyde Thomas photograph burnished in golds and oranges, entitled "Time and the River Flowing." In particular, Holly fixated on an ominous canyon outcrop. During Peter's 12-hour birth she had chosen a random set of keys as her focus object. The more she concentrated on the keys, the more significant they became, representing the doors in their lives— doors to a house, two cars, a big storage shed, and the new door to parenthood. Like the keys, the longer Holly stared at the canyon outcrop the more it seemed a symbol of the ledge from which she was about to jump. Inhale, exhale. Ignore the sweaty fear. Ignore the lack of contingency plan with no job, no lawyer, no custody defense. Inhale, exhale. Just tell the secret. Jump.

Holly sat once again on the edge of the bed, and before Ted had even set down his paper, she blurted, "I lied about calling State Farm. I was scared to call because the truth is, the accident wasn't fully an accident." Inhale, exhale. "I thought it was an accident until yesterday. You know how I couldn't remember part of the car trip, right before the van went into the lake?"

"Mm-hmm." He folded the newspaper and set it on the floor.

"Well it turns out Peter remembered, and as he and I re-traced those moments I realized that for a brief, insane moment, I meant to drive into the lake. I meant to kill myself. I meant to kill…them." The words, spoken out loud for the first time, lashed against her ears. "For one millisecond I meant to kill myself and the boys."

Ted combed through his hair with his hands and held the back of his head, but his face remained unreadable. Holly's tears began quietly.

"They'd been fighting all morning while I was trying to get ready for my reunion. I was sweating and I had a terrible zit. The morning had been so full of interruptions and stress." She omitted the incident with the green Victoria's Secret bra. "We hadn't been gone fifteen minutes when Ethan threw a Pokemon figure at my head right as I tried to pass a tractor. I swerved onto the other side of the road, and there was an oncoming car. Initially, I thought this was the moment when we drove into the lake, but what really happened is I quickly jerked the minivan back into my lane just in time before the oncoming car swished past. I yelled at the boys for almost making us crash, and the boys started bickering about why they'd been bickering. I called them 'horrible pieces of crap' and told them I hated them." Holly wiped her cheeks with the lapel of her blouse. "The van got so deathly quiet, and I realized what abuse had just spewed out of my mouth. I saw the lake up ahead, and it looked so, I don't know, inviting. I thought we would all be better off dead, like what kind of chance do my kids have with a mother who yells such awful things? But then a train whistle blew, and Peter sung, 'Ah-chooo! God bless you,' and I snapped out of my crazy thoughts. I knew Peter wasn't damaged beyond hope. I knew we had good qualities, even along with the bad. I knew our family had many more traditions and car trips to come, even along with the fighting and those damn Pokemon figures." A choked laugh-cry escaped Holly's throat. "Peter's train rhyme snapped me out of my trance, and so I immediately stomped on the brakes. But it was too late."

Ted leaned back against his pillow with his hands underneath his head, and in silence he focused on the tray ceiling.

"I'm so sorry, Ted."

Holly's nose began running, so she mirrored Ted's supine position with her head tilted back. They lay there, staring at the brass and fake-wood ceiling fan, stumped as to how they should feel. The human psyche had built-in responses to infidelity—rage and drawer-throwing for the slighted, guilt and penance-seeking for the unfaithful—but this latest revelation held no pre-wired emotions. The emotional slate was as blank as their white popcorn ceiling. At first the blankness rendered Ted completely still, but soon his eyes began darting to various points on the ceiling, as if competing emotions were shooting up and ricocheting off the white surfaces, not knowing where to land. His busy eyes looked like Holly's whenever she stared at the tray ceiling and composed the mural she hoped to one day paint.

When Ted finally spoke, he continued staring upward. "I was so sure I'd caused the accident. I read the letter about the recalled tires, but I never did anything about it."

"Your initial response is about tires?"

"No." Ted turned on his side and propped himself on his elbow. "Have you felt suicidal before?"

The word "suicidal" sounded overly dramatic, but if she could only pick a yes or no answer, without any qualifications, the answer was yes, she had felt suicidal, once at Lake Odell and once in the garage just the night before. But never had she entertained the thought for longer than a few seconds. Never had she plotted ahead of time, bought the necessary equipment, written the goodbye note, given away her possessions.

"No, never for more than a brief moment," Holly said. "I never premeditated anything. I've just sometimes felt so trapped in this tedious, never-ending mommy world."

"Why didn't you tell me? We could have found a counselor or something."

Holly turned to look at Ted's face to see if he realized the absurdity of what he'd just said, but an amnesiac's innocence stared back at her. Forgotten were all their past conversations in which she'd expressed her frustrations only to have Ted make her feel like a whiny little girl. Forgotten were all Ted's condescending budget lectures, which she could extrapolate to the $100/hour counselor.

"What?" Ted asked stupidly.

"I've told you a million times that I felt trapped and alone, like a single mom, and counseling never once came up. And even if it had come up, I'm quite sure it wouldn't have fit your budget."

"For God's sake. Have I seemed that awful? Of course I'd have fit it in the budget, if I'd known how bad it was."

Their conversation had quickly veered from humble confession to the same old argument, like a drainpipe always channeling water in the same direction. They so often wound up at this impasse of Holly's needs vs. Ted's insensitivity. Holly hadn't meant to argue. She had no right to get pissy.

"Look," she said, "counseling or no counseling, it's no excuse for what I did. I'm not excusing myself. I'm just saying I don't think either one of us knew enough to take me seriously. What I want to say is I'm really sorry. I wish I had been a stronger person. I know that compared to many people, I don't have any real complaints. I know I have a lot to be thankful for—a husband with a good job, healthy kids, a nice house. But the truth is, motherhood has whipped me." Her voice faltered and new tears began. "I'm at a loss. I can't get anything done. When we first had Peter, I went into a fog and I've never quite come out. I stopped seeing the future. I lost my appetite for beauty. I lost myself."

Ted's eyes glistened. "How did you get so sad?" He reached for her shoulder awkwardly. "I guess you tried to tell me."

"It's not your fault.

"It's partly my fault." He let his arm drop. "I didn't listen. I just wanted you to snap out of it. Work has been hard and I needed you to be okay. When I got home from work, I just wanted a nice, peaceful house. I haven't wanted to hear about your problems. I didn't tell you, but I've been on a kind of probation at work. I got a bad first quarter review, and Peterson said he was starting to wonder if I'd lost my edge. I thought I might get the ax. We should be fine now since I won Clearwater and Douglass, but I was pretty worried for a while. I've been self-absorbed."

"Other people make it all look so easy. I wish I were more of a supermom."

"I never fully grasped how hard your job at home was until I had to solo-parent after your wreck. It takes so long to accomplish anything. I thought buying car seats would take one hour tops, but the boys and I spent three hours. We tried Kids R Us, but they didn't have any. So we had to drive out to the Baby Superstore and got lost on the way. They had 50 million choices. We had to take twenty bathroom breaks; the boys kept arguing about dumb stuff; Ethan pulled down a rack of DVD's."

"Oh no, not the Baby Superstore," Holly said.

"It's only for the most advanced parent. I know this now." Ted got quiet. He picked at the frayed edge of the sheet, pulling on the threads that had broken free from the weave.

"Holly? Have you wanted to hurt the boys before?"

"No," she said definitively. "I've never wanted to hurt them, but in the heat of the moment I can sometimes get so mad, I yell and lose my composure. That day in the minivan I couldn't deal with myself for not being able to deal with them, and I didn't want for Peter and Ethan to have to deal with me anymore. It doesn't even make sense. It's crazy. I can be a scary, horrible mother. I don't deserve Peter and Ethan. I probably deserve jail, and honestly I'll understand if you want to call Officer Jackson. And I'll understand if you want a divorce with full custody."

Ted remained silent. His hand moved from the frayed edge of the sheet to the satin piping, which he kept pinching and pushing back and forth. Holly imagined a jail with dirty toilets

209

and stiff cots and scary showers. She wondered how often they'd let the boys visit.

"You slammed on the brakes," Ted said. His eyebrows crinkled in pensiveness. "That's huge. You slammed on the brakes, Holly, because you're not crazy and because you love our boys." He stroked the stubble on his cheeks and swallowed audibly. "You had a crazy moment, but you fought it."

Graciousness was one response Holly hadn't anticipated, and she didn't know if she even wanted it. It seemed too easy.

"But Ted, I had another crazy moment when I woke up in the hospital and thought Ethan was dead. I kept picturing him in a morgue drawer." The flutter returned to her stomach. "I couldn't bear it. I gave up again, escaped, left you with all our troubles."

"I never gave up," he whispered.

He twisted towards his nightstand drawer and pulled out a stack of papers. In bold, san serif letters, Missing Person blared across the top, and on the rest of the page, Holly's vitals and a photo of her with longer hair. The flyer offered a $500 reward for anyone who had seen Holly Reese since the night of 5/26/98.

"I used the little photo we'd taken for that church directory thing. I went to Kinko's the morning after you disappeared and planned to hand these out all around town."

Ted hated that kind of solicitation. Although he didn't mind cold-calling potential clients all day long, he refused to go to people's homes. When his friend Donald Pickerel ran for town commissioner and asked him to canvas the neighborhood, and when Peter was supposed to sell wrapping paper for his elementary school, Ted refused. And yet he'd been willing to hand out flyers for Holly.

"I never ended up handing them out," Ted said, "because Officer Jackson traced your whereabouts to Atlanta. I guess it was a good thing; you would've been embarrassed later on."

"I would have died of embarrassment, but I'm so touched you were willing to do all that for me. Thank you. I'm sorry I made you worry."

Ted returned the flyers to his nightstand and turned to face Holly. He sat up and crossed his legs Indian-style. Holly also pulled herself to a sitting position and straightened her back against the headboard.

"Did you plan on seeing Alex when you first walked out of the hospital?" he asked.

Of all Ted's concerns about her, whether she was a fit parent, whether she still had her sanity, his greatest concern centered on her affair with Alex. Minus the contempt and the rage, Ted was still asking about the maroon teddy.

"No, I didn't plan on seeing Alex," Holly answered. "All I thought about was getting far away from the hospital morgue. I hitched a ride with a trucker who happened to walk into the same convenience store and who happened to be heading to Atlanta." Ted shook his head. "He was a decent guy, and I slept the whole way. At the Holiday Inn in Atlanta, I realized Alex was the only person who might take me in and not force me to go home. It's true that we'd been exchanging e-mails and that I bought that teddy on the off chance something might happen between us. But at that point, when I was in Atlanta, I wasn't in any condition to pursue an affair. I still felt dizzy and disoriented and completely unable to cope with Ethan's supposed death. When I got to Alex's college, I..."

"Holly?" Ted interrupted.

"Yes?"

"I think I just want you to answer one question." His cheeks drooped sadly yet his eyes blazed with determination. "Who do you want to be with, Alex or me?"

Ted didn't want to know the sordid details of her time in Henrietta; he only wanted to know who had won her heart. That he even cared about the winner surprised and moved her, but because she hadn't expected the question, she wasn't prepared to answer. She didn't know the simple Scantron answer. A. Alex or B. Ted. To concentrate Holly shielded her peripheral vision with her hands, blocking out Ted's imploring face and his tacky Americas Cup poster and the clothes that he'd laid out for tomorrow. She pretended that someone else had asked the question, perhaps a talk show host or Sue. She tried to answer as objectively as possible.

"Alex is sensitive, which has always been a draw. We have a long history together. He knows the artistic side of me, which I've squelched over the years. Seeing him again helped me reconnect with this side of me. But the thing is, Alex lacks something, which I've never known how to define. He's just sort of passive, sort of…squishy."

"Alex Meyers is squishy?"

Holly nodded. "He and his wife have been living in separate towns for years. He got a teaching job in Henrietta, and she wouldn't leave her job in Atlanta. Then she got a project in Hawaii, building some big shot hotel. Do you know Alex never even tried to go visit her? She said she was too busy. Now she wants a divorce, and Alex has made zero effort to rectify anything. He contends that Emily 'never bends once she's made up her mind.' He sounds just like my dad."

Holly stopped talking and grabbed Ted's knee. "Oh my gosh. That's it. That's just what my dad said. You know the day my mom left, after her diatribe about cooking and cleaning like a slave and giving her life to a bloodsucking chauvinist, and blah blah blah? Well, my dad and I watched her pull out of our driveway, and I told him to go after her. But do you know what he said? 'She won't change her mind. Your mother's stubborn as a mule.' Oh my gosh, I just figured it out: Alex is squishy just like my dad. Alex used almost the exact words…"

Holly stopped herself. Alex used almost the exact words when Holly refused once again to call Ted or Sue from Henrietta. "I know I can't change your mind," he had said on their last night together.

Holly's father was a wonderful man, but he didn't actively go after her mother, not then and probably not during all their years of marriage. He didn't put on scuba gear and go for the deep dive. He just said, Oh well, that treasure is just too far down. Her father was like the crystal pendant, which hung down helplessly, limited to the movement of the minivan; it could listen—she would still swear to the pendant's supernatural ability to listen—but it couldn't act. Like Alex, her father resigned himself to relational deterioration.

While Holly believed Alex truly treasured their soul-connection, she knew he wouldn't fight for it. What Holly needed was a man who would fight for her like her heavenly father who on April 24, 1998, rearranged the course of the universe so that a train whistle and a man named Milton Benson would come along at the exact time she needed saving.

"I think I can compete with squishy," Ted said, matter-of-fact.

Holly laughed. "You are definitely not squishy. You make Missing Person flyers. You keep after obnoxious clients like Master Nye. You drop-knee proposed, right in the middle of Mama Lucia's, the second after I told you I was pregnant."

"Our waiter was so annoyed when he almost tripped over my leg. 'Please sir, you need to stay in your chair.'"

"We drank a lot of wine that night, out of celebration and sheer terror."

"I don't know," Ted said. "I honestly wasn't terrified. I knew what I wanted. I was exhilarated."

"Because you're not squishy. You're assertive."

"I'm assertive in some cases. Lately I've wondered if I'm really assertive enough for sales."

"You definitely are. You're not always sensitive, but you're definitely assertive." The ideal man, she thought, would be both assertive and sensitive, but given the two choices at hand, an assertive man was probably better for Holly than a sensitive, pillow-tossing one. "I need assertive. I need someone strong to walk with me through this grown-up life. I'm so different than the competent woman you once dated. I've become a needy thing." Holly looked down at her lap. "I don't blame you if you want to leave."

Holly was saying she needed him. She said it indirectly, and he had to use the transitive property from tenth grade geometry to tease out her meaning. When she said she found Ted assertive and said she needed someone assertive, she was saying that she needed Ted. And her need melted away any lingering desire Ted had for payback. Though he might never erase the recurring images he had in his head of Alex and Holly rocking and moaning, he knew he could forgive her. Right or wrong, smart or stupid, sage or sucker, he only wanted to hold his wife who needed him. Her face, puffy and make-up-less from the crying, and her short, messy hair made her look so vulnerable. He rearranged his legs, scooted over, and brought Holly into his arms. She felt good and warm against his chest.

"I'm not leaving," he said.

Holly cried until her shoulders shook and her tears soaked the front of his shirt. Ted stroked the back of her head.

"I'm going to stick by you," Ted cooed.

Abruptly Holly raised her head from Ted's chest. "Sticking by you" set off a loud, obnoxious alarm. Beep. Beep. Beep. Although she would have liked to stay cushioned by Ted's kind words and although his graciousness was more than she could have hoped for, Ted's words were like the Candyland card that sent you back to square one. She could not go back to an obligatory, sticking-by-you marriage.

"What?" Ted said.

"I'm sticking by you. You said that in Mama Lucia's when I first told you I was pregnant."

"Why do you hate that phrase?"

"I don't hate it." She so wanted to be conciliatory.

"But…" he said, waiting for her rejoinder.

"Sticking around is admirable, but it can be very 'let's do lunch.' I don't want you to stick around out of some Boy Scout obligation. If I hadn't gotten pregnant, I wonder if you would have stuck around and married me? I wasn't exactly your ideal woman like what's-her-name with the quilted Bible cover, all prim and proper and dying to wash your socks."

"Margaret Fulton, and she was boring and annoying. But you, I wanted to marry you after our first date—your probing questions, your laugh, your artistic mind. I've told you so many times that I had already been looking at rings before you told me you were pregnant. Why won't you ever believe me?"

"Because you never talked about engagement until I told you I was pregnant. And because once you married me and found out I was a lousy housekeeper, wife, and mother, you seemed to just be toughing it out like a good Boy Scout."

"I haven't been just toughing it out. I like having a wife who can make up stories about Milton Benson and draw pictures of him."

Holly raised her eyebrows.

"I saw your drawings in the laundry closet, but I didn't know what they were until I eavesdropped on bedtime tonight. I liked the Milton Benson story. You should make a book."

"Thanks. That's really nice…"

"But…"

"But if I take the time to make a book or paint or any other creative endeavor, the laundry might pile up even more than usual, and your coffee might go milkless even more often. I definitely wouldn't be able to be your June Cleaver."

"Who's June Cleaver again?"

Holly rolled her eyes. Sometimes she forgot that Ted didn't speak the language of television. When Ted's father was around, they only watched TV sports, and after the divorce, they didn't even own a TV until their neighbors gave them their old 14-inch black and white.

"June is a 1950's T.V. character," she said. "She suppressed her own life for her husband, Ward, and their two sons. She spent all her time putting on lipstick and dusting. June is every man's fantasy."

"Ward can have her," Ted replied.

Holly hooted, and snot launched onto her upper lip.

"What?" Ted asked.

Holly gestured for him to wait a minute while she went to the bathroom for a tissue. When she returned, she asked, "Are you sure you don't want poor ol' June?"

"She sounds as boring as Margaret Fulton. She's not *my* fantasy. I like having a wife who does more than clean and put on lipstick. I like having a wife who's an artist."

Holly stopped smiling and folded her arms skeptically. She didn't want to be contentious, but his compliments floated weightless, ungrounded by the reality of their lives. "Ted, how can I possibly be an artist when you always want our house standing at attention and the laundry up-to-date at all times. I can't meet your expectations and take care of kids *and* be an artist."

"I know, I know," he admitted. "I'm not saying I know how to make it all work, but I think it's possible. I think we can figure out how to set you up to make a book or paint or whatever you want to do. We'll just need to problem-solve about the laundry and milk. I could take care of my own dry-cleaning. I could get more underwear. We could buy a cow."

Holly smiled for a second. "But I would need a space to work. A messy space. I'd probably need to change Ethan's room into a studio because it has great light, and we'd have to move Ethan in with Peter, and they might kill each other. We'd have to strip Ethan's wallpaper. I couldn't concentrate with those yellow stripes."

"O.K."

"O.K.?"

Ted put his hand on Holly's shoulder. "Wait here, I'll be right back."

Ted found a small flashlight in his office and brought it to Ethan's doorway. Carefully he turned the doorknob. Ethan was sleeping with his back towards the door. Opposite his bed beside his closet, Ted shined the flashlight on the yellow and white striped wallpaper. He walked across the room, kicking aside a sippie cup, and knelt down in front of the closet. With his fingernail he scraped the corner tip of the wallpaper and cleanly peeled it upward until he'd gone about two feet and the wallpaper began fraying into ragged bands. Ted ripped away the two-foot section.

In the light of the hallway Ted proudly examined his wallpaper plunder. Though he had never seen Mr. Ward Cleaver, Ted was sure a dictator like him, or a squishy man like Alex, would never rip up wallpaper for his wife's studio. Ted couldn't wait to rip more. He could borrow Judith and Joe's dolly to move the furniture. The boys' beds would fit fine in Peter's room if they took out Peter's long dresser and put in Ethan's tall dresser. Possibly he could squeeze Peter's dresser into his office. The boys might enjoy having all their toys in one closet. Ethan's room had no overhead lighting, but he'd seen an inexpensive floor lamp at Lowe's with three adjustable lights. Ted hadn't taken on a big home improvement project since the fall when he'd set up his workspace in the garage.

He rushed into their bedroom and presented Holly with the floppy, two-foot strip, holding it out to her as if it were a mink stole.

"I started your studio!" he said. "Here, hold out your hands." He laid the wallpaper onto her outstretched palms and she held it stiffly, like a butler balancing a tray of wine glasses.

"It's from Ethan's room," he explained. "The wallpaper came off real easily. It shouldn't be a problem. There may be a few sticky spots, but a little hot water should do the trick, or I could rent a steamer."

Holly started at the wallpaper, then stared up at him. Ted realized then that he should have asked her before he tore up Ethan's wall. The studio conversion was probably a passing idea that Holly had no intention of pursuing.

"I can fix it," he said.

Possibly he could patch the torn piece with wallpaper glue, although the ragged seam would surely show. They could put something in front of the seam—Ethan's giant purple bear

Holly's mother had bought him. Or he could replace the whole wallpaper strip if there were enough left on the remnant roll, which he'd recently noticed, still tucked behind the paint cans in the garage.

"I can't believe you just did that." She laid the wallpaper on the bed and smoothed it out.

"I just thought…"

Holly smiled. "This is my favorite gift ever."

The wallpaper scrap in Holly's hands symbolized the bold nature of this man she'd married. Ted had taken action on her vague, artist dreams, which had never before amounted to more than words. He'd taken her cake-batter desires, scraped them into a pan, and turned on the oven. Even after all the horrible things she'd done. His gift of an art studio went way beyond Boy Scout obligation, and it surpassed Alex's Van Gogh book as her favorite gift ever. She didn't just want to just look at the beauty created by other people; she wanted to create beauty herself. The humble scrap cost so much more than the art book, too, because it was down payment on a huge investment, guaranteed by the fact that Ted never started what he couldn't finish. It was a promise to scrape walls, move furniture, and remodel their very lives.

Ted's wallpaper gift was not terribly sexy, it's true. He offered spackle not spritzer, and a month ago Holly would have dismissed his gift as overly practical, un-poetic, and unemotional. But she could appreciate it now. Like an Andrew Wyeth landscape, simple and uncluttered, his gift held great emotional depth, though it could be easily dismissed by an uppity hater of realism. Holly liked simple and uncluttered. Growing up, her mother had filled every surface of every wall and every table with knick knacks, do-dads, and hoo-has, so that any noteworthy objects got lost in the traffic. Maybe in the clutter of parenthood, she'd lost sight of Ted's beautiful straightforwardness.

As Holly stood up, the wallpaper swatch dropped to the floor with a whap. She kicked it out of the way and reached around Ted's neck to kiss him. It was a long delicious kiss, seasoned with salt from her tears. They kissed for a long time, neither one knowing the next step, Holly not believing that Ted really wanted her after all she'd just told him. Staying was one thing but wanting was another. They lingered in this zone of sweet uncertainty, where they flirted with the point of no return, as they had when they'd first started dating, pressing but not gyrating, caressing near but not on. Finally, when they could stand it no longer, Ted unbuttoned her jeans. And for the first time in ages, Holly didn't just give sex to Ted like alms to the poor, but she took it also.

6

The morning after did not begin with a leisurely breakfast in bed, wearing little panties and one of Ted's shirts. No, the morning after at the Reese home began with loud children, a major home improvement project, and laundry. Holly stood before the fertile laundry closet, which during the past month had birthed a colorful litter of school announcements and mail, each yipping for attention. To the paper pile, Holly added a new document entitled, Counselors Covered by Blue Cross, which Ted had printed out that morning before he started stripping wallpaper. He had asked her as they brushed their teeth if she would consider seeing a counselor, and she said yes. Although good sex had repaired one of the gaping holes in their fallen nest, Ted wanted to address some of the other holes. Eight counselors were listed, their names followed by various letters of the alphabet, L.P.C., N.C.C., L.M.F.T. Two were women. All sounded wonderfully unfamiliar, strangers with whom she might be able to discuss her life.

Holly turned from the laundry closet to the load of dirty clothes on the kitchen table. With her stain stick set on attack mode, she applied the powerful enzymes demanded by Peter and Ethan's clothes. The task was wonderfully simple, requiring no analysis or decision-making; find stain and dab. She knew after she cleaned these shirts and shorts, they'd get dirty in a week's time, when she'd have to wield her stain stick once again, yet this Sisyphean task warmed her with its sense of normalcy. Through crisis and triumph, plague and pestilence, there was always laundry.

A gray flutter outside took Holly's attention from Ethan's

dinosaur shirt. The magnolia sparrow had flown onto the patio table and now hippity-hopped on top of the black iron mesh. She pecked at some crumbs before decorating the black metal with a purple and white excretion. Now that her babies had left the nest, taking with them the springtime excitement and the genes to perpetuate the same ordinary sparrow life, the mother sparrow was back to her life of eating and pooping until the following spring.

"To hell with the sparrow," Holly said out loud.

"What did you say, Mommy?"

Holly whipped around; she hadn't noticed Peter walk into the kitchen. He wore a cape made of yellow and white striped wallpaper.

"Hey Peter, look at the sparrow." Peter walked over to the window in front of Holly's thighs, and she patted down his stick-up hair. "The little bird found some potato chip crumbs to peck at. She's very glad you and Ethan are sloppy eaters. She also just went potty right on our table. See on the right?"

"Gross."

"I know. Her life is pretty quiet compared to the raptors we saw. Remember the movie we saw on your Raptor Center field trip?" Peter nodded. "Do you remember what the fastest birds are called?"

"Green Falcons!" he said.

"Pere-grine falcons," she corrected. "They can fly way faster than a car."

In tandem, the two warrior-birds had shot by the camera so fast the footage made her dizzy. No hippity-hopping there. The Peregrines left the frame for a moment while the camera focused on a doomed gray bird flapping in the distance. Then back into the frame the two hunters swooped, followed by a mad flurry of feathers, squawking, and aerial magic. Within seconds, they had killed the gray bird, packed it neatly in one hunter's talons, and started moseying homeward like it was just another day at the office. They soared effortlessly on the breeze over impressionistic sweeps of color and shape, two deities enjoying their domain. The next frame changed dramatically again. Back at their nest, the birds fed the prey to their three hungry fledglings, fussing over this domestic chore.

That day in the Raptor Center theatre, Holly remained in her seat until the last kindergartner filed out, strangely moved by these two Peregrines. How seamlessly the falcon mates experienced both the thrill of the flight and the joy of the nest.

Holly patted Peter's cape. "Were you helping Daddy take down Ethan's wallpaper?"

"Yes, but Ethan started throwing wallpaper balls, so Daddy said we couldn't help anymore."

"You can help me later when I start making my studio, okay?"

"Can we use markers in your studio?"

Several months ago Holly had hidden all markers at the top of her closet after Peter and his friend Justin drew red and black roads on the patio rockers, using permanent Sharpies. They said they were just trying to help direct the passerby ants and couldn't understand why Holly had gotten so angry. The roads were now faded from rain and sun, yet the markers remained off limits.

"You could use markers only in the studio but nowhere else. I guess we could leave Ethan's table in there, stocked with your watercolors and glitter glue and stuff like that. But mostly the room will be Mommy's art studio. Are you excited to share a room with Ethan?"

"Can we get bunk beds? I get the top!"

"Bunk beds—that's not a bad idea. We might do that. Want to go with me upstairs to the attic? I want to bring down the rest of my art supplies."

"Yes!"

Holly left the wad of laundry on the kitchen table and walked upstairs with Peter.

From the attic stairs, Holly handed things down to Peter—sketchpads, portfolio, canvases, French easel, tackle boxes. Ethan wandered upstairs to check out the commotion, and together the three of them carried everything into Holly and Ted's bedroom.

"Who's this?" Peter asked as he held up a charcoal nude.

"A model from an art class."

"Why did he take off his clothes?"

"So the artists could learn about his muscles. Hey look." Holly held up a papier découpé. "Can you guess what this is?"

"Soup?" Ethan asked.

"Tinker toys," Peter said definitively.

When Holly told them it was a pot of flowers, Ethan squealed, "I see it!" but Peter looked skeptical.

The boys fingered the brushes, incredulous that some had come from real horse tails. Peter asked about the name "H. Dover" written in black magic marker across a tool box. "That was my name back when I was an artist," Holly explained.

"H. Dover," Ted said from the doorway. He wore his grubby project clothes and his hair was flecked with bits of wallpaper. He looked around at all her stuff. "You have more art supplies than I remembered. You really do need a studio."

"After she makes her studio," Peter said, "me and Ethan are going to get bunk beds, and I get the top."

"Nuh-uh," Ethan protested.

"No," Holly said, "I didn't say we're definitely getting bunk beds. That's just an idea. Your dad and I will need to talk about it."

Ted said, "We may not be able to afford bunk beds right now because we're going to have to buy a new car."

"I want bunk beds!" Ethan said.

Peter held up the papier découpé. "Daddy, look at Mommy's artwork. Can you see the flower pot?"

Ted took the picture. He turned it upside down and sideways. "I'm not very good at art. Your mom is, though, isn't she?"

"Yep."

"Mom said me and Ethan can have our own art table in her studio, and we can use markers in there."

"Sounds good. Holly, did you see my list of Blue Cross counselors?"

"Yes. Thanks. I'll call Monday."

"I'm going to go make myself a sandwich," Ted said.

"I left a bunch of laundry on the kitchen table. Sorry. Just push it out of the way."

By the time Ted left for Knoxville on Monday morning, Ethan's walls were stripped, patched and primed, and the upstairs was in a state of upheaval. Tools, knick-knacks, and art supplies lined the hallway and specks of wallpaper littered the carpet. After chauffeur duties for Peter, Holly drove with Ethan to Lowe's to find paint for the adobe walls she envisioned. She settled on Laura Ashley Apricot 3 for the base coat and Laura Ashley Taupe 5 for the glaze. In addition to fresh roller covers, Holly splurged on brown edging tape, a Purdy angled brush, and EZ furniture sliders.

Holly and Ethan carried the supplies upstairs and added them to the hallway chaos. In Ethan's doorway, Holly grimaced at the pile of furniture in the center of the room. Ted had managed to work in the 2-foot swath around the periphery, but the narrow workspace made Holly feel claustrophobic. She also had an aesthetic and psychological need to see a blank slate. So she pulled off the old sheets that covered the furniture and with her EZ sliders and the patience of a beaver began to drag out the furniture, piece by piece. The mattress and box springs were difficult, especially around the corners and with all the junk in the hallway, but through a combination of sliding, pushing, pulling and tipping, along with great enthusiasm and the absence of any single-mom self-pity, she eventually got Ethan's twin bed set up in Peter's room. In the fray, Ethan discovered many lost treasures—missing puzzle pieces, the remote control to his drag racer, a Power Ranger's leg, and several microscopic guns—all of which kept him thoroughly entertained. Peter's room looked cramped and Holly wasn't sure where to put Ethan's toy box and chest of drawers, so she moved them temporarily into Ted's office.

By the time she went to pick up Peter at school, her studio

was officially Ethan-free. The boys played in "their room" from after school all the way until bedtime. They jumped from bed to bed, built a fort between the beds, and set up opposing armies that launched objects across the gulf. Falling asleep in the new arrangement required an hour of shushing and pleading, but it was a small price to pay for the Brigadoon later that evening.

At 9:00, the time she'd normally be putting on pajamas and crawling into bed, she gathered up rollers, brushes, tarps, and the gallon of Apricot 3 and set up these supplies inside her empty studio. When she slipped into her painting clothes—the khaki pants and navy t-shirt from her road trip, which she'd decided not to give to Goodwill after all—she felt a small, folded paper in her right-hand pocket. She didn't even have to look at it to know that the right-slanting, uppercase words spoke of Langston Hughes, her beauty, and the directions to Professor Zoë's art studio. Alex had written the note the morning she'd left Henrietta. She stroked the smooth paper but didn't take it out, leaving it in her pocket as her studio muse.

She stuck trim tape along the baseboards and poured Apricot 3 into the metal tray. Before proceeding, she paused to admire the gleaming, white-primed walls, beautiful in their own right, free of scuff marks and handprints. The dutiful Mrs. Reese hesitated. It wasn't too late to move Ethan back into this white-walled room and forget all about her studio. Once she painted the Apricot 3, which Peter and Ethan had deemed a girl color, she would irrevocably claim her stake on the room and on her life as an artist, and her claim would definitely inconvenience her family. Not only would Peter and Ethan sacrifice space and privacy in a shared room, but all three of her men would sacrifice some of her time and attention. The dutiful Mrs. Reese crossed her arms across her chest. Wasn't her studio just another selfish act, like running off with Alex? But Holly Dover Reese answered this question with another: Weren't these smaller sacrifices better than Lake Odell?

Holly Dover Reese dipped the roller into the paint tray and applied the first shocking stroke of orange, throwing caution and resale value to the wind. The stripe of color seemed to flip off the dutiful Mrs. Reese. It was Screw You Orange 3, by Laura Ashley.

At midnight when she finished the base coat and edging, Holly lay on the tarp with her arms spread eagle. Her shoulders and back ached, but as she breathed in the paint fumes, her all-time favorite smell, she basked in the terra cotta warmth of her own space and whispered towards the ceiling, "Thank you, Father."

The next morning, her muscles still ached, but the minute she returned from dropping off both boys at kindergarten and preschool—finally it was Ethan's preschool day—she returned to her walls. She mixed glaze, white primer, and Apricot 3, and with a crumpled, plastic grocery bag she dabbed this lighter color onto her pure Apricot 3 base coat. After the light-colored wrinkles dried, she mixed glaze and Taupe 5. She rolled out a section and smudged the glaze with a scrunched-up old t-shirt, working fast before the glaze dried and left behind stripes. Right before she had to pick up Ethan at preschool, she finished glazing the last wall.

"You'll have to go look at your old room," Holly said to Ethan when they pulled into the garage.

They ran up together. "Mommy's art room!" Ethan said. "Hey, what's the brown?"

"Painting tape. You want to help me pull it off?"

Her invitation tumbled out before she'd thought it through, and before she could stop him, Ethan bent over the baseboard and yanked up a long piece of painting tape, which ripped in two and left behind Rice Krispie-sized, brown remnants that would have to be scraped off one by one from the white trim. Holly pulled Ethan away from the wall. The job of pulling up trim tape was normally so satisfying to her, a great reward after a long painting project.

Ethan glared at her with angry green eyes and matching pout. The last time Holly had really studied his green eyes she'd been painting his eulogy in Zoë's studio. She pulled Ethan into her arms.

"Sweetheart, thank you so much for your willingness to

help, but I can't explain how to pull up the tape without leaving behind pieces. I'm going to need to do the tape, okay?"

"But mo-om, it's my job. You said."

"Ethan, I'm going to do the tape."

"No fair!" Ethan yelled. He tried to throw down the wad of tape in his hand, but it stuck to his shorts. He stomped out of the room with a brown paint ball protruding from his thigh, shouting, "No fair, no fair, no fair."

Holly resisted the urge to laugh and to immediately go talk to him. Instead she scraped off the tape remnants with her fingernail. Then, with perfect tension and angle, she pulled up the next brown strip from the baseboard, revealing a satisfying band of unblemished baseboard. She had overestimated Ethan's three-year old capabilities and underestimated her own need for precision. But she didn't need to blame Ethan or herself. Recalibration was in order, not blame. Of course the integration of flight and nest involved some squawking.

After Holly pulled off the last strip of tape, cleaned up all the painting remnants, and vacuumed the carpet, she stood in the doorway and marveled at the perfect horizontal lines that shot across every plane. The old adobe walls and white trim looked exactly how she'd imagined them. The walls had perfectly submitted to her will, as would the paintings she planned to create here. In her studio, in this one corner of her life, no one could boss her. Here, Holly would be a woman king.

Only after she'd gotten her fill of admiring her accomplishment did she go check on Ethan. He was sticking paint tape across his forehead. "Hey bud," she said. "I don't like the way you yelled at me. What do you need to say to me?"

"Sorry."

"That's alright. Listen, I'm sorry I gave you the wrong job. The trim tape is really a grown-up job, but I have a better job that's a three-year old job. No, actually it's a five-year old job, but I think you can handle it. Do you think you want to try a five-year old job?"

"What job?"

"There's a white basket in the hallway. I want you to use it to gather up all the art supplies from around the house—the crayons and coloring books in Peter's closet, the stickers in your nightstand drawer, some pencils and pens from the laundry closet. Then we'll put the basket in my studio, and I'll set up your table."

"That's easy!" Ethan said.

While he busied himself with his new job, Holly set up her tarp and easel by the window, along with Ethan's old changing table, which she had cleared of books and puzzles and now began loading with art supplies. When she got to the Etienne Aigner shoe box, she couldn't remember what was inside. The box had been hidden behind two canvases in the attic. Using an old exacto knife she cut the tape off the lid and discovered among some random clay tools a stack of photographs she one day planned to paint. The collection included photos of her mother's silverware, clouds, birds, hands, and to her delight the aerial photo of her house, taken by her former colleague, Dave the copywriter. Holly took some tape from the shoebox lid and taped the "Home" photo to her easel. "Home" would be the first painting produced from the Holly Dover Reese art studio.

Next she opened her H. Dover tool box, inhaling the intoxicating scent, a strong magic marker bouquet of Xylene with a slight hint of paper mill. Her pencil set, ranging from 8B to 8H, remained complete, but her kneaded eraser was black with graphite. She started a list of supplies to buy: 1) Much-Needed Kneaded Eraser. With real pencils she could refine her Milton Benson drawings. Holly inventoried her tubes of paint. The translucent colors like alizarin crimson and French ultramarine had remained juicy, but the more opaque colors had hardened. To her supply list she added: cadmium yellow, burnt umber, titanium white, and the specialty colors for her "Home" painting, chartreuse and lilac.

Holly pulled from her pile the strip of wallpaper Ted had given her, which deserved a special place of honor as the yellow and white seed from which the entire studio sprung. She tried taping it to the side of the old changing table, then to the bottom of her easel, but she finally saw its rightful spot, centered on the wall beside the window. She tacked the wallpaper strip straight into the pristine adobe wall.

"Ta-dah," Ethan said as he walked into the room.

He dropped the loaded white basket onto the carpet. Along with some of the craft supplies she'd suggested, Ethan had included pennies, foil gum wrappers, a beaded bracelet, two empty juice boxes, a Diet Coke can, and Obi Wan Kenobi. And these were just some of the random items she could see on the top layer. No telling what lay on the bottom of the basket. Holly picked up the Obi Wan figure. Mary Engelbreit hadn't addressed the storage of action figures in her magazine issue about art studio design.

The absurdity of Ethan's items reminded Holly of the peanut butter incident when Peter was two. It was lunchtime and Holly had looked everywhere for the jar of peanut butter—the pantry, the refrigerator, the cabinets, even the freezer. Off-handedly, she asked Peter if he'd seen it. He nodded, led her to the master bedroom, and pointed to the mauve dust ruffle. Underneath the bed lay the missing peanut butter jar. As rationale, Peter said something about monsters, a less than satisfying explanation he could not expound upon given his verbal limitations as a toddler. Thankfully the monsters didn't need the jar opened.

Back then Holly lamented the fact that peanut butter jars turned up underneath beds no matter how carefully she'd organized the pantry. "Why bother with planning?" she used to think. Perhaps now she would learn to dance between the need for planning and the absurdity of planning. Yes, design a studio where she was the supreme boss. But why not welcome the random action figure?

Her art studio would be like the bird's nest she once saw at Ramsey Creek Park, with Styrofoam cup woven into twigs and leaves; the crazy amalgam wasn't pretty or conventional, but it got the job done.

"Excellent work, Ethan!" Holly exclaimed as she set the basket on top of the little table.

"Peter's glitter glue spilled a little," Ethan confessed.

"Peter!" Holly yelled. "Oh geez, I forgot Peter!"

She dove for her watch, which she'd laid on a step stool in the hallway to avoid getting paint on it. She was 15 minutes late picking up Peter from school. At least she was no longer carpooling with Sharon and Ann, so Justin and Frank weren't waiting on her too. She ran with Ethan to the car, not taking the time to change out of her painting clothes.

The carpool line had completely dissipated by the time she got to the school, and Peter was one of only six stragglers left waiting on their delinquent caretakers. While Peter walked to the car, Holly looked in her visor mirror. Umber glaze streaked her hair and the side of her cheek.

"Mo-om," Peter said after he got in the car, "why were you late? And why do you look so dirty?"

"Sorry, bud. I've been busy working on the studio. These are my painting clothes."

"I don't like it when you wear your painting clothes to my school." As if she'd been doing it for years.

As their after school snack Holly and her boys made their famous parmesan butter popcorn. Holly ate while she read the three school announcements from Peter's book bag: the green sheet asked for PTA nominations, the blue one asked for help cleaning mold in the library, and the white one solicited volunteers for field day. All three she stained with popcorn grease before stacking them on top of the Milton Benson drawings inside the laundry closet. By putting the school papers here she was not saying yes or no to volunteering but was letting the laundry closet shoulder these requests until the deadlines passed.

Holly wiped her hands and then gathered the Milton Benson drawings from the pile, rescuing these laundry closet captives from their humid purgatory. She also un-tacked her "Home" sketch from the laundry wall. "Home" was the only drawing actually done on drawing paper. The Milton Bensons she'd drawn on make-shift envelopes, lined school paper, and flimsy printer paper. All these stray drawings would have a new gathering spot, in her studio, away from household demands.

The boys went outside to the swing set and Holly whisked her sketches upstairs. She taped the "Home" sketch to the easel just below the aerial photo and stood back from it. Out from the laundry closet in the light of day the sketch looked lifeless. Just as she suspected the composition needed a bird's wing, both to add movement and to balance out the driveways. Holly untaped the sketch and gathered her oil pastels. Sitting on the floor, using a thick art book as a drawing board, she added sweeps of white in the lower right-hand corner, building up the greasy surface and scraping parts of it away. The wing that emerged unified the entire composition and added the whole idea of flight. She decided that this work, formerly called "Home," would now be called "Flying Home."

7

The first product from the Holly Dover Reese art studio was not the "Flying Home" painting, though she was raring to start it. The finished sketch with the bird's wing hung on the wall; a fresh canvas nestled between upper and lower canvas trays of her easel; and tubes of paint marched along the edge of the changing table turned taboret. The boys were in bed, and Ted was still in Knoxville. Yet, on this first night in her completed studio, instead of painting, she knew she needed to produce a long-overdue goodbye letter to Alex.

Sitting at the boys' miniature table, she cut a piece of drawing paper into two stationery-sized sheets, and on the first sheet, she designed an elaborate salutation. With colored Micron pens and Peter's glitter glue Holly created tiny acrobats, vines, and flowers that formed the words, Dear Alex. The straight line of the D was a thick vine, and the D's curve was a woman arched backwards, holding the top of the vine with her hands and the bottom with her pointed feet. The A was another woman in a yoga position—the downward-facing dog—with her scarf forming the crossbeam. Vines flowed in and out of all the letters. On a separate piece of notebook paper, in pencil, she wrote a draft of her letter to Alex. For half an hour she erased and crossed out and tweaked until she felt ready to write the words with a Micron pen onto her one-of-a-kind stationery:

> Dear Alex,
>   I came to you in Henrietta because I was running away from my family, just when they needed me most, which was so crazy and wrong

and cowardly regardless of my grief. I also came to you in Henrietta because you held a piece of me that I lost for a while, the piece of me that is fun and artistic and interesting. I can never thank you enough for helping me rediscover this piece. You were right about the dutiful Mrs. Reese, and I plan to no longer let her boss me around. Thank you for inspiring me. I've set up an art studio in my house so I can start painting again. Thank you also for letting me paint in Zoë's studio. Keep the painting if you'd like, as payment for cleaning up the mess I left behind. Sorry for all the messes I've left in your life.

You and I share a unique connection that I will always cherish. But I can't abandon my family. Ted and the boys and I share a beautiful interdependence I can not undo, no matter how far I run. We have the greatest power to heal one another (though also the greatest power to disappoint). I am choosing to stay with Ted, not out of sheer duty, but because I need him.

I'm sorry to once again have to end things. You are a wonderful person—so funny, sensitive, intelligent, and kind—and you deserve a much better woman than me.

This letter will be my last communication so that we can both move on. I promise not to show up at the English building if you promise not to leave beverages on my doorstep.
With gratitude,
Holly

Holly wiped her eyes. "Two roads diverged in a yellow wood, and sorry she could not travel both and be one traveler," decided to leave the road that led to Alex and never return. The decision saddened her, even though she felt sure of her path. Judith recently pointed out that the word "decide" contained the same murderous root as "homicide" and "suicide"; to decide required the killing of one option in favor of another. Holly grieved the dead option lying lifeless before her in the form of a goodbye letter.

She also grieved the rejection Alex would feel after this fourth break-up. Never had she intended to hurt him so many times over the past 20 years. He really did deserve better.

The best way she could think of to care for Alex would be to make this rejection stick, and the best way to make it stick would be to truly purge his presence. So after getting her letter ready to mail, Holly began filling a cardboard box with Alex memorabilia, plucked from various caches. For starters she removed the Van Gogh book from her nightstand and dropped it into the box, letting it slap loudly against the bottom. Next came the Catatonic State t-shirt, wadded up in the back of her underwear drawer and still smelling of Alex. From the storage compartment of her French easel, she pulled out the swatch of Alex's old soccer jersey (number ten) and a bundle of his old love letters, ignoring her intense desire to reread each one. In the kitchen, camouflaged behind her grandmother's tea set on a top cabinet shelf, she found the final two items: the cranberry spritzer wine glasses. Although she thought about Alex's note in her khaki painting pants, she did not add it to the box. Maybe she could keep this one vestige.

Holly set her box down on Judith's front stoop. It was 8:30, and she tapped on the door instead of ringing the bell, in case Joe was asleep.

"Hello, Holly," Joe Farrell said when he answered the door.

"Oh hi, Joe. You're still up. Is Judith around?" Holly asked.

"Yes. She's baking. Come in. What's in the box?"

"Oh, it's the equivalent to Judith's liquor bottles—stuff I need to get rid of in my life. Smells delicious."

"Yep, chocolate chip cookies. Can't wait. I'm carving a duck in the garage. Good to see you, Holly."

In the kitchen Judith was transferring cookies from pan to cooling rack. "Hey missy," she said, "What ya got there?"

Holly clunked her box down on the kitchen table. "It's a

bunch of Alex memories. Some of them I've actually been hoarding for 20 years. This is Alex's soccer number from the twelfth grade." Holly showed Judith the shiny, black number 10 on the frayed swatch of green. "Look at this craziness: here is every letter he ever wrote me. I'm wondering if you would take this box to your apartment dumpster where you threw all your liquor. Don't tell me which apartments, and you may need to do it soon before I change my mind." Holly dug out the Van Gogh book from the bottom of the box. "Actually, this book doesn't need to go. Who cares if Alex gave it to me. It's a great reference book, and I adore Van Gogh."

"Can I see the book?" Judith wiped her hands on a dishcloth and fanned through the book backwards until she came to Alex's inscription in the front. "If he had just signed on a page, you could tear out the page and keep the book, but he had to sign on the inside cover. You can get another Van Gogh book. A dime a dozen, honey."

"The book was expensive," Holly said, taking back the book, slightly annoyed by Judith's bossiness.

"Expensive like my Lagavulin Scotch." Judith put her hand on her hip.

Holly opened the book to Alex's note. "We're destined to gaze upon beauty together for the rest of our lives." The line still whispered seductively to her artistic soul, wooing her from her resolution. She shut the book and flung it in the box. "You're right."

"I'm proud of you, Holly. There'll be moments when the least little remnant can pull you backwards. For this young man in my AA group, it was an almost-empty bottle of rum he'd forgotten about in his box of garden tools. That one little bottle set him on a two-month relapse."

Holly reached in her pocket for Alex's note and unfolded it: "I can hardly stand leaving you to teach my classes. You are so beautiful lying in my bed." This little note, if Ted ever discovered it, could devastate him all over again. The tremendous risk was not worth the small comfort and inspiration it brought her. Besides, the bulk of the note's inspiration came from Langston

Hughes, and she could always look up the quote: "If dreams die, life is a broken-winged bird that cannot fly."

"I guess I'd better include this, too," Holly said. She crumpled up the note and dropped it in the box.

"I'm not even going to ask," Judith said.

"Also, will you mail this letter? It's my goodbye note. I might chicken out over night."

When Holly walked back across Judith's front lawn in the cool night air, she didn't feel like she had hoped, as if a tremendous weight had been lifted. Instead she felt like a weight had been added, the weight of deciding. She had boxed up and thrown away her soulmate and muse, had "killed" their relationship, and the pocket of her khaki pants felt empty.

Alex requested a booth in the corner of O'Leary's, a dark little pub in downtown Henrietta where he sometimes met colleagues. That afternoon he wanted to drink alone. He ordered a gin and tonic, a departure from his usual Amstel Light, because he predicted that he would need something stronger to face the letter he'd received from Holly. He pulled the unopened envelope from the pocket of his windbreaker and set it on the table. The letter was a departure from Holly's typical e-mails, and its formality felt cold and ominous.

Gillian the waitress dropped off his drink, and Alex gulped half of it in two swallows. He put on his reading glasses but decided not to open the envelope just yet. He feared that after he read the letter, his relationship with Holly would be over forever, and he wanted to linger with her just a little while longer. He ran his finger along the names and addresses written in Holly's pretty cursive: *Dr. Alex Caleb Meyers*, the lonely professor she'd loved for a moment; *605 Londonshire Street*, the place where she'd lain with him on his futon; *4316 Gilead Knob Court*, her home where she'd stood in her doorway wearing his t-shirt. The date stamped on the letter, *21 May 1998*, he committed to memory because it was likely the day the love of his life decided to leave him.

One more sip of gin and Alex felt buzzed enough to open the envelope. The first quarter of the note was covered in a flowery and intricate "Dear Alex," and he studied each elegant pen mark. Specks of glitter caught the sad, ochre light. This had to be the most beautiful Dear John letter in the history of mankind. Earlier that week he'd gotten a much plainer letter from Emily's lawyer, which began "Dear Respondent."

Holly's was a charitable dismissal, thanking him for his inspiration, apologizing for the mess she'd left him, acknowledging their unique connection. It made clear, however, that she'd chosen Ted, with whom she had an "interdependence" and "need," not exactly the stuff of poetry. Clearly the dutiful Mrs. Reese still lingered, but at least Holly had decided to pursue her art. Her painting of Ethan now leaned against the wall of his bedroom, a disturbing reminder of the time they'd spent together.

Alex chugged the rest of his gin and tonic and asked Gillian for another.

Two components of Holly's letter annoyed him. Holly's comment about how he "deserved a better woman than her" seemed condescending, like she were writing to a simpleton who would take easy comfort from her flattery. If he were so great, she wouldn't be rejecting him for the fourth time. Also, her closing, "With Gratitude," bothered him, not just because of its stiffness, not just because it didn't say "Love," but also because, again, if she were so grateful, why the rejection? Softening the blow was one thing, but insulting someone's intelligence was another.

When Gillian the waitress brought him a third round, he slurred to her, "I must get my soul back from her, you know?" He was quoting Sylvia Plath but the reference didn't register with Gillian.

"You will," Gillian said. "Just give it some time."

"How we need another soul to cling to." More Plath.

Gillian cocked her head and gave him a look. "I gotta deliver this order, but I'll come back to check on you in a minute."

Alex got out a pen and scrawled on the back of the Holly's envelope: "What did my arms do before they held you?" Or something like that. Good ol' Sylvia really knew how to come alongside someone during a break-up. He raised his glass and said to no one in particular, "To Sylvia."

A golf tournament played on the pub's TV up above the bar. During a commercial a little blonde boy sat with his dad in a golf cart while the fantastical promise of a financial planning company flashed across the screen. "Georgia Trust: Security for Generations to Come." He was pretty sure the boy was Ethan.

He said towards the TV, "Who cares, Ethan."

Who the hell cared about Ethan and the generations to come? Everyone was working so damn hard for the damn generations to come. What about love?

Gillian walked back to his booth and asked Alex if he was okay. He asked for another drink, but she talked him out of it. Apparently Gillian was the only woman left on the whole damn earth who cared whether or not Alex drank himself into a bloody coma.

8

All school year long George Finley bragged about going to Carowinds Amusement Park. He went like 50 million times last summer. And now Peter was at Carowinds!

Peter's favorite ride so far was the old timey cars. He could drive them himself. They went on them three, count em, three times. The black car was best. The first time they went, Peter got to drive the black car with his daddy. Ethan tried to get on it but Daddy told him No. Ethan had to ride the purple car with Mommy. Ha, Ha. Purple was a girl color. Ethan got to ride the black car on their second turn. But on the third turn, guess who?

After the cars, Peter's mommy wanted to go on the Scooby Doo rollercoaster, and Peter had to stand next to Scooby to see if he was tall enough. Just barely. He was the tallest kid in Mrs. Jamison's class. He was kind of hoping he wasn't tall enough because the ride looked super scary.

"Mommy, we're going to fall out around those turns. See? They go sideways."

"No," she said. "the seatbelts keep you glued to the seat."

"Seatbelts can burn," he reminded her.

"These seatbelts won't, I promise. They're more like metal bars, totally different than the ones in a car. But we don't have to go if you don't want to. We can just go straight to the water park."

George Finley always talked about the water park, how you could shoot people with water guns and slide down water tubes that were miles long. But George never mentioned Scooby Doo, and now Peter knew why. George was the shortest boy in Mrs. Jamison's class, and he wasn't tall enough to ride Scooby Doo.

"I'll do it!" Peter said to his mommy. He couldn't wait until next school year to tell George all about riding Scooby Doo.

Ted and Ethan waited on a park bench while Holly and Peter rode the Scooby Doo. Ethan happily licked his rainbow-flavored ice cream cone, a small splurge that had prevented a tantrum after Ethan's indignation at being too short for the Scooby Doo. They were already spending a fortune on this end-of-the-school-year celebration, and Holly had worked hard packing a car picnic so as to avoid the exorbitant price of park food, yet the $3.25 ice cream was a worthwhile investment that protected their larger investment of $119.80 for all 4 tickets. More and more, Ted understood the small compromises Holly endured on a minute-by-minute basis. With the boys you had to, at lightning speed, weigh imperfect solution against imperfect solution: spending money on a bribe but maintaining your sanity vs. parenting wisely through a tantrum but sacrificing the enjoyment of a long-planned event.

Even though they'd just taken on a new car payment, Ted felt strongly that they all needed this extravagant outing. Not only had Peter finished kindergarten, Ted landed 2 new accounts, and Holly finished her studio, but most importantly their family had survived the spring of '98.

"Yummy, yummy, yummy," Ethan said as he happily licked his ice cream cone and pumped his dangling legs.

"Your lips are blue," Ted said. "Let me see your tongue."

Ethan stuck out his tongue in between licks of ice cream.

"You have a blue tongue just like a giraffe."

"Giraffes have blue tongues?"

"Yep." Ted put his arm around Ethan. "Hey, little giraffe."

In the serpentine line feeding into the Scooby Doo ride, Ted caught sight of Holly and Peter. Holly wore a long purple skirt, sleeveless shirt, and scarf, hippie clothing more typical of her pre-motherhood wardrobe. Ted liked her rekindled Bohemia, especially in the bedroom, and yet the bedroom had been the hardest place to forgive. The first time had been fueled by an intense gratefulness that they had not lost one another, but the last time Ted had been unable to exorcise from his mind the image of Alex kissing the same spot he was kissing, the hollow between Holly's collar bones. The last time, Ted had abruptly halted the kissing and said good night.

Of all topics, Pastor Johnson preached about forgiveness when they attended Tom Jarvis' church. Tom had invited Ted to his rock-n-roll Presbyterian church when they ran into each other at Walgreen's. He also told Ted he'd finally found another job, 3 months after getting fired from Ted's company. A guy at his new company had told him about the church. Without thinking twice, Ted agreed to go out of gratefulness to God for saving his family. Holly had agreed to church in theory, but rallying the troops was another matter. There'd been spilled orange juice and outfit changes and yelling, but once they were finally sitting in the pew, they loved the rock music and the self-deprecating pastor. During his sermon, Pastor Johnson looked straight at Ted as if he knew his situation and said, "A happy marriage is the union of two good forgivers." How did Pastor Johnson know Ted was struggling with forgiveness? Forgiveness was like young Master Nye in Knoxville, a wavering and demanding client.

Ted still had his difficult moments, but most of the time he was thankful and proud to have held his family together. If he hit another dry spell at his job, Network One might easily replace him like they did Ted Jarvis—in less than a week with a hot shot college grad—but no one could replace Ted in his family. Because of him they'd made Holly's art studio, gone to church, and now were experiencing this fun family adventure. This was the life he'd sworn himself to back when his father left.

Ted looked down at Ethan's rainbow-colored mouth and smiled.

Once the metal safety bar locked into place over their laps, Peter kept yanking on it to make sure it was secure.

"You're very brave," Holly said to him. "Your first rollercoaster! I'm proud of you."

Holly loved rollercoasters, even though she hadn't ridden one in a decade and even though she balked when Ted proposed a day at Carowinds. The outing seemed a lavish way to celebrate in light of their new car payments, which required careful belt-tightening in the budget. They had replaced the Dodge Caravan, now nothing more than a parts donor, with a used Mazda 626 sedan in sage green mica. Ted had argued for the carpooling and hauling capabilities of a replacement minivan and the dirt-hiding virtues of tan, but in the end he said it was Holly's choice, and she was adamant about a car that didn't remind her of Lake Odell. Ted gallantly handled negotiations with the Mazda dealership and with State Farm, which ended up covering almost all the rental car expenses.

During their budget discussions as they talked about getting rid of cable, not eating out, and home-laundering Ted's shirts instead of dry cleaning them, Holly cried, not because she'd miss these luxuries but because she felt bad all over again about the mess she'd made of their lives. That's when Ted said for the first time, "I forgive you." Oh, he'd said "I'm sticking by you" and had acted on his commitment, but he seemed to have purposefully waited to utter these words of forgiveness until he really meant them.

"Why aren't we moving?" Peter asked.

"They're making sure everything is absolutely safe and sound."

Even that morning Holly tried to back out of their Carowinds excursion, not only because of the expense, but also because she was exhausted from staying up until 1:30 the previous night to finish her "Flying Home" painting. She'd set the goal of finishing by the last day of Peter's school, which was yesterday. Technically midnight was the deadline, but an hour and a half past midnight wasn't bad.

When Holly first began the painting, she loved it; halfway

through, she hated it, deeming it the worst painting in all of Western civilization; then last night when she signed her name to it, she loved it again. The bird wing was the hardest part, at first so disastrously gaudy in bright white but then so perfect once she'd overlaid it in browns and blues. The wing ended up being her favorite part.

Her signature had required a ludicrous amount of thought. H. D. Reese was nice and androgynous, deflecting any bias a buyer might have against women artists, yet H. D. Reese over-emphasized Ted's name. Her maiden name, Holly Dover, or H. Dover if she went with the androgyny angle, though it expressed independence, simply didn't exist anymore. There was no bank account or driver's license under the name Holly Dover. So she finally settled on Holly Dover Reese, the best representation of the artist formerly known as H. Dover, though the three names took up an entire corner of canvas.

Holly pried Peter's hand off the safety bar, entwined her fingers around his, and kissed his knuckles.

"It's going to be okay, sweetie, I promise."

Peter's hand felt so solid and warm, God's mercy made visceral. Holly's hand was dry from the mineral spirits, as if her skin had a layer of white crackle paint. Traces of chartreuse remained along her cuticles. Their two hands fit perfectly together, her disheveled artist's hand and his soft, smooth six-year old hand. Together they formed a yin and yang very much like the past 12 hours: late last night she was a mother attending to her art; this morning she was a tired artist attending to her mothering. The thrill of the flight and the joy of the nest. Holly's therapist, Barbara Cooley, would have gone ape over this picture of integration.

In their first therapy session, Holly and Barbara had been talking about expectations from Ted, from the boys, from the supermoms. Barbara stroked her chin in a typical therapist way and asked, "What are *your* expectations?"

Holly wanted to respond in a typical mental patient way, "That's what I'm paying *you* to figure out *for* me," but instead she thought for a few seconds and said, "I expect to be a good mother *and* a good artist, without feeling guilty. I want to weave together the two parts of me and enjoy them both."

Barbara clapped her hands. "Brilliant!" she said. "Forget expectations. Forget the supermoms. Focus on integrating the different parts of your own unique life. Integration, Holly, integration."

The Scooby train finally began moving, and Peter took his hand back in order to grip the safety bar. The rollercoaster began its slow ascent up the first hill with an ominous, metallic clicking that sounded like the chains of a medieval torture device, laboriously dragging them up to the death drop.

"I changed my mind," Peter said. "I feel sick."

"It's too late, baby. You'll be okay. Just close your eyes."

Peter squeezed his eyes shut, leaned over the safety bar, and proceeded to vomit one projectile burst that splattered the hem of Holly's skirt, ran down her ankle, and oozed into her sandal. She could smell the bile.

"You've gotta be kidding," she said.

Holly had no Kleenex, no napkins, no baby wipes, no water bottle. Her bag of tricks was currently hanging off Ted's shoulder. Even if she had clean-up options, she had no time; they'd almost reached the apex of the hill. All she could do was stare down at the orange vomit. She started to feel bad that she'd encouraged Peter to ride the rollercoaster; any good mom would have predicted his nausea. She started to hyperbolize about how *every* fun thing was *always* ruined. She started to feel sorry for the absurdity, filth, and bad timing of her mommy life. Then Holly paused and thought of Barbara Cooley's other mantra: "Perspective, Holly, perspective." Peter happened to get sick at an inopportune time—that's how life rolled sometimes. His nausea didn't testify for or against her ability as a mom; it didn't attest to a universe bent against her. She had two choices: to enjoy the ride or not enjoy the ride.

She chose to enjoy the ride with her son who had survived a car crash. Holly threw her head back and laughed.

"It's not funny," Peter said.

"I know, sweetie. Don't worry. We'll take care of everything

244

after the ride. Hang on! Here we go!"

Whoosh. Holly's stomach dropped and the g-forces whipped her head back, pinning her cheeks to her ears. Warm tears shot across her face. Or was it spit? It didn't matter. She had vomit on her leg, this other bodily fluid on her cheek, and a good chance of whiplash. She was out of control, and she liked it. With the speed of a Peregrine, she shot down and rose again, screeched around a turn, and before regaining her equilibrium, dropped down once more. Holly let go of the safety bar and raised her hands in the air. In a few minutes she'd be cleaning and consoling, but for now she was flying.

Made in the USA
Lexington, KY
01 December 2012